Also by Robert Olen Butler

The Alleys of Eden

Sun Dogs

Countrymen of Bones

On Distant Ground

WABASH

WABASH

a novel by

Robert Olen Butler

Alfred A. Knopf, Inc. New York 1 9 8 7

This Is a Borzoi Book Published by
Alfred A. Knopf, Inc.

Copyright © 1987 by Robert Olen Butler
All rights reserved under International and
Pan-American Copyright Conventions.
Published in the United States by Alfred A.
Knopf, Inc., New York, and simultaneously in
Canada by Random House of Canada Limited,
Toronto. Distributed by Random House, Inc.,
New York.
Library of Congress
Cataloging-in-Publication Data
Butler, Robert Olen.
Wabash.
I. Title.
PS3552.U8278W3   1987   813'.54   86-46003
ISBN 0-394-55597-X

Manufactured in the United States of America
First Edition

For Joshua

A bar of steel—it is only
Smoke at the heart of it, smoke and the blood of a man.
—Carl Sandburg

Do not abandon me, O Lady most holy, to the mercy of men.
—Greek votive office to the Virgin Mary

WABASH

Whang Wabash Steel had orders and there was work, the fine, black soot from the mill lay on the porch steps each morning like an overnight snow. Deborah Cole was sweeping it away on a June morning in 1932 when her mother appeared before her, panting, saying, "Come on now, hon. Maybe you can help with Aunt Berenice." Deborah leaned her broom against the front screen and followed her mother along the street, running, past the narrow shotgun houses and then the semidetached flats, into her mother's own street of clapboard two-stories and on down toward Aunt Berenice's place.

As she approached, Deborah could see Aunt Della and Aunt Adah beneath the sugar maple on the verge of Berenice's lawn. They were looking up into the tree until Deborah was very near and they turned.

"Maybe you can talk to her," Della said to Deborah.

"Miriam," Adah said to Deborah's mother, who came up now, breathing heavily, "she's going too far."

"Yes," Della said with a sharp little laugh, "she's ignoring Adah."

Deborah watched Adah's face pinch in irritation like a child's and then her hand rise to push with a defiant pride at her newly marcelled hair, the flaxen waves turned almost completely white.

Deborah looked into the tree. Ten feet up, Aunt Berenice sat straddling a limb that looked too thin to hold her. She was wearing a flower-print housedress which she'd tucked modestly around her legs that dangled down with one foot slippered, one foot bare. Deborah glanced at the ground and Della seemed to read her thoughts. "Over there," Della said. By the trunk was Berenice's other slipper. "Adah threw a rock," Della said.

"We had to get her attention," Adah said. "It was a little rock."

"Bunny, come on down now," Deborah's mother called.

Berenice did not look down. Deborah stepped back to see her face. Her aunt's chin was lifted slightly; her eyes were closed. She seemed peaceful. Deborah had two opposing feelings that tugged her into silence: she was sad for her aunt, for the fearful impulses that sometimes drove her; and she was happy for her aunt, for her perch there above the hard times.

Deborah thought she could even see a faint smile on her face.

"Talk to her," Miriam said to Deborah.

"She seems so peaceful, Mama."

"She could lose her balance."

"Not Berenice," Della said. "She could always outclimb us all."

Miriam said in an intense whisper, "I don't think talk like that is going to help with the present problem."

"That's right," Adah said. "Be quiet, Della. Let Debby talk."

The three sisters turned their faces in expectation, all three bearing the wide-set, unwavering eyes, the high cheeks, of Grandma Birney. Della, the youngest, had a narrow, pointed chin and her habitual faint smile; Adah's lips were enlarged by her own hand by a red butterfly of lipstick, and her eyebrows were plucked into thin lines; Miriam, Deborah's mother, had Grandpa Birney's square chin, and it was her gaze that forced Deborah's eyes back into the tree. Aunt Berenice looked less like Grandma Birney than the others; but perhaps it was just the distraction she carried with her, the furtive sadness, that set her apart, transformed her face. She had her sisters' high cheeks. Next to Adah she was the oldest, and her hair had darkened into the color of the pig iron of the mill. Her hair was pulled tightly back into a bun. She seemed at once out of place and perfectly at home in the tree.

"Aunt Berenice," Deborah said. She thought she'd spoken too softly, but her aunt opened her eyes and looked down at her. The three sisters on the ground stirred and murmured and this drew Berenice's attention to them and she raised her face once more and closed her eyes.

"Aunt Berenice," Deborah said. "Are you all right?"

"I'm fine," Berenice said gently, without moving.

"Do you want to come down?"

"If I wanted to come down, I'd do it."

"Mama and Adah and Della were just concerned."

"They don't have to concern themselves about me."

"Is the limb you're on strong enough to hold you?"

"If it hasn't broken yet, it's strong enough," Della interjected. "She's not gaining weight while she's on it."

"Be quiet," Miriam said.

Deborah looked at the sisters and Adah was gone. She was walking quickly up the street.

"I'm just fine," Berenice said. "I'm real good."

Deborah listened hard for a tone in her aunt's voice that was saying the opposite of the words, but she could hear nothing of the sort. The words sounded true. Deborah was of a mind just to walk away, to wish Aunt Berenice a good day and to let her sit in the tree. Aunt Berenice was happy. She was better off in the tree than on the porch swing at Deborah's mother's house, where the sisters sat to talk. There, her face was not placid. Her eyes could not close like this, in apparent peace. But Deborah felt the silent urging of her mother and she said, "Is there anything you need?"

"Yes," Berenice said. "I'd like all of you to leave me so I can listen."

"Listen?"

"I can hear children up here. And the mill. I can hear the trains going in and I can even hear the furnaces." Berenice kept her eyes shut and she cocked her head slightly.

Deborah looked at her mother and said softly, "Why don't we let her be?"

"She's not your sister," her mother said, her voice hard. "She's my aunt."

Della said, "It's easier to have a crazy aunt than a crazy sister. People start looking at *us* funny."

There was a squall of sound up the street, children's voices shooting at each other—imitating a tommy gun and a pistol—and Miriam said, "Della, keep the kids away." Della moved off toward the sound.

"Where's Uncle Joe?" Deborah asked, though the question carried its own understood answer: Uncle Joe, Berenice's husband, was in a speakeasy or in a culvert or if he was sober he was running errands for a bootleg gang in East St. Louis. If he was here, he was in bed, tight, unconscious till he would demand a fresh shirt and he'd tie his bow tie and go off again. Miriam shrugged.

Deborah looked up and though the faint smile was still on Berenice's face, Deborah found that she was looking at her aunt in a slightly different way, conscious now of more, and Berenice suddenly seemed very vulnerable: the limb was bent and trembling, her bare foot was bony and gray, her escape was futile, doomed. Was it the thought of Uncle Joe that stirred this fear for her aunt? Most of the time the sisters blamed Joe for all of Berenice's problems. Deborah didn't quite believe that.

"My gosh!" A child's voice.

"Della," Miriam said sharply.

"What did you want me to do?" Della said. "Wrestle them to the ground?"

Two little boys were standing beneath the tree observing Berenice. One held a rusty try square by its short end, like a pistol; the other held a length of tree branch across his chest with both hands.

"Hey, lady!" the boy with the branch cried.

"Listen, kid . . . " Miriam began.

Della said, "He won't answer you unless you call him G-man. He's J. Edgar Hoover, see."

The child called to Berenice, "You need the government to rescue you?"

The children made Deborah feel a running inside her, like water, warm, too warm; her lungs felt like they were filling. She wanted to climb up with Berenice. She knew clearly what this was all about inside her. Her own daughter, dead almost three years now. How could she turn away from a living child just because her own was dead? She made herself speak. "And who's this with the pistol?"

"I'm Al Capone," the second child said.

"Now's your chance to escape," Deborah whispered. "J. Edgar's distracted by other things."

The little boy looked up at Berenice; his eyes squinted. Deborah felt him weighing the relative attractions of a grown woman in a tree and escaping back into his game of gangsters and G-men.

"Now's your chance to take it on the lam," Deborah said.

The boy dashed off.

"Capone's made a break for it," Deborah said to the first boy. He studied the woman in the tree for a moment more. Deborah followed his gaze. Berenice was very still. Her eyes remained closed. But her mouth had drawn tight, as if she were dreaming a faintly unpleasant dream. Deborah felt a flutter of fear, like the leaves around Berenice that fluttered in a hot breeze now. Berenice's dress rippled. The boy ran off. Deborah said, "Aunt Berenice?" She wanted to say something to bring her down, but her concern cut off any further words.

Deborah felt her mother come up beside her and Della behind. They stood together for a time in silence watching Berenice's face, her still face, tight now in an unspoken pain. The breeze faded, the leaves grew still. Berenice's eyes wrinkled slightly as she pressed them more tightly shut. No one moved. Deborah and her mother and her aunt Della stood looking up and Berenice sat on the tree limb and they were all motionless for a long while. Then there was a rumbling sound up the block, wooden wheels on the brick street.

Deborah looked and it was Adah leading the hot tamale man, who was pushing his cart. Adah turned and said something to the man as they approached and he began his vowel-stretched cry. "Hot tamales!" Della set her fists on her hips and laughed. Deborah and her mother looked up at Berenice. Her eyes were open.

"Hot tamales! Get 'em hot!"

Adah was under the tree now. "Bunny, why don't you come down and have a tamale? You know how you love tamales."

The tamale man was quietly cursing as he poked at his pot of coals. It was morning and Adah had found him somehow and dragged him here. He was wearing a nightshirt under his apron. The tamales were wrapped in corn shucks bleached pure white and there was a smell beginning of the burning coals and the corn.

Berenice was looking down from the tree and Miriam joined Adah in pushing the idea of hot tamales. They both smacked their lips and sang the praises of tamales. Adah hissed at the tamale man. "Norman. Norman," she said.

"Hot tamales!" Norman cried.

Deborah couldn't imagine that this trick would move Aunt Berenice, but when she looked up into the tree, her aunt was coming down, hugging the trunk and stepping down on the branches and nodules of bark, moving rapidly, in expert control of her descent, though the sisters were frantic now in concern at the foot of the tree, shouting cautions and stretching up to break her fall. Berenice looked over her shoulder and stopped and said, "Get out of my way." The three sisters lowered their arms and fell silent but they did not move. "Get out of my way, please," Berenice said, more gently. Adah and Della and Miriam stepped back and Berenice came down. The others kept their distance as Berenice briskly brushed her hands and then smoothed her dress.

Finally Adah said, in a tiny, put-on, sweet-talking voice, "Bunny, do you want chili on your tamale?"

"Come on, Adah," Norman said with undisguised irritation. "There's no chili this time of day."

Adah said, "How about some ketchup then, Bunny?"

Berenice sighed and drew the back of her hand slowly across her forehead. "Adah dear, I didn't come down to eat hot tamales. I came down because it was clear to me that no one was going to leave me alone." And then Berenice turned and walked up her sidewalk, climbed her porch steps, and disappeared into the house.

Beneath the tree no one spoke for a long moment and then the sisters began to stir and make sounds of relief and bafflement and the wooden wheels began to roll and Adah said, "Wait, Norman," and she went after him. Deborah moved partway up the walk and looked at the wavy blankness of the screen door. Berenice's house was still, placid-seeming. But Deborah felt a scrabbling sadness before it, as if she stood before a sick child, a child's cough, untouchable. Deborah turned away and she saw Berenice's slipper on the ground beneath the tree and she felt for a moment as if her aunt had fallen there, she'd fallen and was dead.

When Jeremy Cole saw Nicholas Brenner edging over to him in the locker room at the mill, he knew already that Brenner was a radical, even maybe a Red, a man who could endanger Jeremy's work—under thirty hours a week now—a man who'd be on the breadlines by Friday, if he was starting to agitate, or maybe beat up and dumped at the levee. Spud would see what Brenner was and there was no foreman at Wabash Steel tougher on agitators than Spud. Beyond the mill, even. Spud could get things done. Spud was a dangerous man; and so this Brenner was a danger. But Jeremy sat with his face forward and he thought of how he once had used this time to change. He would come to the mill in street clothes and carefully undress, folding his shirt, his pants, rolling each sock, putting on his flannel shirt, his overalls, his kersey cap. He had a chance to ready his mind, his body, for the work. But it'd been three years now since the country went crazy and he was lucky to be working at all and if he couldn't afford a change of clothes to keep the street separate from his work each day, that was the least of his problems. If he had to go to the furnaces still a little distracted, not quite ready, he could accept that because there was worse on the outside. There was much worse and maybe he could understand an agitator. Not a Red, but an agitator. Something maybe had to be done.

Jeremy looked down the bench. Brenner was sitting more than an arm's length off and he was looking the other way. He was watching Turpin, who always wore an immaculate white shirt and changed at the end locker. Turpin was close to sixty, was bald and thick-necked; no one ever heard him speak of his wife, but there was always a fresh white shirt every day, even now, though as he took the shirt off before his open locker, the fraying at the cuffs and the collar was visible from where Jeremy sat. Brenner turned his head and smiled at Jeremy and slid closer.

He was a wiry man, not a steelworker to look at him, but his thinness was hard. He was no more than Jeremy's age—about thirty—and his face was round and Irish-boyish. But the face was minutely wrinkled and often the wrinkles would sharpen and his eyes would shift away as if he was in pain, as if he had the hot-mill cramps and was trying to cover it up. And this thinness made Jeremy vaguely nervous, made his own body restless. Jeremy was hard too, but large, hard and powerful enough that he moved with what seemed a kind of thoughtfulness, slowly, in careful control. Brenner was quick and brittle and it made Jeremy nervous.

"Cole?" Brenner said.

"Yes?"

"I'm Brenner."

"I know."

"Nick." He offered his first name in a low voice, as if it were a secret.

Jeremy waited. Brenner looked around.

"You're not careful enough," Jeremy said.

Brenner's head snapped back at this. "What do you mean?"

"I haven't talked to you yet and I know already you're . . . stirring things up."

Brenner laughed. "How'd you know that?"

Now Jeremy looked around. There was only Turpin in the locker room and he was the last man who'd be a company spy. "I heard you talking to Gus. I've seen you watching people, sizing them up."

"You're a smart man, Cole."

"It wasn't so hard."

"I'm not as careful as I used to be." Brenner's eyes shifted away, he seemed to turn his attention to his own thoughts. Jeremy pushed his locker door shut.

Brenner said, "You're a lot smarter than most of these guys, Cole. You educated?"

"I even had a year at Champaign."

"College? How'd you end up back here?"

Jeremy grew very still. He thought of the reasons. There was no money, even in the good years; there were always others to care for beyond himself—first his mother, since his father was long dead, and then his mother was dead and there was Deborah. That was all right. There was no regret over Deborah. She was worth the mill. And for a time there'd been another to care for. He felt a stirring now, in his strongest places—his arms, his shoulders, his back—a futile stirring: if only he still had one more to care for, even in these tough times. His daughter, Elizabeth, was dead, dead too soon, and he wondered how his thoughts had come to her. She had nothing to do with his leaving school. There was one other reason, one that he half believed in. This one he spoke as an answer. "You grow up in Wabash, Illinois, watching the mill, and someday it draws you in. Wabash won't let its boys go away for long."

"Now that attitude scares me on both ends of it," Brenner said.

"What do you mean?"

"On one end you're passive before the power of this company that some capitalist owns and sucks all the juice out of. If the mill's got its teeth in you, then John J. Hagemeyer's got his teeth in you."

"Hagemeyer owns a lot more than me and this mill."

"That's right . . . But the other thing in what you say scares me too. You shouldn't mind coming back to a steel mill. To work as part of the proletariat—the real producers of the world—this is the highest goal of all."

Jeremy raised one hand—just a little—and Brenner stopped. "I don't think much of the slogans, Nick."

"I understand."

"And as soon as you heard I'd gone to college for a while, you were the one who asked me what I was doing back here."

Brenner's face rumpled in a laugh. "You're okay, Cole. That's great . . . I don't go for the slogans so much either, by the way. But ideas have to be gotten across somehow."

"Did Gus go for your slogans?"

"Gus." Brenner shook his head. "I don't understand. He's probably the last Hungarian left at the blast furnace."

Jeremy lifted his head slightly. He liked Brenner's calling Gus a Hungarian. Jeremy had heard the Hungarians called only Hunky for as long as he'd been working in the mill. He thought the Hungarians were good men; as a group, they were better workers, stronger, than anyone else.

Brenner shook his head again. "And still he doesn't see who the real enemy is. The management. They're using the hard times to eliminate the ones they never wanted anyway. The weak, the sick, the Negroes and the Hungarians and the rest . . . Hagemeyer's not hurt by this thing. His personal fortune's intact. He's even buying up more of Wabash Steel. Taking the stock back, now that it's way down. And the workers he doesn't want, he gets rid of."

Jeremy felt a twist of anger over one of the laid-off workers. A man named Cronin. Not a Negro or a Hungarian or weak, really, though he'd had a nagging knee injury that kept him out a little too often. But mostly he'd gotten on the wrong side of Spud. He never could look the other way when Spud got mean. Cronin was gone only a week and Jeremy missed him. But instead of talking about the man, he said to Brenner, "Why haven't they gotten rid of you?"

"I was real careful when I worked over at the tin-plate rolling operation. But since I'm over here, well, it's just time, is all. The time's come to get people moving. We gotta move as fast as possible now. Listen, things are gonna happen soon in this mill. And in this town and this state and this whole country. The world, even . . ."

Jeremy stopped Brenner with a frown.

"Okay," Brenner said. "Forget the world. But I'm telling you there are more guys at this mill, more in this town, who are listening to the truth than you'd ever imagine. People are too hungry to ignore it now."

Jeremy had an abrupt sense of the time. He was still measuring it, unconsciously, by the preparations of other men in the locker room. Men like Cronin. But the crews were cut so far down from the layoffs and the spread-work program that there was not enough movement to alert him. He stood up. Brenner stood up, too, and they went down the row of lockers and past the showers. Jeremy decided to stop at Cronin's house after the shift to see how he was doing.

"Before the week is out," Brenner said, "Hoover's going to be nominated and then—"

Jeremy cut him off. "What is it you want from me?"

"You won't let me preach at all, huh, Cole?"

They stepped out of the locker room and into the smell of ammonia and naphthalene and sulfur, into the grip of the plant. The dark mass of the mill pressed at Jeremy's face, his chest, but he did not look. He kept his head down as he moved with Brenner at his side toward the labor shack.

"Jeremy, wait just a moment," Brenner said, slowing them down. "I'm sorry if I danced you around. I've been watching people. You're right. And I think you're the guy who can make a big difference. You're tougher than any two Hungarians and the men respect you, they make way for you. Even Spud's a little afraid of you, I think."

Jeremy laughed at this.

Brenner said, "I mean it," and his face pinched and he looked around. No one was near. The labor shack—where Spud probably was at this hour—was still a hundred yards away. Brenner said, "What's going to happen is this. We've got a big meeting on Monday night. An unemployment council. It's for the suffering working people—the unemployed—and those who care about the unemployed. We've got to figure out how to change things so that people can get something to eat, a place to live, some dignity. Come to the meeting."

Jeremy felt stirred by the invocation of the hungry and the homeless. He'd seen too damn much of that already. He was afraid he and Deborah were heading for that themselves. But Brenner made him nervous, and Jeremy still wasn't sure if the man was just a radical thinker, a Socialist maybe, or if he was actually a Red. Jeremy didn't know if there was a difference, really, but he suspected there was. He just didn't want to get into the explanations of all that. So he turned and moved off toward the labor shack. Brenner caught up with him and walked beside him and he didn't say another word and his silence impressed Jeremy. A real Red couldn't hold his tongue, he figured.

When they got to the labor shack, Jeremy stopped. He wanted a moment to himself, and he said to Brenner, "I'll think it over."

Brenner nodded and said, "Thanks." He didn't linger but went on into the labor shack alone.

Jeremy turned and let himself look now at the mill that had been pressing at him, shaping his walk, his bearing, since he emerged from the locker room. Before him was the clustering of buildings of the gas recovery section, the uneven rising of the cooling towers and storage tanks. To the right was the long bed where the pusher machine ran before the ovens, the bell on the pusher ringing now as the machine's broad facade began to slide this way along the tracks. Above the bed the thick pipes of a collection main linked the gas recovery plant to each of the three coke oven batteries: no matter how tangled or sprawling the mill became there were always connections. And, except for the hardness of the sky, there was never a scrap of the outer world to be seen here; there was nothing but the mill's own unyielding mass. Not even a bird wheeled in the slab of sky over the ovens. Ever. Around the fringes of the plant, out by the slag dump, near the ore bridge, there were a feeble few birds. But not here, not near the ovens. Jeremy looked at the long row of the three batteries, looked at the even, narrow line of doors. The seepage of smoke in a dozen ovens along the length curled away, stressing the bulk of the doors. The pusher stopped before an oven on A-battery but the door extractor did not ease forward. Jeremy felt a prickle of pleasure at this. The work waited. There was work to be done and he turned and opened the door to the labor shack.

The room was small and hot and smelled of sulfur. Turpin was against one wall with his arms folded, waiting for the shift to start. Above his head was a faded sign: SAFETY FIRST. Near him on a wooden bench sat Gus, his thick forearms laid along his thighs, his hands folded. There was a space on the bench next to Gus, and Brenner was crossing to it. Three other men slouched against a wall, new faces, men from other departments, other shifts, here now from the spread-work. Everyone in the room was quiet, edgy, as if they were the survivors of a shipwreck waiting on a sandbar. Only Spud was calm. He stood by the window. He was a short man but his chest and shoulders and arms were massive. A furnace stoker had made a private joke to a few other workers about Spud being Mae West's dad, that she got her pumps from him, and the man didn't show up the next day and his name was on the laid-off list the day after. Spud was over fifty now and maybe could be had in a fight, but no one felt sure of that, not even the couple of East St. Louis guys who'd come and gone and thought they were specially tough. Nobody tried Spud. They went off to the breadlines without getting even a punch in. Jeremy looked at Brenner sitting next to Gus and Brenner's face was wrinkled in a faint smile and Jeremy knew that there was going to be trouble in Wabash soon and nobody was going to be able to keep out of it.

To the east of the blast furnace operations of Wabash Steel were horseradish fields, a slash of Illinois Central tracks, two miles more of river-bottom farmland and then the massive ten-story-high earthen mound left from a pre-Columbian Indian empire once centered there. To the north of the mill, past the slag dumps, was a shallow depression with a clustering of tar-paper shotgun houses owned mostly by the mill and holding the poorest of the workers, the mass of the cheapest labor that changed its dominant nationality slowly over the years—German to Irish to Welsh to Slav, mostly Hungarian now—and its local name seemed to be sticking: Hunky Hollow. Beyond the Hollow, toward the North Plant, where the open hearth was, lay another neighborhood of shotgun houses but with asbestos shingles instead of tar paper, and with small yards, and many of them were owned by the workers. It was there that Jeremy and Deborah lived, two blocks from the North Plant. In the same area, but nearer the boundary of Hunky Hollow, was Cronin's house.

After work, Jeremy turned into Cronin's street. He had more energy than he wanted. The shift had been five hours today and that wasn't enough, not nearly enough, to stretch him, to vent off the strength of his body. He felt taut still, he felt like the afternoon: the air was hot and it had grown tight with humidity, but there was no promise of rain, only the tension of the unseen moisture, unreleased. He pitied Cronin even more now for his joblessness. And for worse: Cronin's family. He had a wife and an infant son and a daughter who was five, and they had no money beyond Cronin's paycheck. Jeremy stopped. What could he do? What could he bring to the man? Jeremy felt in his pocket, but payday wasn't until Monday. He had less than a quarter with him, and Cronin wouldn't take the money anyway. Damn this whole thing. "Damn," he said.

Jeremy moved on up the street, beneath the stunted maples, past the sounds of women shouting, a broom whisking, chickens clucking. He crossed the street, the tar sticky in the heat. Cronin's house was gray-shingled, three end-to-end rooms where he said the man who'd lived there before had once actually fired a shotgun clear through, from front door to back, filling his wife's lover's behind with buckshot as he was going out the door in his skivvies. These places were built right for something, Cronin had laughed.

Coming up on Cronin's house, Jeremy could hear a child crying. It was just another sound of the neighborhood, of the afternoon, a child crying. But as Jeremy moved, he listened to it more carefully: it was rising and falling and dry-sounding; tearless, as if it had been going on for a long time. He turned in at the worn, dirt trough of a path to Cronin's front steps. He went up the steps and stood at the screen door and the child's dry wail came from inside. It was not the little girl's voice crying, it was the piping sound of the infant. Jeremy felt a quick gathering in him, a reflex of his body as if to danger. And the tears of a child scraped at him, behind his eyes, even though his own child had shed no tears in dying. The sound within this house made Jeremy open the screen door without knocking. He stepped inside.

The first room was empty and dark and the child's cries stuttered into a brief silence and then resumed. Jeremy went forward, pushed a half-open door, and in the second room, the bedroom, he was in the presence of the sound. Three thin mattresses lay on the floor, the bedclothes knotted there; one mattress was stripped. The crib sat among them and, inside, the infant cried on.

Jeremy looked toward the door to the third room. It was open and there was a shadow and he approached it and in the kitchen, near the wooden sink, from a roof beam, on a twisted bedsheet, Cronin hung by the neck, his head angled sharply, his mouth open, his eyes gaping, his feet dangling, a chair knocked over beneath him. Jeremy stepped into the room. He stared for a moment at Cronin. The face was only faintly recognizable. Jeremy had known the movement there of laughter, anger, stubbornness—damn willful stubbornness, not this fixed stare. Jeremy felt a dangling in his chest, like Cronin's body. Then his fists clenched, his body flexed in anger, he was pumped full of enough power to beat the crap out of the two East St. Louis guys and Spud and any two others, right now, right in the yard, he was full of anger and power that had no object. Spud maybe. But Jeremy thought of Spud as a nothing in this, a little man with only a clipboard and somebody telling him what to do. Wabash Steel, then. Hagemeyer. Brenner flashed into Jeremy's head, whispering targets for this anger. The businessmen, banks, the government. But they were all faceless, vague. Distant. His arms were here, his fists were here, jumping up before him. "Dammit, Cronin," he said, and when he spoke he realized that he'd been hearing a sound. The baby was crying in the other room, but this was another sound, low, a panting. He turned. He was not alone in the room.

Sitting on a chair against the wall was Cronin's wife. She was facing the body and she was leaning forward, leaning toward the body and she was panting and standing beside her was the little girl. The little girl. Elizabeth's age. Cronin's little girl was standing with her body twisted behind her mother's chair and she too was watching her father. She was very quiet and she looked at Jeremy and then back at the dead man and her face was very still, very quiet, just like Elizabeth's face as she lay dying, her lungs packed tight with fluid, so tight that even the coughing had stopped. Cronin's child was watching her father hang from the roof beam and her mother let her watch, did not protect her, did not hold her, did not cover her eyes from this terrible thing and Jeremy's anger spun inside him and lunged at this woman. Jeremy could barely control his body now. He moved very carefully. He separated the girl from the woman. The child did not resist. She let him guide her to the bedroom and he was very conscious of how light his touch was on her, even as he wanted to release all of his strength. "Your brother needs you," he whispered to the girl. She continued into the dimness, toward the crying.

Jeremy turned and he moved to the woman in the chair. He knew how she'd hurt the child by letting her see this and he was angry only at her. She was here and his right arm was very strong and his fist squeezed but he knew that there was something wrong in what he wanted to do. His breathing was very fast, very hard. Cronin's wife was still panting, fixed on the body.

Jeremy stepped in front of her. Her eyes did not acknowledge him. He held back, held back, he opened his fist, made it open, made his hand flat, and he hit the woman hard across the face.

Aunt Adah grinned. She was proud of herself and she pushed at a wave in her hair. Deborah's mother had remarked on how Adah had gotten the tamale man out of bed and behind his cart so quickly.

"Norman does what I want," Adah said.

"Except marry you," Aunt Della said.

The two sisters were sitting beside each other on the swing on Miriam's porch. Deborah was sitting on a wicker chair and her mother was in a straight cane-bottom for her back.

Adah lifted her chin. "I don't have any intention of getting married again. I've done much better than tamale men in my life."

"At least we'd be sure to eat," Della said softly, suddenly serious.

Deborah watched her mother straighten in concern at this.

Deborah herself felt a ripple of helplessness. It was hard to hear these soft, serious turns in Della. Especially in her. She wasn't a complainer.

"Della?" Miriam said, and no more. Deborah understood this to mean: Are you hungry? Do you need something now?

Aunt Adah and Aunt Della lived together in the house left Adah by her first husband, dead in the Great War. They had a house but there was only a little money between them from an insurance policy from Adah's second husband, dead just before the stock market crash. Miriam was somewhat better off, Deborah's father having left this house and some money beyond the stocks that were worthless now. She'd resisted investing the cash in the real good times a few years ago and her hesitance had saved a bit of what she had. But she didn't have an excess, and Deborah knew her mother would be helpless, too, if Della and Adah developed pressing needs. With Jeremy working less than half the hours he had three years ago, Deborah could only watch and shudder when even Della turned serious over all this.

Adah said to Della, "If you didn't think about food so much, you'd have more of it. You envy me a man like Norman. But you'll never get him because you're not making yourself pretty anymore."

Miriam said, "Hush up, Adah. What are you saying? Della's hurting. Can't you see that?"

"I appreciate your defending me," Della said to Miriam in a voice flinty with unappreciation. "But do butt out. I'm not ready for pity yet. I'm not hurting at all." She turned on Adah. "Don't *you* ever get hungry? I've seen you just push our measly meal around the plate like you were a little queen. Hard times don't mean a thing to you, do they?"

"I live on love," Adah said, her hand rising to her hair.

"That's a hoot," Della said.

"Butt out?" Miriam had apparently been fuming.

"Miriam's right," Adah said. "You need pity, Della honey. Like Berenice."

"Adah," Miriam said sharply.

Deborah looked away into the yard as the three sisters sniped at each other. Deborah didn't want to hear any more for now. She watched a dragonfly flitting and hovering out in the sunlight and she wished she had a power over these women to stroke their heads and stop their words, to make them be gentle with each other. The voices slowed and then there was a silence and Deborah began to listen again. The swing chain creaked. Adah and Della had to have made at least a surface truce for this to be happening—they had to push in concert to swing together.

Deborah looked and the two women were swinging high, their feet rising simultaneously off the porch at each push. Their faces were set, Adah's arms were folded, Della's hands were gripping the edge of the seat. Deborah looked at her mother and she was looking out into the yard. Her mother closed her eyes, as if in pain. Deborah asked, "What is it, Mama?"

"I'm just thinking of Berenice . . . I don't know what to do for her."

"Stop talking about her so much, for one thing," Adah said.

Deborah jerked her face toward Adah. The swing was swooping away, as if Adah were running off after this remark. Then the swing stopped and began to rush forward and Deborah almost spoke, almost told her aunt off for her hardness, her vanity; Adah wanted less talk about Aunt Berenice because she wanted more talk about herself. But Deborah did not speak. Instead, her mother said, "Do be quiet, Adah," and that was enough. Adah began to pout and Deborah's anger was mitigated. Adah was a child. Her daddy had made her—the first of his daughters—a little bauble, Adah the ornament, and she felt she could never please anyone as she had pleased him, Deborah knew.

They all fell silent for a while and then Miriam smiled and said, "You were right, Della, about Bunny's being able to out-climb us all."

"She was a climber, all right," Della said.

Miriam laughed softly. "I remember every morning in the summer she was in black bloomers. And she'd go up anything . . . You were pretty little then, Della. Do you remember?"

"Sure. Clothes posts."

"That's right. She'd go up the line pegs . . . And somebody taught her—some boy on the street, she said, but she never said who—some boy taught her to go up the doorjamb and she'd sit on the transom."

"Mama hated that," Della said. "Bunny would scare the dickens out of her from up there."

"I don't remember Bunny so much as the climber," Adah said. "But she really liked the mud."

Deborah watched her mother as she paused and studied Adah. She seemed to be deciding—as Deborah tried now to decide—whether this was a way for Adah to attack Berenice.

"Don't you remember that?" Adah said in a voice tiny with flamboyant innocence.

"Yes," Deborah's mother said.

"That's why Mama was always happy to give her black bloomers," Della said.

"At lunch each day," Adah said, "I never saw her face without dirt on it or streaks of mud in her sweat."

"That's true, Adah," Miriam said. "But then it came to about two o'clock. Do you remember the transformation? Berenice would come in on her own every afternoon at two o'clock and she'd have a bath and she'd put on a dress—she had one little white dress with a ruffle at the bodice—and she'd sit on the porch to wait for Papa. All of a sudden the muddy little climber was the prissiest little girl in Wabash. She'd watch and watch and when she heard the shift whistle blow at the North Plant, she could hardly hold still. Finally Papa would come walking down the street and she'd run her legs off to get to him and they'd walk that last half block together."

The sisters paused, the chain creaked, and Deborah wondered why it was that Adah and Della and her mother had never competed with Berenice for their father's attention as he walked home from the mill. It sounded as if Berenice had had that honor to herself. But Deborah could never ask this question, for fear it would cause an argument. The bickering of these women, the niggling little competitions and jealousies between them, were a source of constant distress for Deborah.

"This is terrible," Miriam said. "We're sounding as if Bunny was dead or something."

"You started it," Adah said.

"Why shouldn't we talk like that?" Della said. "I like to talk about the times when we weren't so terribly afraid of what was going to happen next."

Adah nodded. "I like it too."

"We were five swell sisters," Della said and eyes were full of tears.

Adah's face turned sharply to Della and for a moment Deborah didn't know why. Then she realized that it was Della's numbering of the sisters that was the offense. The number implied the existence of a fifth sister, Effie, who was never mentioned among the other four. Deborah couldn't remember how she had learned that a fifth sister existed, but when she did, her mother was very vague about her. Effie was dead, Deborah came to understand, and the death must have been horrible, for it seemed such a painful subject that Deborah had always respected the silence that her mother and aunts desired.

"Sure we were swell," Miriam said.

"Some of us still are," Adah said.

Della wiped at her eyes, wiped away the nostalgic tears, and she said, "Mama never did slap your face enough, Adah honey."

Deborah clutched the arms of her chair, ready to rise. She expected the talk to get openly angry now, and she would just walk away from it. But Adah surprised her. Instead of attacking Della, she said softly, "She hit me plenty. That's why she's not in our house, Della. That's why she lives alone and spends her time worrying about rats in her house from the dump. She'd rather live with rats than her Adah."

"Don't talk like that," Miriam said, but faintly.

A silence rolled over the women, and Deborah found it as painful as the bickering. She rose from her chair and the faces of the three sisters turned to her. She felt powerless before them.

She was the ornament, not Adah. She could only sit and watch and listen as these women she loved hurt each other and themselves.

"Are you going, Debby?" Adah said, her voice stripped of its affectations, the voice suddenly—unexpectedly—pretty, like a blue jay's nesting call.

"I'm going to wait for Jeremy," she said. "His shift is over soon."

"You're blessed with a good man," Della said. "You go on home now."

Deborah's mother said, "Debby? Is everything going okay?" Deborah understood the question as her mother's apology for having paid no attention to her on the porch, for having gotten caught up in the bickering that she too didn't like.

"I'm okay," Deborah said and she went down the steps and into the yard. The voices quickly resumed behind her but she couldn't hear any words. She turned into the street and she passed under a sugar maple and she wondered if Aunt Berenice would teach her how to climb a tree.

J eremy didn't show up at the time he usually did. The house was clean. Deborah had cleaned it twice today. Even though the soot from the mill came inside now that the windows were open, she could always stay ahead of the cleaning. She alone was in the house. The house was still when she was.

She sat at the table under the kitchen window. The sun was behind the split trunk of the old pin oak across the alley and so Jeremy was undeniably late. The concern this gave her sharpened the regard she had for her husband. Two things she knew: he was not with a woman; he was not drunk. What was left was the unknown, and she began to tremble faintly. If he'd been hurt at the mill, there would have been someone here already to tell her, she reasoned. She moved to the front porch and sat on the step and tucked her legs up to her chest, spreading her skirt out uniformly at her ankles.

After a long while she saw him coming up the street. She rose but she did not run to him as she wanted to do. Now that he was approaching her and she knew he was safe, her regard for him drooped into sadness. She knew his reserve, how little he would say and how hard it would be for her to enter the events of his life away from her. She knew, as well—though only as a vague lethargy in her limbs, an uneasiness on the surface of her skin—that he would not touch her tonight. She didn't blame him for that; so much so that this unease was accepted without a conscious awareness of its source. But as Jeremy approached, she grew physically conscious of him, keenly conscious. He was a large man, a powerful man, a man who preserved for Deborah the comforting physical proportion of father to child. And more: other women she knew had husbands of physical power; but their power carried what for her was a disquieting element. Those men were rough-skinned, matted with body hair. Jeremy was as smooth-skinned as a mother—his arms, his chest, his back, his legs. She was more conscious now of the unease that had begun when she first saw him approaching, she was conscious now of wanting him to fill her up, of the long time it had been since he'd made love to her.

He turned in at their gate and his face was before her, his eyes black and flat as coke. She wiped a smudge of dirt from his cheek, which was unstubbled even at this hour of the afternoon. "Are you all right?" she said.

"Yes," Jeremy said and he felt empty at last, he felt tired even, though the tiredness wasn't physical enough to satisfy him. Her hand that brushed his face felt cold. He wondered if she was all right. He didn't want her to be sick. This thought surprised him, but maybe Cronin's death had made him sensitive.

The police had come; the wife had wept bitterly and she had said nothing to anyone about the bruise spreading on her cheek; the little girl never shed a tear, even when she saw her mother crying. The child perhaps made him worry now about Deborah's

health, her cold hand. All this swirled through him as shapeless
as oven smoke. He had no idea how to speak his feelings and he
went past Deborah and into the house. He passed through the
living room, the bedroom, and into the kitchen where he went
to the sink and ran a basin full of water and he took off his shirt.

Deborah stood at the kitchen door, and when his back was
bared she crossed to the table and looked into the yard, seeing
nothing, holding back her desire for him. "Did something happen?" she said.

Jeremy turned to her, his face and forearms wet. Her profile
against the window brushed him like her hand on his face a few
minutes ago. But her profile was warm. The line of her brow
was long, her eyes and mouth were soft-edged, soft, but her chin
was strong, as strong and square as a man's, and it made her
beautiful; Jeremy knew she was beautiful, she was very beautiful
to him as he watched her, even now, and the beauty made him
weary and sad and he felt cold, felt Cronin dangling in the center
of the room. "Do you know Cronin?" he said.

"Cronin?"

"Did I mention him?"

"No," she said, thinking: You never talk, almost never;
there's so much I don't know. But she thought this with no anger.
This was the man she'd always known.

"He was a man I was friendly with at work." He paused.

"Yes?"

"He killed himself today."

This chilled Deborah, though she'd never heard of the man;
and it wasn't for him, exactly, that she was moved. It was for
everyone who was desperate now. She looked at her hands lying
on the table.

Jeremy had already said more than he'd expected to. The
hard words, the feelings suggested by them: Deborah was too
fragile for these things; she was a woman and the soft yielding
that was her nature made him restless, awkward. He needed
flint to strike his feelings against. Her softness sucked his words
in and he could not steel himself, could not harden and flex

himself before her. He dipped his hands and wrists into the water.

"Are you okay?" Deborah said.

"Yes."

"I worry," she said. She herself didn't expect these words. She couldn't even really say what they were about. Certainly Jeremy. She worried about him, his safety, his happiness, even. But the words were meek, she knew, a reflex that she disliked in herself. And Jeremy was standing over her.

"Are *you* okay?" he said. Freed from speaking about himself, freed from his own feelings, he felt focused once more, he felt strong, though he didn't know how to use his strength, how to wipe away this tremor in Deborah's voice.

"I'm okay," she said.

"You shouldn't worry."

"It's nothing. I didn't mean it."

"I'm here."

She rose before him. "I know that. You know how much I like that." She put her hands on his shoulders. His arms came around her and she felt tiny. Part of her let go, eased into this dependency. But her mind broke away, stalked back to the porch of her mother, looked at the timid, bickering lives there, cried out in impotent anger. Only Jeremy's arms, her own hands flat on his bare back, his smooth back, only her cheek turned now against his hairless chest, made her mind fade. And just before it did, she thought: If he were to make love to me again, if we could love each other physically as we once did, I'd just be one of them, I'd be just like my mother and my aunts. A crazy thought; but she held it for a moment, the irony of it even shaping a faint smile on her lips, very briefly, and then she let it go.

That night they lay together in the dark and Deborah had no expectations anymore, either of touching or of sleep. For the first few minutes it was the touching she missed the most. But soon that faded and then it was the sleep that swelled her yearning. As always it would be deep into the dark early morning before she would sleep. Not that her restless mind would accomplish anything. There would only be slivers of the day, like broken glass, tumbling in her head, bits of her aunts' conversation, glimpses of housework and of moving through the streets and, on this night, of Berenice in a tree. Deborah would be anxious but unable to focus her feelings. Even as Berenice came now—her legs dangling from the tree, her face still—Deborah didn't know whether to be amused or fearful. And she fought off the thoughts of her child. That was what took her strength in the nights of her sleeplessness. She could not give way to the grief that waited in her as restless as her passion for Jeremy. And it was more than grief. Elizabeth's death, in a room just like this one, her death coming quietly so that Deborah yearned even for her daughter to cough again, to make a sound again: that death had given her more than grief; it had given her a keen sense of her own powerlessness. It had always been that way. Her father had died of pneumonia too, his chest full of the sound of locusts, a terrible scraping, a rattling, brittle feet, dry wings in him. She'd been twelve and she'd wondered at this: her father's soul was surely a light and beautiful thing and would extricate itself with a sound like the breeze moving through the tops of the trees or perhaps, at the end, a rushing wind as on the day of Pentecost; but not this sound, not this ugly nesting insect sound. And she'd had no power then, either. No way to protect the one she loved. She turned her face to the wall and Jeremy heard her, knew she was awake, sensed her waiting.

He wanted in his mind to make love to her. He could will himself to extend his hands, to stroke her, kiss her, and there'd been a time after his daughter's death when he'd done that, night after night. But night after night his flesh had recoiled, had shriveled and grown cold, even as he'd touched her, even as he'd widened his eyes, taken in what he could clearly see as the taut beauty of Deborah's body. He could touch her now, but he remembered touching her, perhaps the first time after Elizabeth's death: running under his hands was the skin of his wife but all that filled him was a pale light, the memory of a light bulb on a wire from the ceiling, dangling from the ceiling, slack, like a hanged man, its light pale from a newspaper wrapped around the bulb to mask the glare for his daughter's eyes. His hands were his measure of her sickness, her skin was hot beneath his hands, her forehead, her cheek. The child's fever pulsed in his palms and there was a smell of burning. The newspaper had begun to scorch and he rose and unwrapped the bulb and wrapped it again. Lizzy was dying. Then Lizzy was dead. And Jeremy couldn't make love. He had never actually craved to enter a woman. He had always been plucked there unexpectedly, and not often. He had felt like his father. Abraham Jeremiah Cole. His father had been an old man. Dead early in Jeremy's life, but by his death already an old man and sexless, in Jeremy's eyes. He'd never seen his father touch his mother. His father had had the astringency of death. Jeremy's skin felt the astringency now. His daughter was dead and he'd been very angry for a time. But there had been no one to turn against. God had been as distant to him as the banks and big business and the government were today at Cronin's. To receive his anger there had only been this impulse to touch; he had grown angry at that. It had brought him a child that made him cry, him, the man worth two Hungarians at the coke ovens. All this was a welter in him, was as hot and shapeless as a flame, and he turned his face the opposite way from his wife. He was sorry. But his hands clenched and tightened and they could not move.

Jeremy woke the next day with a bleary regret, like the sour morning taste in his mouth. He stared at the pale foxing of the blinds and then closed his eyes, and it was his father that he felt bad about. Last night he'd thought of his father as if the only memories of the man were of his withering. His father had been a quiet man and though his silence seemed passionless, the woman he never touched never said a word against him.

Jeremy himself could remember moments when it was clear

that his father was trying to be good to him, trying to love. Jeremy had come to believe that there was some sadness in his father that could not express itself. Sparks rose up like panicky insects and his father was on the opposite side of a camp fire. Jeremy was fifteen. His father would soon be dead, but this night they were together in the Ozark Mountains. Jeremy's father had always made sure Jeremy could handle guns, though he almost never fired a gun himself, even when they were hunting. At age ten Jeremy could hit birds in flight with an air rifle and his father's hand would always come and rest on his shoulder after a good shot. This day in the Ozarks he'd let Jeremy practice with his long-barrel Colt revolver, the one he'd carried as a young man. Jeremy had shot well with the revolver, his arm already strong and steady, but in the dark by the fire Jeremy could feel his father's unspoken sadness. Jeremy wanted the sadness to be cast into an animal—like the demons into the pigs in the Bible story his mother had read to him—and then he could shoot it. The sadness would fly into a squirrel or into a pheasant and he could kill the thing. A simple target, a simple act.

Instead, his father began to speak. He talked about another camp fire. Back in the seventies. He left the Ozarks on horseback in early fall and headed north and came out on the prairie near the Kansas border. Late in the afternoon on the first day out of the hills, in a stretch of prairie that still had not been plowed over or grazed off, that still had its turkey-foot grass with its purple claws clutching as high as a man's head, he saw a yellow haze off in the west. He knew at once it was a fire. By dusk he could feel the smoke faintly in his eyes. He had just reached the trail to St. Louis and he could see the smoke, dark blue now, filling the western sky. The air was thickening and it smelled ropy. He turned east and he rode hard for as long as he could and then finally he stopped and built a camp fire in a dry gully. He sat awake most of that night before his own fire and he remembered the stories of the Indians. Before the war, they would set fires in the autumn. They would torch the prairies in a great ring to drive the buffaloes into a killing ground. They would hunt with fire, barely able to control this force they used, sometimes swept away by it themselves. Jeremy's father stopped speaking for a time and Jeremy wanted no more of these words; he wanted silence now, wanted to be alone. His father frightened him, the man's face drawn near the flames. Indian fire, his father said, and Jeremy could see all the animals rushing to the center. But as if his father had sensed his son's wish, the man said no more. If the sadness was part of this tale, it had been driven deep inside by the flames and only the face remained, the silent, flickering face.

Jeremy sat up in the bed and he felt the circle around him, burning. But awake now, he knew it was all right. The circle did not move. It held its place like the fires of the mill and he was calm in the center. The mill waited for him and he rose up.

Gus walked silently beside Jeremy and finally the man glanced over and Jeremy gave him a nod. Gus nodded in return. They entered the alleyway under the front of the A-battery and turned at once to mount the steps to the bench level that ran the length of the ovens at their base. Jeremy paused at the top of the steps. Gus paused, too. He caught Jeremy's eye and nodded once more. There was no apparent meaning in this but a second hello. The man's round, blond, pocked face waited and Jeremy returned the nod. He knew what Gus was saying: Thanks, these other bastards don't talk to Hungarians.

They moved to a narrow door. The heat from the battery pressed against them but they paused. Gus waited as well. Jeremy wasn't surprised. The man knew how to work. This couldn't be rushed. When they worked up on the coke ovens, this, at least, was left to them as a transition from the outer world. After a moment Jeremy opened the door and they stepped into a tight, metallic room. Gus went farther inside and Jeremy put the other man out of his mind for now. From a hook he removed a heavy jacket and put his right arm in the sleeve, pulled the jacket upwards and inserted his left arm. He fastened the jacket from the top but left the neck button for last. He pulled the collar up slightly at the back. He picked a pair of goggles from a shelf near the hook. He fastened the clasp of the goggles at the back of his neck but he did not pull it over his eyes. He put on his gloves. Every movement was unconscious now; the deliberation was a reflex. His body moved with the necessary reserve to prepare for the work it would do.

Suddenly Brenner was in the room. Jeremy looked at him but he felt no resentment at his rush. He should, he knew, but the man had other things on his mind and Jeremy understood that. Brenner looked at Jeremy and his eyes were alert and steady, waiting. Jeremy realized an answer was expected about the unemployed council meeting; he realized, too, with a faint surprise, that he hadn't even thought about it since yesterday. Brenner waited and Jeremy thought, instead, about Cronin. What would Brenner say about that? Come to the meeting, he'd say. The answers are there.

Brenner nodded at Jeremy as if to release him from an answer for now. Brenner went on into the room and greeted Gus with a cuff on the arm and loud words. "How ya doin', Gus, how ya doin'?" Gus's neck stiffened a little. He smiled and nodded in return but Jeremy could see it was forced, could see the suspicion in Gus's eyes.

Jeremy stepped from the room. He would isolate himself now. It was good, working the pusher-side doors. His actions were independent except when it was time to latch or unlatch a door. Eleven years he'd worked at the mill and the job still fit him. He thought of his mother holding his hands, speaking in a moth-soft voice about his hands, their hardness, the traces of mill grit around his fingernails, and she was sorry, she said, so sorry that her needs had brought him back from college. She closed her eyes in sadness and Jeremy wanted to explain exactly how it was all right so she'd believe him once and for all. He was happy to take care of her. And he liked the work at the mill.

You could have friends but you didn't have to fill the air between you with talk; and when something came over you—you got angry or full of desperate energy or you felt like there was nothing inside you but a lump of slag in your chest—you could be alone, truly alone. But these were things that could never find words when his mother was like this. He would just turn his hands and hold hers and he would say it was okay, he was happy. And he was. For when she was dead, he remained. By then there was Deborah to care for, but it was for himself that he stayed at the mill. College had made him restless. He wanted the fire around him, like Indian fire, and in the center he wanted to act, not think.

Jeremy moved out onto the metal bench platform that ran along the base of the tall, slender oven doors, door after door stretching far away, before the pusher machine track that lay over the rail and twenty feet below. The whistle began. The flow of its sound did not modulate. The sounds of the mill fell off slightly when it was done, and Jeremy heard Brenner and Gus coming up behind him, their steps clattering on the platform.

Jeremy picked up a shovel from where it leaned against the rail and he waited for the pusher machine to come to life again. Up the narrow columns of doors, beyond the top of the battery, the sky was the color of an alcohol flame.

The pusher began to whine, its engine caught and grumbled, and Jeremy took his shovel and stood beside the door of the oven that was next on the discharge schedule. Gus and Brenner helped the extractor ease forward, its tangle of latch linkage and lifters pressing now at the door. Then Jeremy bent with the other two men and the connections were made and he straightened and the extractor pivoted the latch, lifted the door, and drew back. A breaker of heat rolled over Jeremy. He did not move and the heat churned at his face, pummeled his body, pulled his muscles taut. The door hung near him, its brick belly glowing at the edges, its center mottled gray. For a brief moment door, oven, and man were suspended, then the great head of the pusher's ram slid silently from the machine, across the billowing space, and into the corridor of the oven. The press of heat eased slightly on Jeremy's face as the ram went deeper in, pushing.

He could see in his mind the coke falling on the other side, could see the coke moving through the oven as a vast, burning column, then stretching over the train car and crumbling, turning fluid in its fall, the only image of the mill that made him vaguely uneasy.

The ram stopped and began its withdrawal. Jeremy tightened his hands on the shovel and watched as the head of the pusher emerged and a stream of burning coke rushed out of the floor of the oven. The coke fell in flameless burning, exploded soundlessly into dust, flared, then smoked on the bench. When the ram was gone, Jeremy stepped in front of the open doorway, into the battering heat. He drove his shovel beneath the pile of coke, felt the gritless scrape of metal under the pile, lifted the shovel, and looked into the oven.

There was no periphery in his gaze. He felt as if he had entered the oven: the corridor burned without flame, with no possibility of ending; in the path through, the heat was visible, rolling like the sea. Jeremy threw the shovelful of coke deep into the oven and lowered his face, numb now from the heat, to retrieve the remainder of the coke on the bench. He took it all in a swoop of the shovel and lifted his eyes once more into the narrow corridor stretching away as if infinitely, as if the forms of buildings and sky beyond the open far end existed only as an image within the oven, a world burned clean. He felt tightly bound by his clothing, safe within the wrappings of his clothing, for the corridor plucked at him. This was the balance he expected, this was the fine balance of a moment that would be repeated a hundred times today. But suddenly, in the oven, in the image there, a dark silhouette was projected from his mind, a dangling body, an angled head, two figures watching, one a child. He flung the coke from his shovel and did not wait to see it fall. He pulled back and stood motionless as the door came forward and covered the opening. He bent to the latches with the others and he rose and Cronin always gave him a wink at this moment.

The latch turned and Jeremy picked up a hose. He knew the seal on this oven was imperfect. The flames burst through the thin gap at the rim of the door. He sprayed water on the fire. Where the water touched, the flame was transformed into yellow smoke, heavy with tar, that rolled up from the oven and at last sealed the door.

After the fires were quenched, the door sealed, Jeremy remained before the oven. The bell on the pusher began to ring as the machine moved down the line. But Jeremy lingered. This was usually another fine little moment in the rhythm of his work: he would hold the vision of the oven in his mind. He alone was allowed the moments before the open door; he alone saw its world, burned pure. He was separated, but the separation implied a connection that had once existed and would exist again.

But it had changed this time. The outside world had intruded. Cronin, dead. He'd intruded because his death had flowed from the mill.

Jeremy moved down the platform, caught up to Brenner. "Nick," he said.

Nick turned.

Jeremy said, "I'm coming on Monday to the meeting."

That night Deborah knew she wouldn't sleep and when Jeremy had been still for a long time and his breath was slow and faint, she rose up and dressed and went out the back door and into the yard. The night was thick and passionless. She moved into the alley. The impulse that brought her here had promised her contentment in the loneliness of the night, but she knew at once it had been a lie. Her skin prickled with a chill though the air was warm, and she found tears in her eyes, purposeless tears. Then she heard a distant sound, voices, taunting voices uttering wordless syllables of mock sympathy, taunting her for her tears, she knew. The voices approached and they were overhead, high overhead, and they grew more distinct: the voices of geese. She looked up and was surprised to find that the sky was clear. There were stars. No moon, but the stars were there, and somewhere above her, invisible in the night, geese were flying over and the put-on sympathy of their cries turned now to feigned surprise, phony wonder. Ah, they cried with the nasal voices of adolescents. Ahh.

Deborah lowered her head and walked down the alley. She pressed any thoughts from her mind. She walked to make herself weary so she could sleep. But her body would not yield; it kept its vigor, and finally she found herself in West Wabash, not far from Grandma Birney's house. She decided at least to go to the house and look. If it was dark, she'd turn back. Her grandmother had always been a strong-willed, even eccentric, woman with her own patterns of doing things, and it was possible that she too was still awake.

Deborah turned down a gravel road that skirted the edge of an open field. Out across the field, in the dark, was the levee. Ahead, along the levee, were a few flickering lights. Fires at the shantytown, Deborah guessed. She turned off the gravel onto a dirt street, and as she drew near to her grandmother's house, the impulse she'd followed to go out into the night carried another promise: not solitary contentment now, but some time with her grandmother and maybe an understanding of this circle of women that Deborah was kin to. She held back her eagerness as she walked. Grandmother Birney might be asleep. Deborah had to stop and turn around in a full circle, peering at the few dark houses to find the right one. She saw no lights. She smelled the rot of the dump nearby, though she couldn't decide from what direction the smell came.

She moved farther east, along the street, and she could make out in the starlight a side-gabled hall-and-parlor house that she knew was her grandmother's. At first the place looked dark. But she kept moving toward it and the angle of her sight shifted and she saw an isolated light through a window. She let herself hope now. Her grandmother was awake. Deborah crossed the front yard, which was ragged with weeds.

She did not knock but moved, instead, to the window. The light was faint and she wanted to see her grandmother inside, awake, before she disturbed her. The house was two rooms wide and one room deep and this was the parlor side. Deborah looked in. Beyond the old fan-backed couch and chairs, in the far corner of the room, Grandma Birney sat at a desk with a coal-oil lamp. She was writing on a piece of paper. Deborah returned to the front door and knocked.

There was no answer. Deborah knew that her grandmother's hearing was still acute and then it occurred to her to call through the door. She knocked again and called, "Grandma," thinking: Why am I so timid here?

"Debby?" her grandmother said. "Is that you?" Her voice came from the hallway.

"Yes."

"Come in, honey. You don't need to knock here. Just walk on in."

Deborah opened the door and stepped in and from the darkness her grandmother's arms came out and the two women hugged. Then Grandmother Birney hooked her arm in Deborah's and guided her into the living room. She said, "Debby, is everything okay? That boy hasn't left you, has he?"

Deborah laughed. "No, Grandma. He's not left me."

"You're welcome here anytime, you know. It's just that it's so late I thought maybe something had happened."

"I'm just having trouble sleeping. I've always had that problem. Since I was a girl."

Grandma Birney stopped. They were in the center of the parlor floor, and her brow furrowed in thought. Deborah was so often, and so recently, conscious of the faces of her aunts and mother that looking now at her grandmother it seemed as if the likeness had flowed the other way, as if Grandma Birney had gotten her high-cheeked face from them. She looked most like Adah, in spite of Adah's attempts to make herself younger. Behind Adah's primping and Grandma Birney's deep-creased age, there was a kinship of bone that was very clear. Even as Grandma Birney turned thoughtful now in a way Deborah could never imagine in Adah, the dominant impression about the old woman's eyes was not that thinking was going on behind them but that they were set wide apart, almost wide enough for Deborah to lay three fingers cleanly between them, this feature fixed and unchangeable, and in this she was just like her first daughter. "You never could sleep well?" she said. "Why can't I remember that about you?"

"Maybe you never knew."

"That seems unlikely."

"There's a lot we don't know about people we love," Deborah said. "I was sort of aware of that just today."

"It's so good to see you though, Debby." Grandma Birney cupped Deborah's elbow and guided her onto a seat on the couch. "Can I get you some coffee?" She instantly answered her own question with a shake of the head. "No, not that," she said. "That would keep you awake even longer."

"I'm okay, Grandma. I don't need anything."

"I've got the opposite problem. Lately I always want to sleep. That makes me nervous."

"I'd gladly trade you problems," Deborah said.

Her grandmother sat down beside her on the couch and leaned to her with an air of urgency. "Don't say that. I'm an old woman. You don't want an old woman's problems. You stay awake. That's okay."

Suddenly her grandmother's words, her manner, fit together, and Deborah felt she understood the woman's fear. The increasing need to sleep was leading to the sleep of death: that was what her grandmother was afraid of. Deborah felt herself pitying her grandmother in silence. But she forced herself to speak. "Now, Grandma, you don't have to think that wanting to sleep is . . ." Then the words stopped. She couldn't bring herself to state the fear. Surely this was a private matter for her grandmother.

But Deborah stammered only briefly, for Grandma Birney seemed already to know what was meant. "That's not how a person dies," the woman said. "I'm not afraid of sleep."

Deborah caught the denial—Oh, I didn't mean that—in her own throat and did not let it out.

And Grandma Birney didn't seem offended. She patted Deborah's hand and said, "I've watched a lot of people get old and die and I've noticed something about them. They all start forgetting things. Have you noticed that?" She paused, as if the question needed an answer.

"Yes."

"*That's* the way it happens. You start by forgetting where you put your eyeglasses. Then you forget to close the windows in a blowing rain. Then you forget—you can't remember no matter how hard you try—what day of the week it is. Then you go out one day and forget the way home. Then you forget one of your daughters. Entirely. Somebody—a stranger you meet—asks you how many daughters you have and you say four when you really have five . . ."

Deborah was struck that there was something she wanted to ask her grandmother, but it didn't quite reveal itself and her grandmother continued in her point and Deborah let it go.

" . . . Then you wake up one morning and you don't quite remember the room or the house, even . . . This is how it happens, Debby. I'm sure of it. You just keep forgetting. It gets worse and worse until one morning, just before waking up, you forget it all. You just forget that there's anything to wake up to . . . You see what I mean? That's what I'm fighting here."

Deborah didn't know what to say to all this. She was distracted by the thought she had a few moments ago; what was she going to ask her grandmother?

"But maybe you're right, Debby. Maybe sleep has something to do with it. I have been awful anxious to stay awake. And it's in sleep that you don't have control of your mind. There may be something to what you say." Grandma Birney fell silent for a moment and her thoughtfulness changed abruptly to cheer. She patted Deborah's hand again. "It's so good to see you. You walk in and I'm filled with wonderful memories, Debby . . . How's your mama?"

The image of her mother brought back the front porch conversation of the afternoon and Deborah realized what she wanted to ask. About Effie. "Grandma . . . your memories, what if they're sad? Do you mind remembering them?"

"No. The sad ones are sometimes the best for keeping you alive. They don't go away so easily."

"Then can I ask you a question?"

"Of course."

"How did Effie die?"

Grandma Birney grew very still. Her eyes grew still like her daughters' eyes, though there was nothing that looked like sadness in them. Then she said, "Who told you Effie is dead?"

"No one . . . That is, I guess I must have assumed it. She seemed to be such a painful subject for everyone. Nobody wanted to talk about her. I thought she surely must have died a terrible death."

Grandma Birney laughed a faint, dry laugh. "The truth of it is that your Aunt Effie is alive and living in St. Louis. Just over the McKinley Bridge, in fact. But she's as good as dead, as far as this family is concerned."

"What did she do?"

"She became a Cat-licker."

"A what?"

"A Roman Catholic. Your Aunt Effie left the True God and the circle of her family and got caught up in all that black magic. And that was that."

Deborah felt blank. She'd always heard that Catholics were different somehow, but the intensity of feeling that these differences seemed to prompt baffled her. They'd never been explained and she'd never had any Catholic friends for her to learn something on her own. She was embarrassed by her ignorance now. "So Aunt Effie didn't want to see us anymore?"

"Let's just say that the decision was mutual."

Deborah almost asked her grandmother what the Catholics did that was so bad, but she didn't want any more conflict today. Aunt Effie was alive. That was enough for the time being. It intrigued her and now that she had another living aunt, she didn't want her to be immediately turned into the brunt of more gossip and criticism. She wanted to hear her grandmother's pity, not her anger. "Aunt Berenice had a spell yesterday."

"Poor little Bunny," Grandma Birney said at once, with no condescension at all, only a mother's tenderness. This tone made Deborah's breath catch in gratitude, and her grandmother asked, "What happened?"

"She climbed a tree in the yard. She wanted to have some peace, I guess. She certainly looked peaceful when I first arrived."

Grandma Birney shook her head slowly. "I'm not sure she'll ever have much of that." But she said no more. She folded her hands on her lap and looked toward the darkness at the window. Deborah waited for her to share the memories she was obviously having, but no words came. The memories had another purpose for her grandmother now, Deborah knew, one that did not have to include the telling of them.

"Grandma, can you explain something that puzzles me? I know how Aunt Berenice used to dress up for her daddy every afternoon."

"That's true."

"Why was it she could sort of have Grandpa Birney to herself as he came down the street? The way the others act now . . . I mean, I just wonder why there wasn't any jealousy over that. Why did they let her have him all alone?"

"Because I'd've jerked a knot in their tails if they didn't."

"You kept them . . . ?"

"The little ones were manageable. Your mother and Della."

"And Effie."

Grandma Birney's face grew unexpectedly hard. But just briefly. "Effie was still in diapers. The young ones were happy to stay with me if I said so."

"And Adah?"

"Adah." That was all Grandma Birney said. Nothing followed the name, spoken like a dropped pot.

"Why did you stop Adah? She and Grandpa were real close, weren't they?"

"They were." Again Deborah's grandmother paused. But this

time, after a moment, her voice loosened a bit. Not that she seemed warm, or even reminiscent; rather, she was matter-of-fact. "Adah knew how to handle her father. Berenice needed help. She needed something. So I made sure she had that little time, if she wanted it, even if I had to lock Adah in the cellar, which I did once."

Her grandmother grew silent again and Deborah was relieved by that. The talk had grown both bitter and sad and Deborah had come here to escape that. A naive expectation, she realized. The house, the night, were very still. There was only a tiny scrabbling sound somewhere, a dry splintery sound that Deborah was about to identify when her grandmother said, "Adah was always a willful girl. Willful and foolish."

"She's suffering now, I think," Deborah said, searching for the same little spot of pity in her grandmother that she'd shown earlier over Berenice.

"Oh, I'm sure she is." But there was nothing in her grandmother's voice to suggest sympathy. Then she sighed and softened. "She and Della are taking in other people's laundry, I hear. Della wouldn't let Adah get away without helping her. Maybe that's all for the best. There was a pretty good little nest egg for them from that sick old man of a second husband Adah married. An insurance policy. But I'm glad to see they realize it won't keep them both fed to the end of their lives. Adah hanging a yardful of other people's clothes at a dollar a household so she can eat. Maybe that's the best thing that could happen to her."

With another silence the brittle little sound was instantly clear to Deborah. It came from inside the walls. "Grandma, do you really have rats?"

"What's that?" Grandma Birney seemed faintly confused by the abrupt change in the subject.

"I'm sorry. I just heard that sound. Are they rats?"

"Rats. Yes, that's right." This was spoken not with fear or revulsion but with a vigor that seemed almost playful.

"Have you seen them?"

"Coming and going. Yes. And I find things chewed on in the house."

"Are you doing anything?"

"My mama had a remedy for rats and I'm just beginning to try it. She saw it work when she was growing up, though she never had to use it herself, thank God."

"Are they dangerous to you, Grandma?"

"It's where they put the dump now. And those hoboes down the levee. Maybe the water, too. River rats. The few I've caught sight of are black as a crow's eye."

"What are you doing?"

"Rats are smart animals, you know. Now, this sounds a little odd, but my mama said she saw it work in the Ozarks over and over . . . You write the rats a letter. You write to them courteously at first, but you make it real clear that they're not wanted and you tell them why. It's good, too, to offer them a suggestion as to where to go and why that'd be a good place for them. Then you roll the letter up and grease it with lard and you put it where they can find it. I figure it's worth a try. My mama was no fool and she believed in it."

Deborah was surprised to find herself caught up in this idea. Her grandmother had frankly conceded how odd this sounded and then had opened her own mind to it. So it didn't seem to be an act of craziness. Spilled salt over the shoulder, bless a sneeze. Why not? Deborah even found that the idea appealed to her. Write to the darn things. Tell them to go to hell. Plenty of times people talk to other people just knowing that they're not going to listen. Why not write to the rats? "Do you think it'll work, Grandma?"

"If I say the right things." She sounded serious. "Rats are smart animals and maybe they can understand."

Deborah listened for the sound of the rats in the walls, but it had stopped.

Grandma Birney said, "I was just finishing a letter when you knocked." She got up and crossed to her desk and returned with several sheets of paper. "You know," she said, "you used to be quite a letter writer, Debby."

"Me?"

"Yes. The summer when you were eight you wrote me a letter every day."

"I remember that."

"And you'd sneak up to the mailbox—I was in the frame house on Quincy then—you'd sneak up and put it in the box and run and hide behind a tree and wait for me to come out and find my mail."

"You always made a big show of that for me," Deborah said and she leaned to her grandmother and kissed her on the cheek.

"You were such a smart little girl." Grandma Birney seemed to forget the letter in her hand and she gazed away, out the window. Deborah was curious now about the letter, but she didn't want to disturb her grandmother's thoughts. The reverie ended abruptly and had gone in a direction Deborah hadn't expected; her grandmother said, "You're a smart *woman* too."

"What have you written to the rats?"

"I was going to start off, 'Pay attention now, you filthy little turd eaters.' " Grandma Birney giggled. "Excuse me, Debby honey."

"They maybe need some rough talk."

"No. I decided that wasn't the way to do it. Not in a first letter, at least. Here's what I came up with . . . Can you read my writing?"

"I think so." Deborah took the letter and read Grandma Birney's large, loopy hand:

Dear River Rats,

I assume you're river rats because I caught sight of you a few times and I'm giving you the benefit of the doubt. You look too refined to be dump rats and that's why I think you'll understand it if I write to you in a reasonable tone. Here's how things are. I'm a cranky old lady with a real tough streak and not above buying strong poison to make an end of you. Maybe that doesn't sound reasonable after I said I was going to be so, but I figured you might as well know the worst of it right off. I've always been tough. Ask any of my daughters and they'll tell you. They'd even say *too* tough probably. But I don't care about that. I did what I thought was right and they always deserved it. It means you don't love them only if they don't deserve it. Not that love's got anything to do with what *you* deserve. I'm just saying I'm a tough old gal which you should have figured out by finding me living all alone in a grubby depressing part of town like this with the levee so close and all the bad things that happen out there. So if you want to have some good advice you better go elsewhere for food and lodging and leave my house before sundown on Saturday or things will get real unpleasant for you and even fatal. I would suggest you go on down the levee aways to the hobo jungle. They're real dirty down there and you're sure to find plenty to eat because they're just drunken men who can't keep watch on what they've got, which is unlike me who keeps things in tins and is real clean. So be on your way by Saturday sundown at the latest if you know what's good for you.

Your friend for the time being,
Mrs. Carl Birney

Deborah felt like a schoolchild watching the teacher stand some other kid up for discipline—a sneaky, pleasant little feeling—happy it's not her. "If I was a rat," she said, "this letter would make me very nervous."

"You think so?"

"I'd get out by *tomorrow* night and not even wait till Saturday."

"Oh, I'm glad to hear it." Grandma Birney yawned. "I'm so glad to hear it." She closed her eyes and though she was still sitting upright, she seemed to sleep.

"Grandma?" Deborah said it softly. There was no response.

Whether Grandma Birney was sleeping or remembering or forgetting, Deborah couldn't say. But she felt it was time to go.

"I'm going now, Grandma," she said, standing up. There was still no answer, but she could see her grandmother's eyes scanning slowly back and forth beneath her closed lids. Deborah bent and kissed her on the forehead and went out into the night. She was more at ease now in the darkness, and she smiled as she sensed that this had something to do with her grandmother's letter.

D eborah fell quickly asleep when she got home and the next day, after Jeremy left for the mill, she decided to go see Berenice. She felt guilty for not having done it sooner. But it was Berenice who'd walked away from her sisters and from Deborah, too, and she'd seemed perfectly lucid and Deborah just hadn't wanted to intrude. But it was two days later now, and Deborah yearned to see Aunt Berenice normal, to talk with her for a while about the weather and sewing and the neighborhood children and Deborah's plot in the community garden. Nothing fearful, nothing intense; as if everything was all right again.

Deborah's ears had begun to ring as she walked and her arms and legs and cheeks felt puffed up, as if with sticky hot air. She rubbed her eyes and concentrated on her walking. These were the effects of the night of little sleep. With luck, by noon she would simply feel tired. She turned onto Aunt Berenice's street and in addition to the bloating in her face and limbs, stray thoughts rattled around in her, unresolved because of insufficient sleep. Her grandmother's letter: would the rats read it directly or eat it and absorb its contents that way? Words from the letter: go on down to the hobo jungle, it's full of drunken men. Deborah wondered if her grandmother was right. She'd understood that there were families down there, that it was more shantytown for the dispossessed than hobo jungle for the drunken.

Ahead was the sugar maple in Berenice's front yard. Deborah tried to focus her thoughts on the visit. Conscious of the tree, she now grew conscious of the air—heavy but beginning to move—and the sky. She looked back over her shoulder, west, where the late spring weather came from, and the sky there had turned the color of wet concrete. Soon it would rain. She was before Berenice's house and she went up the walk without looking at the tree.

She climbed the porch steps and knocked at the screen door. The inner door was standing open. There was no response. Deborah blinkered her eyes with her hands and put her face against the screen. A bump in the screen yielded, giving Deborah a tiny pleasure, like popping a soap bubble, and she felt a bit like a child, coming to visit her aunt on a day of summer vacation. "Aunt Berenice," she called but there was no sound. She touched the handle on the screen door and hesitated briefly. There was a faint fear in her that told her to go in, quickly even. She opened the door, but she brushed the fear aside, thinking instead of her grandmother's chiding her last night: Walk right in, you don't need to knock here. Aunt Berenice, too, had always made Deborah welcome.

The front room was dim. The curtains were closed and the furniture was just an arrangement of dark shapes. Deborah knew what her Aunt Berenice's living room was like. The upholstery was worn very thin and the room was immaculately clean. To look at this would be difficult for Deborah, like looking at her aunt's bony gray foot, and she was glad the place was dim. "Aunt Berenice?" she said once more, but she couldn't raise her voice much above a whisper.

Deborah listened. The room buzzed with silence. She listened harder. The house ticked, a gutter somewhere hummed faintly with the wind. But these tiny sounds simply intensified the silence. Nothing from outside could come in here: that was the feeling she had. Not even a sound. Now she could no longer put aside a worry. Where was her aunt? Was she having another spell?

Deborah moved through the dining room and into the kitchen. The table was bare, the sink was empty; there was no sign of the fine soot, even on the windowsill. Her aunt had cleaned this morning. Deborah looked into the backyard, but no one was in it. She turned. The house had an inside stairway to the cellar and Deborah was drawn to it. She stepped through the door and onto the first step and there was a smell of earth and concrete and something else. Starch. She moved down the steps, slowly, thinking to speak her aunt's name once more but unable to shape it, feeling a little shaky. There was a light bulb burning down here and the smell of laundry.

"Debby." A muffled voice.

Deborah started.

"I didn't mean to scare you." It was her aunt's voice.

Deborah came down the steps quickly and her aunt was standing in the basement, lines strung all around, laundry hung there—Uncle Joe's shirts, some of Berenice's underthings, a dress. Deborah's heart was still pounding and she felt foolish. Aunt Berenice took a clothespin out of her mouth and pinned the shoulder of a shirt. "I'm almost done," she said. "I hate to hang the laundry down here, but we're going to have some rain soon."

"That's right," Deborah said, breathless now with relief and thankful for this invitation to small talk, just what she'd desired. "The sky out to the west looks pretty dark."

"And we've still got a month or so to go in tornado season," Berenice said.

"Yes," Deborah said, but with a diminished enthusiasm. It was not the kind of weather she'd been eager to talk about.

"Living in Tornado Alley is an education. It keeps your head straight in the spring, and I think that's a real gift. Just at the time the world is waking up after winter and things are starting to bud and grow and everybody feels like there's hope in the world, *bam*." Berenice slapped her hands together. "One of those monsters comes roaring through to remind you of what's what."

Berenice paused and Deborah's mind thrashed about for a

way to change the subject. She could only think of the laundry but she didn't know what to say. She was surrounded by Berenice's underwear and drunken Uncle Joe's shirts.

"Did you ever see the sky just before a tornado arrives?" Berenice asked.

"Yes."

"The sky turns green. This ghastly green that seems to stain everything. You start rubbing hard at your skin, thinking the green from the sky is going to color your skin."

"Is Friday always your laundry day?" Deborah blurted, her mind a little slow in finding this gambit but thankful now that it had.

Berenice looked puzzled for a moment as she apparently tried to follow the abrupt conversational turn. "No," she said. "I don't really have a set wash day like some. When you've got a man who comes and goes with no set pattern, you really can't get your wash day settled."

Deborah struggled to repress a sigh. She thought: I can't blame myself for Uncle Joe's coming into this.

Aunt Berenice narrowed her eyes, looked intently at Deborah. "But enough about that," she said. "How have you been, Debby?"

"I'm okay, Aunt Berenice. I'm okay."

"And Jeremy?"

"He's okay. He's still working, at least. Not so many hours, but he's working."

"You've got food on the table?"

"Most times. I'm putting some things in the community garden."

"You can always use my yard too."

"Thanks. I appreciate that. But so far we're all right."

"Why don't we go upstairs to talk," Aunt Berenice said. "The little bit left to do here can wait."

Aunt Berenice led Deborah up the steps, but instead of sitting down in the kitchen, she went on through the dining room and into the living room. Deborah followed and sat on the couch and Berenice sat on a chair opposite her without turning on a light or opening the curtains. Deborah thought that perhaps her aunt, too, was sensitive about her worn furniture, but she would have expected the solution to be to talk in the kitchen. Deborah's eyes adjusted quickly to the light, and though the room was dim she could clearly see her aunt's face.

For a time the conversation went as Deborah had wanted it to go. They talked about what Deborah was planting in the garden and Berenice's own garden and how she still had to put more tomatoes in as soon as she could get some seed. They talked about the sewing Berenice was doing for a family down the block. "They're paying me a little bit for it," Berenice said.

"That's good."

"I don't mind doing it. It helps out."

"People are getting by," Deborah said, but her cheerfulness sounded phony to herself.

"Joe doesn't know about it."

Deborah ran out of words. Aunt Berenice closed her eyes briefly and said no more. The voices left no trace in the dim room; the silence hissed in Deborah's ears. She could not move her mind to find more things to say. A thump of thunder made her start. Aunt Berenice cocked her head slightly. "You see?" she said.

"What?"

"The rain."

"Yes."

"Do you think I hurt his feelings?" Aunt Berenice said.

"Hurt his feelings?" Deborah wasn't sure, but she thought her aunt meant her husband. Would it hurt his feelings that she was taking in sewing.

"Adah's friend."

"Who?"

"Adah's friend the hot tamale man. I think I treated him rather rudely. I didn't want a tamale, but I should have made it clear to him that I generally like tamales and I'm sure he makes an excellent one."

There was a gathering rush of sound now. Deborah found it welcome. It masked her inability to respond to this odd turn in her aunt's thoughts. And it was a relief from the silence of this house that clung to her like the green of a tornado sky. The rain blurred from a cluttering of first drops into a hard, steady roar. The thunder cracked again and then again and Deborah liked the hardness of it, the decisiveness. She was tempted to close her eyes, withdraw into the strength of the storm sounds, but she felt herself turning away from Aunt Berenice and that made her feel guilty. "It's a hard one," she said to her aunt.

"Yes," Berenice said, her voice crimped at once by another stroke of thunder.

The two women sat together and said no more and soon the initial burst of the storm was spent. It remained insistent but with less strength. The rain slobbered against the house like a drunkard's kisses and Deborah wanted to leave now. She didn't know what to do or what to say.

When the rain faded into a gutter trickle, Deborah rose and said, "I better be going now, Aunt Berenice."

Her aunt nodded and said, "Bye bye, Debby. You don't mind if I just sit here, do you?"

"Of course not."

"Debby." Aunt Berenice reached up and took Deborah's hand. There seemed to be nothing desperate in the gesture, as might have been expected. Berenice held Deborah's hand firmly, and with a self-possessed voice, she said, "Thank you for coming to visit me."

N ick looked and smiled and broke away from a little group of men when Jeremy came in on Monday night. The unemployed council meeting was being held in a large, empty work shed of the long-defunct Wabash Packing Company, a meat packer dead on its own several years before the market crash.

Jeremy decided the place still faintly held a chill smell of raw meat. A spur off the main railway line between St. Louis and Chicago lay just outside, and Jeremy figured this had been the killing shed. He'd just come in through a large barnlike door. Nick was before him now and pumping his hand with both of his.

"I knew you'd make it, *Jeremy.*" Nick stopped abruptly and smiled. "Listen, don't get nervous if somebody calls you comrade tonight, okay? *I* had sense enough not to. Right? It's just words."

Jeremy looked past Nick at the gathering. There were maybe two hundred people. A few women at the periphery, some children, but most of them were men. They were standing, though there were wooden benches and crates and chairs set up in the middle of the floor. The light was patchy and dim from the gas lamps burning on the walls. Jeremy smelled the gas and maybe the meat smell had been his imagination, for the gas smell was strong, as was the smell of men, musty, sweaty, a breadline smell. The men were talking; there was a din of voices, some rising loud and then fading.

"It's a good turnout," Nick said, "and they're still coming in."

Two men moved past just then. Nick nodded at them, greeted them as they drifted toward the crowd. Jeremy peered into the dim light, looking for familiar faces. There were men that he recognized from the mill, but he didn't see Gus or Turpin or anyone else from his own gang. Except one. A man standing apart at the far side of the crowd, a large man in work clothes with a handlebar mustache like a turn-of-the-century boxer, a mustache that fit his bulbous nose but made his eyes look ridiculously small. Even as the eyes worked hard. Jeremy could see them darting and straining and darting again, though the man held his body stiffly upright and still. His name was Skinner, and Jeremy always associated him in his mind with Spud, though there was no formal connection. Skinner was just another furnace worker, and Jeremy didn't have much contact with him, but he had a general sense of Skinner and Spud being allies.

"I don't know exactly how he found out about the meeting," Nick said. Jeremy glanced at him and he was looking where Jeremy had been looking—at Skinner.

"I don't know much about him, myself," Jeremy said.

"We have to take chances," Nick said. Then after a moment he added, "Maybe he's fed up."

Jeremy turned back to Skinner, who was looking this way now. The man nodded at Jeremy and bodies crossed in the space between and Nick said, "It's good. It's good. There's enough here already to do something."

"Like what?"

"A hunger march, for one thing... Listen, Jeremy. I've got to move around the hall now. Make sure things are going okay. There's only a few of us who's actually running the thing and I've got to get it started. I'll be back to you."

Jeremy nodded as Nick went off and he looked once more toward Skinner, but the man had disappeared. Jeremy thought to turn and leave. If Skinner was here as a company spy, there could be trouble for the ones who were still working. But Jeremy looked at the men in the room. Most of them were jobless, with families to support; all of them were hungry. Jeremy was always hungry himself, even though he could eat every day. Something had to be done, and this guy Skinner wasn't going to chase him away. Besides, Jeremy was just here to listen for now.

He moved into the hall, among the men, picking up bits of conversation as he passed. Been down to the Sally. Get some clothes there? Hoover again. He'll never win this time. My boy coughs his head off all night.

Jeremy veered out of the crowd and he thought of the empty house he'd been in just an hour ago. He'd gone to Cronin's house to see if his family needed anything he could give. But the place had been dark and he'd opened the door without knocking and stepped in and stood in the silence for a long time, listening, wondering if there were more dead inside, but not moving, not wanting to find out. Finally, he'd backed out the door and gone down the walk and he'd found a woman on a porch next door and she'd said that Cronin's wife had taken the kids and gone off with a suitcase in her hand.

Men drifted near to where Jeremy stood. One man said, "It's Pet Milk keeps the mill open. Everybody knows that."

"One customer keeps it open," another man said, "one customer can close it down."

"What are they gonna put their milk in, then?"

"There's other mills to go to."

"Hagemeyer's a bastard, but he's a tough businessman, at least. He wouldn't let that happen." There was a clear tone of respect in the man's voice and Jeremy smiled. He was glad that Nick hadn't heard the remark. Jeremy figured a remark like that would drive Nick crazy.

A loud voice called for attention. Not Nick's voice. An older man in a suit and tie and bowler hat was standing on a box at the front of the crowd and calling for attention, for people to find a place to sit. The men near Jeremy moved toward the benches; people gathered in the center of the shed and began sitting down and Jeremy moved away a bit, leaned against a wall and waited.

"Comrades," the man in the bowler cried. "Every one of you here understands how deep the trouble is, in this country. Every one of you is suffering. But I want you to know tonight that the system that put you in this mess won't be able to hurt you much longer." There was applause and Jeremy felt fidgety. He thought again about skipping out. The man in the bowler resumed: "Every one of you . . . " and Jeremy ignored the words, watched the faces gathered in the center of the floor. They were wide-eyed from hunger, loose-jawed. Skinner was beside Jeremy now. "Didn't expect to see *you* here, Cole," the man said.

Jeremy looked at Skinner. The man seemed to be waiting for an answer, but when none came, his mustache twitched and he said, his voice pitched low, "These're just a bunch of bindle stiffs here."

"You a company spy, Skinner?"

The man drew back slightly. "No. Not me. I'm just at this thing to see what it's all about."

"And you found a bunch of bindle stiffs."

"Yeah."

Jeremy looked away, toward the speaker, who was talking about the conservative elements that were as stiff-necked as Hoover, protecting a status quo of disaster, but Jeremy kept his attention mostly on Skinner, who was still beside him.

Finally Skinner said, "The boss likes you a lot, Cole."

"The boss?"

"Spud."

Jeremy thought: Maybe Nick was right; maybe Spud's afraid of me a little bit.

Skinner said, "How 'bout you? What are you doing here?"

Jeremy had the urge to tell Skinner to go to hell and take Spud with him, but he held back. He waited a moment and he considered Deborah and his job and this guy in the bowler throwing the leftist slogans around, attacking the liberals now, who he said were weeping over Sacco and Vanzetti and never doing a damn thing for the masses. Jeremy felt aligned with no one. "I'm like you, Skinner. Just seeing what it's all about."

Skinner looked blank and Jeremy lowered his voice, gave it a conspiratorial edge. "Like you."

The man squinted at Jeremy for a moment and then his mustache expanded. There was a smile beneath it, Jeremy guessed. "I get you," Skinner said. Teeth finally appeared at the bottom of the mustache: unquestionably a smile.

Jeremy wasn't quite sure what conclusion Skinner had drawn, but at least Jeremy seemed to have distanced himself in the man's mind from the speaker in the bowler, who now directed his wrath on the Socialists. "Debs has been betrayed by a wealthy lawyer and an ex-clergyman," the man cried.

Skinner winked and edged away, his eyes returning intently to the others in the hall. Jeremy understood the man in the bowler: if he was ridiculing even the Socialists, there was only one group left. So these guys—Nick, too—were probably Reds after all. That wasn't the worst thing, maybe. Jeremy moved off along the wall in the opposite direction from Skinner. He headed for the great door, open to the night. Not because they were Reds but because there was too much sloganeering. Capitalist tyrants, now. Workers needing to unite.

Outside, Jeremy could hear only the ring of the voice, no words, and he went down the slope of the loading platform and stood by the railroad track. The night air was as thick as mill air and Jeremy set a foot on the steel rail and he resisted thought. Here at the edge of the light and sound from the building, he keenly felt his isolation from everyone who would seek his attention—the Reds, the managers of the mill, even Deborah. He regretted his isolation from Deborah. She wasn't outwardly insistent anymore, but as his wife she insisted without saying anything, without meaning to. Even having thought this, he could put her out of his mind again. The clamor was all contained in the empty killing shed, out of earshot from where he stood. He felt alone and silent and that was good.

He stood this way for a long time. Silent and unthinking, contained by the thick air as if he were before the ovens, as if he were ringed by fire. Then gradually the silence itself began to draw his attention. It grew recognizable: it was the silence of those who did not seek his attention but deserved it. Like those faces inside, turned to the speaker. And a dead man. A dead child. Their silence spoke to him without slogans, without selfishness, without demands. They were what they were: hungry, fearful, vulnerable, dead. There was applause.

Jeremy turned his face toward the shed. The applause went on and then faded. Was it over? He'd been standing for a long while, he realized. He took a step toward the building and another voice started up. Still the words were not distinguishable, but the voice was unmistakably Nick's. Nick was speaking and Jeremy went up the ramp and approached the door and stepped inside the shed. Nick was saying: "You will eat again. You will work again. You will have your dignity as human beings again." He paused and looked around the hall.

Is he looking for me? Jeremy wondered. It's now that I'd tell him to be careful of the slogans.

Nick said, "And there are things that you will never do again. You will never again look at chimneys in winter and see no smoke. You will never again put your hand on your child's stomach, before he sleeps, to quiet the hunger pains. You will never envy another crow picking at a dead squirrel in the weeds and wish you were a different kind of animal with different needs, different skills."

Nick spoke on as Jeremy snagged on the image of a hungry child, a father's hand trying to press away a pain that was too deep inside, beyond reach. But that pain was a new one, a pain of the last three years, and there was a cold comfort in that Lizzy had died before the bad times came. She never went hungry. Jeremy had never been forced to face the hunger of his child.

"Do you think," Nick said, "that you'll ever be free of this burden if you just slink off to your homes and wait for the lights to go out, wait for the landlord to throw you out, wait for the light in your children's eyes to go out because of hunger? Can you just wait for that?"

"No!" A voice shouted from the crowd.

"Can you wait?" Nick cried again.

"No!" More voices.

"Can you wait?"

"No!" People were on their feet, arms waving.

"No!" Nick picked up the cry of the crowd.

"No!" All the voices shouted, all the voices in the hall, it seemed, but Jeremy's. And Jeremy felt the word shape in his throat, felt a rush of strength.

"You're powerful together!" Nick raised his fists before him. "You're powerful in your weakness. You have the power together, as the workers of the world. You are what makes this country strong. Not the fancy men whose cuffs are clean. *You* own Wabash Steel. *You* do. Not John J. Hagemeyer. Hagemeyer doesn't stoke the ovens. Hagemeyer doesn't clean the furnaces. Hagemeyer doesn't run the shears or tap the open hearths or any other thing that makes that mill breathe and live and produce. You do. You and your kin and your friends and now you're dying off. You're being left out, put down, thrown away, run over. You're being starved and evicted and humiliated by John J. Hagemeyer and all the men like him. Hagemeyer."

"Hagemeyer!" a man shouted from the crowd.

"Ha-ge-meyer!" Nick stretched out the name.

"Ha-ge-meyer!" the crowd repeated.

"We're lucky in Wabash! We can see things clearly here. There's a man. One man, and he can't hide behind a company name or a boardroom door. Wabash Illinois is Wabash Steel and Wabash Steel has a man who sucks its blood. One man. Ha-ge-meyer."

"Ha-ge-meyer!" the crowd roared and Jeremy cried out the name too. He heard his own voice and then he smiled. Nick got him caught up in this. But Nick was right. Jeremy could see that. Old man Hagemeyer did control these lives.

"Just two weeks, comrades!" Nick lifted his chin and paused. The "comrades" registered in Jeremy, but it didn't put him off. He smiled again at Nick slipping the word in at the right moment. Then, as if Nick was aware of Jeremy, he said, "Just two weeks, my friends!"

Jeremy laughed aloud but no one heard because a man shouted "Let's march!" and others repeated it. Then Jeremy realized that the man's voice was the same voice that had been the first to pick up the other cries. A ringer, Jeremy guessed, like a carnival midway. One of the organizers was out in the middle of the audience helping to shape the crowd's response. This realization made Jeremy draw back a bit. He felt no impulse to cry out again with the crowd. But Nick's eager, earnest face before the hungry people kept Jeremy from turning and leaving. The organizers had simply hedged their bets. And the crowd was legitimately with them.

"In two weeks," Nick said, "on the Fourth of July, we'll march. A great march of protest to the very gates of Wabash Steel. This Fourth of July we'll declare the independence of the jobless, the independence of the hungry, the independence of the dispossessed, the independence of the workers of Wabash and the U.S.A. and the world!" Nick's voice soared, his arms rose up, and the crowd applauded and stamped their feet and hooted and Jeremy was happy for these people, happy for their hope. He raised his own hands before him and he began to clap, slowly at first and then faster, harder. Okay, Nick, he thought. Okay.

The next day Nick was laid off. At first, when Nick was not on the shift, Jeremy decided he'd been staggered off for a day under the spread-work program. But as Jeremy approached the personnel shack near the front gate to make his daily check of the layoff list, he realized he'd been naive and even a little stupid. He suddenly knew Nick's name was going to be there and it was, halfway down the list that was tacked to the board beside the door. Jeremy felt a rush of strength, angry strength, and his mind groped around for a target. He heard Nick's voice in his head say Hagemeyer, and that was right because Jeremy felt it was Hagemeyer who'd somehow made him so stupid all this day, thinking Nick could run a meeting like last night's and not pay for it. But Hagemeyer was too remote. Nick had no job and Jeremy's angry vigor turned to concern. He pushed into the personnel shack ready to crack heads if they gave him a hard time, but the man there gave him what he wanted without a word—Nick's address—and Jeremy went out again. He hesitated at the front gate. He almost went back in to find Spud and force a confrontation. But there'd be time for that, if it was the right thing to do.

Instead, Jeremy went to the address he'd gotten. Nick's house was up the rise on the eastern edge of Hungry Hollow. It sat on an isthmus of trees and rocks and tar-paper houses that stretched into a sea of horseradish. These fields and all the little houses were owned by Caleb Hart, the Horseradish King of Wabash. Another big business man, Jeremy thought, and he smiled at the way Nick was shaping his thinking.

The schools were out for the summer and there were children

running in the hard-packed dirt street. Jeremy kept his eyes
lifted to the field at the far end. He did not look at the children.
He walked and began to read the numbers on the houses, and
the last one was Nick's. Two crows, then a third, rose up from
the witchgrass between the settlement and the field. They circled, croaking in alarm, but soon fell again, disappearing into
the high grass. There was something dead in there, Jeremy knew.
Food for the crows, the envy of the starving workers. Jeremy
went up the path through the front yard weeds. He knocked at
Nick's screen door.

"Yeah?" Nick's voice from inside. But it was muffled, odd.

"Nick? It's Jeremy."

There was no answer at first. Then Nick said, "Jeremy."
There was something wrong with the voice, the shape of the
word from Nick's voice. "Come in."

Jeremy opened the screen door and stepped into the living
room and Nick was trying to sit up on the couch. He'd apparently
been lying down, for he was pushing himself into a sitting po-
sition, but slowly, painfully. Jeremy saw Nick's face: it was
splashed and streaked with wounds, his eyes black, one swollen
shut, the left side of his face from ear to jaw puffed up. Nick
grabbed quickly at his ribs and barked in pain as he finally sat
straight. The inside of his mouth was very dark.

Jeremy strode across the room. "Oh, shit," he said. "Those
sons of bitches." His hands went out, as if to press away the signs
of Nick's beating, but he knew he couldn't help. Nick was hurt
bad and Jeremy's hands withdrew and clenched. "I'll kill those
sons of bitches."

Nick kept his face turned, his battered face, as if he were a
shy schoolgirl. "Wait," he said, the word as puffy as his face,
almost unrecognizable. "Wait," he said again.

"Which ones did it?" Jeremy asked, leaning close to Nick,
still ready to dash out the door and hurt somebody bad.

"Didn't . . ." Nick paused, swallowed. "Didn't really see
them."

"It's easy to guess."

"Don't do anything dumb," Nick said. "If you want to help me, don't do something dumb."

"What's dumb? What? Beat the shit out of one of them isn't dumb."

"It's dumb. It is." Nick still wouldn't look directly at Jeremy. He leaned away from him, over the arm of the couch. He kept his face angled away. His hand rose and his fingertips gently tapped at his forehead, just above a raw red patch at his right temple. He kept the fingertips there for a long moment, his palm hiding his face. "The only bad thing," Nick said, "is how it scares my kids. I've got two boys. One's eleven, one's nine. It scares them bad. They can't take this shit. They're just kids. That's what makes me fucking mad." Now Nick clenched his fists before him, even though he flinched with the pain of doing it.

"Okay," Jeremy said. "I'll take somebody apart."

"No. I need you on the inside . . . They didn't lay you off, did they?"

"I'm still working."

"Good."

"Fucking Skinner." The words came at the same moment as the thought. Until now, Jeremy had put aside Skinner and his clear purpose at last night's meeting. "It was Skinner."

"I didn't see any of them. It was dark."

"But it was Skinner at least who was the spy."

"Jeremy." Nick paused again. He pulled out a handkerchief and leaned away and spat into it. Then he wiped his mouth very gently and put his handkerchief away. For the first time he turned his face fully toward Jeremy. The visible eye was sunk deep in the swelling. It peered out without luster, without seeming even to see, like an animal's eyes, an animal mortally wounded and aware only of what was happening inside, of its own imminent death. Jeremy looked away.

"You're with me now," Nick said. "Am I right?"

Jeremy turned his face the other way, looked sightlessly around the room.

"Good," Nick said, as if Jeremy had answered. Jeremy thought: I *did* answer.

"Good," Nick said again. "You've got to try to keep your job for as long as you can. Be *our* spy. Seem to play along. Okay?"

Jeremy felt foolish. He wasn't a damn child. He wasn't squeamish about a man's wounds. But he didn't like to see Nick hurt. It made him very angry and he felt as if he had to do something.

"Jeremy."

He turned back to Nick.

"Their time is coming," Nick said. "Do what I tell you."

"All right."

The screen door creaked. Jeremy whirled around in reflexive hope: they'd come back to try to hurt Nick some more and Jeremy would have a chance to fight after all. But there was a boy peeking in at the door. A gangly, round-faced boy, obviously Nick's son. The eleven-year-old, Jeremy guessed. The boy was half inside, half outside. He looked at Jeremy, looked at his father. The boy's face was wide-eyed, stricken. He backed out. The door clapped shut. Footsteps, running, faded away outside. Jeremy had the clear sense that it was not himself, a stranger, that had stopped the boy from entering; it was the father, the father sitting up, the father's battered, conscious face waiting in the room.

Jeremy looked toward the couch. Nick's face was turned sharply away; his eyes were hidden. Nick was hiding more than his bruises now, Jeremy knew. Jeremy could not face his friend's tears. He muttered a good-bye and, like the boy, he fled.

J eremy woke in the night and his anger was renewed. Nick never had a chance. He was no fighter. That was clear just to look at him. Not a fighter with his fists, at least. But he had guts. He had looked at Skinner at the meeting and had known the risks. Skinner. Jeremy sat up. How could he let Skinner, the one clear offender, get away with this?

"Jeremy?" Deborah's voice beside him in the dark. Jeremy was irritated at her consciousness, at her concern. But he held back his words. He knew not to shift his anger from its real target to his wife.

"What are you doing awake?" he said, and he heard the hardness of his own voice.

"I have trouble sleeping. You know that."

"Go to sleep." He tried to say it gently, but he still sounded gruff.

Deborah said no more. Jeremy lay back down. Nick didn't want him to jeopardize his job. Was that really so he could be useful to Nick or was Nick just protecting him? Either way, Jeremy knew he shouldn't do anything to get himself laid off. And that made him want to leap up in anger again. He wanted to act. He had to act. And he couldn't even jump up from the bed because of his wife's solicitousness. He couldn't beat the shit out of a guy like Skinner. Why? Jeremy forced himself to hold still and think this out clearly. He couldn't beat up Skinner in a way that seemed to be an answer to Nick's beating. That was the only danger—to seem to be part of the radicals. A private reason: that would be safe. Jeremy smiled in the dark.

The next day Jeremy waited near the personnel shack after his shift. He'd gotten there quickly, before the other gangs had broken up. The men all lingered after the shift, reluctant to leave, as if there'd be more work if they just hung around. Skinner wasn't on the coke ovens today, but Jeremy figured he'd just been rotated somewhere else, probably onto one of the furnaces.

Jeremy stood at the far corner of the personnel shack and he watched the men coming out, fidgety, swinging by the layoff posting and then moving off—all of them stiff, whether they were on the list or not—those who still had jobs hiding the intensity of their relief, those who didn't, hiding their despair. Neither emotion was a steelworker's emotion. Jeremy saw Turpin go out, and Gus. Gus and Jeremy exchanged a nod and it looked for a moment as if Gus would come over and begin to talk, but Jeremy glanced away, discouraged any approach, and when he looked back, Gus was gone. Jeremy felt bad about that. But he had something more important to do.

Finally Skinner appeared. Jeremy turned half away, whipped his work gloves against his hand—a gesture meant to be nonchalant but which felt angry, provocative. He feared he'd give his intention away, but when he glanced over, Skinner was gone. Skinner must not have paused at all. He hadn't even looked at the layoff list—another suggestion of the man's involvement with management. A company spy wouldn't be laid off. Jeremy stepped around the personnel shack. He saw Skinner's tall, broad frame up ahead, moving out the front gate. Jeremy followed.

Skinner never looked back. He walked east on Collinsville Road, over the Illinois Central tracks, and Jeremy hung behind a little. He knew where Skinner was going—the Blue Moon Restaurant. There were a few other men up ahead going to the same place, though Skinner did nothing to catch up with them; he continued to walk alone.

Off to the left were the horseradish fields, still flecked with white flowers, but on the right now was a marshy flat and then the edges of Green Pond. The pond covered maybe forty acres, and in the afternoon sun its clear water was green from the thick plant growth along its bottom. Between its shore and the blacktop were some tumbledown bait shops, a gas station, and the Blue Moon, a flat-roofed place made of wood that looked as if it had been scrounged from a dozen different houses of different colors and ages that had been torn down by a tornado.

Skinner went in, but Jeremy did not. He went down to the pond's edge and sat on a rock and waited for Skinner to have a chance to get a couple of drinks in him. The Blue Moon was known to have a back room where any man who could show mill grit on his hands could get a shot of clear, pretty-good moonshine for fifteen cents.

Jeremy waited and he thought about how he'd pick a fight.

He didn't know Skinner well enough to make it something very personal. It'd have to be a physical thing. A bump. Whatever. But Jeremy didn't want the fight to happen right away. Inside the Blue Moon there'd be guys to stop the fight. Even calling Skinner outside wouldn't be a sure thing. There'd always be peacemakers around and Jeremy would have to fight three or four guys to get any real damage done to Skinner. He'd have to seem to hold a grudge. To make that believable, he knew he'd have to pretend he'd already had too much to drink himself. That could be plausible. There were plenty of basement stills in Wabash.

Jeremy felt suddenly very calm. He knew exactly how it would happen. He'd wait another few minutes and then he'd go in. He looked out to the pond. The rippled surface was the color of grass. He waited and a pair of ducks rose from the marsh and tore across the lake, their necks stretched out. Jeremy thought: When they're out of sight or settled on the water again, I'll go in.

The ducks kept going and veered east, and Jeremy watched them fly out among the humping of earth, the Indian mounds, the little mounds clustered near the big one, Sun Mound, that stood a half mile off. It was big, even from here—taller than the tallest furnace stacks and broad and long, a great earthen ship, as if stranded in this bottomland by the shrunken Mississippi.

When he could no longer see the birds, Jeremy rose up and turned and faced toward the blacktop. He tucked his shirt in, straightened his cuffs, squared his cap on his head. These were mindless movements, preparations as if he were going before the ovens. But he stopped. He intended to go into the restaurant pretending he'd had too much to drink already. He cocked his cap, opened his collar, concentrated on the plan.

He went up to the road and walked fifty yards east to the Blue Moon. A sign sat on a high pole at the edge of the blacktop: a blue crescent moon with a profiled face in the curve—a pointy nose, wide eyes, a sly grin. Jeremy turned beneath the face and moved to the door. He opened it and stepped in.

There were half a dozen tables and a lunch counter. Only

an old couple sat in the restaurant, at a table near the door. Jeremy looked to a burly man in a white apron behind the counter. Jeremy crossed to him and sat on a stool.

"Howdy," the man said.

Jeremy held back his reaction. The drunks he'd seen were slow to react. He nodded and answered a question that hadn't been asked yet. "I'm fine, thanks."

The man behind the counter concentrated on Jeremy's face. Jeremy knew he shouldn't overplay the role, either. They didn't want a drunk in the back room. He said, "I'm just lucky to be working."

"You work at the mill?"

"Blast furnace." Jeremy lifted his hand in a vague gesture to the west.

The eyes of the burly man followed Jeremy's hand. Then he nodded, a friendly nod. "If you're thirsty, there's a room in back," he said. He angled his head toward the door at the rear.

Jeremy stood and muttered his thanks to the man and went to the door. He paused and knew he had to establish his plan quickly. He opened the door and inside was a room smaller than the outer room but set up in a similar way. There were several tables and a counter—a bar—with a keg behind it and a shelf of unlabeled bottles. Jeremy took a single clear look and let his head loll a little to the side while he considered what he'd seen. Half a dozen men sat at two tables pushed together at the rear. Another burly man—his thick chest and something in his face suggested he was the brother of the man at the outer counter— was behind the bar. And at a table between the door and the bar sat Skinner, alone. Good. Nobody wants to sit with a son-of-a-bitch company spy.

Jeremy closed the door and moved into the room, veering just a bit so he could come near Skinner's table. There might be no better chance than this. He glanced up as he neared the table and he saw Skinner's face turned to him, a broad, eager smile there. "Cole," he said.

Jeremy lurched and hit his foot against Skinner's chair,

bumped into the man's shoulder. "Dammit, Skinner, watch out," Jeremy said, deliberately slurring his words.

"It's okay," Skinner said, his voice friendly.

"It's not okay. You tripped me," Jeremy said.

"No. Hey, I'm sorry. Have a drink with me, Cole." The man half rose, his tiny eyes intently fixed on Jeremy, full of good intentions. Jeremy felt a crazy twist of regret over all this. He groped in his mind for the image of Nick's battered face.

"You're a clumsy son of a bitch," Jeremy said, staggering a little, playing the drunkenness.

"Please," Skinner said, "I'm sorry. Let me buy you a drink." Skinner refused to be provoked and his good-naturedness nagged at Jeremy. He found himself angry at Skinner not for what he did to Nick but for falling in with whoever it was that made him do it. But the man had helped hurt Nick. Hurt him bad. Jeremy fought this damn fool softness in himself. He'd set Skinner up already. No need to keep confronting the oafish friendliness of this company thug. Jeremy cursed his way over to the bar, thinking of Nick's eyes swollen shut, his tears before his son.

The man behind the bar said, "Looks like you've had some pretty good home brew already."

"What's that?" Jeremy said.

"Maybe you've had enough," the bartender said.

Jeremy wanted to leap at this idea. He wanted nothing more than to get out of here right away and wait for Skinner outside. But he had to put up at least a little protest. "Not me," he said.

"Let him have a drink," Skinner said from behind. Jeremy could sense that Skinner had stood up, had moved nearer.

"We don't want any trouble in here," the bartender said.

"He's okay," Skinner said.

"I don't like your damn place anyway," Jeremy said and he turned around and lunged toward the door abruptly enough that Skinner couldn't get out of his way. Jeremy bumped into the man and drew back and said, "I'm tired of you pushing me, you son of a bitch."

Now Skinner clearly seemed to struggle to hold onto his

composure, but he kept his face calm, his hands down, he even managed another little smile. "Just one of those days, Cole. Maybe we can drink together another time. I'd like that."

Jeremy wavered. Skinner was a damn fool. Maybe that was all. But Nick was Jeremy's friend. Nick knew who needed to be helped and it wasn't John J. Hagemeyer. What kind of effort did Skinner make to be patient like this with Nick? He and his friends almost killed him. And for what? Didn't Skinner know anybody who was starving? All this ran fast through Jeremy's head as he stood before this friendly goon. Jeremy pushed past him. "Out of my way," he said and he was through the door, across the restaurant, out the front entrance and he ran along the blacktop and then down to the pond. He'd wait now and finish the work he had to do.

He sat on the rock where he'd sat before, but he kept the pond to his back and he kept his mind empty of everything but the pain of his friend Nick.

The afternoon brightness faded, but there was a long way to dusk on this mid-June day. That was good, because Jeremy would clearly see when Skinner went by on the road. But it also meant that Jeremy had to concentrate on doing his work quickly, once it began. He didn't want it to be a public spectacle. He'd told Deborah he had to visit Nick after work and also see Cronin's family. He didn't want word getting back to her of anything else. No need to worry her.

After a time he grew conscious of the sun pressing heavily at the back of his neck, boring hotly in, as if the rays had been compressed and focused there. But he did not even wipe the sweat from his neck. He did not move. His hands lay on his knees and he waited and waited and then suddenly Skinner passed before him, out on the blacktop, walking slowly west.

Jeremy rose up, compressed himself, his own will, focused himself: there, on the company spy. He moved quickly up to the road and turned and he began to follow Skinner. No one else was in sight and he walked faster, drew near. When he was close, he began to hum to himself and then mutter a tuneless song.

He saw Skinner glance over his shoulder, but he kept his head down for now. Skinner said nothing, did not stop. Jeremy was glad for that. He didn't want to face the man's friendliness again.

Jeremy looked up and Skinner was walking faster. Jeremy said, "Uh oh," as if this were the first time he'd noticed him. "It's you." He said it loud, but Skinner made no acknowledgment. Instead, Skinner walked faster, didn't look back.

"Skinner," Jeremy shouted. "You bump me in a bar but you run away from me out here?"

Skinner stopped, though he did not turn. Jeremy came up to him. Skinner was a big man, a young man, strong. Jeremy realized that these things made what he wanted to do easier. He was ready now. Nick's battered face was before him now. His temples pounded and his arms tightened and he was going to say more, but Skinner spoke instead.

"You're drunk, Cole," Skinner said. "Don't do something stupid."

Jeremy almost denied it, almost said: I'm not drunk, you bastard; this is all for Nick Brenner. But he did not speak and he thought to push Skinner to get it going but before he could, Skinner spun around, crouched, slammed forward headfirst, Jeremy's breath popped, he fell back, Skinner's arms around him, and he was driven against the ground.

Jeremy's arms were free and he grabbed Skinner's head in his hands, yanked it off his stomach, but before he could twist it, Skinner stiffened his neck. The two strained, immobile, Jeremy's breath was coming back and he was twisting Skinner's head to the left, the man's spit spewed up, covered Jeremy's left hand as he twisted and then Skinner drove with his legs, the two men scooted, Jeremy jerked the man's head, and Skinner let go, slipped down, rolled away.

Jeremy got to his feet, a broad circle of pain in his abdomen, fading; he looked toward Skinner. The man was out on the black-top, still sitting, tossing his head, trying to straighten his neck. He glanced at Jeremy and struggled up to his feet.

Jeremy strode to Skinner and the man did not raise his fists but crouched to charge again, and Jeremy had only the top of his head to swing at so he waited and let the lunge come and he jumped to the side, only Skinner's right hand and wrist catching him, and he punched between Skinner's shoulder blades and the man went straight down hard to the blacktop. Jeremy was strong now and very angry again over Nick and he didn't have time to wait and he swung his leg far back and then forward fast into the man's ribs, cracking hard. Skinner cried out, rolled over on his back, clutching his side. Still Jeremy hadn't let off enough through his shoulders and arms and fists, and he waited as Skinner gasped on his back.

"Get up," Jeremy said. "Get up. It's not gonna stop but I don't want to kick you to death. Get up." And he realized he sounded sober. Utterly sober, but Skinner was probably in too much pain to notice. Nick's broken ribs were paid back, but Skinner's face was clean. "Get up, you clumsy bastard," Jeremy said.

Skinner slowly sat up, wincing. Jeremy came close and Skinner lunged, barking in pain, and Jeremy jumped back, disgusted at Skinner, disgusted at his single-minded impulse to wrestle. He wanted Skinner to stand up and punch, but it wasn't going to happen, he knew. Skinner was on all fours now and Jeremy stepped to him, drew his leg back again and kicked hard, the heavy toe of his work shoe catching Skinner somewhere on his face with a crack and the man straightened up, blood pluming in an arc above his rising head and he fell onto his back. Jeremy stepped forward, put one knee on Skinner's chest, pressed down heavily, and he clenched his fists, looked at Skinner's tiny eyes, large now, wide, full of fear, the eyes now: Jeremy coiled his arm back, his fist compacted, and he drove down—left eye, no give to the head, thump, a hard sound—right eye, the thump again—a thick knot of sound snapped in Skinner's throat. Nick's eyes were paid back. A wide, swooping punch into the jaw, crack inside, the sharp pain against Jeremy's fist. Throbbing in both fists now: a good pain; Jeremy expected this to be the good pain of hard work, debts paid. He heard his own breathing. Only that.

Then crows somewhere, out in the field, crying like old women. To hell with them, Jeremy thought. This is done. His fists hurt. He felt released—his body did—but he did not feel relieved.

He stood up and he didn't look at Skinner's face. They were in the middle of the Collinsville Road and he grabbed Skinner by the ankles and dragged him off the blacktop and onto the shoulder. Skinner moaned and stirred and Jeremy resisted the urge again to tell him what the real reason was. Jeremy looked back across Green Pond, out as far as the mounds, and he waited to see what he felt. A faint satisfaction. But even as he grew conscious of it, that little bit was gone. Nobody went back to work at the mill for this; no child was fed. "Dammit," Jeremy said aloud. Something felt wrong and he couldn't figure it out. He walked off, fast, heading west. He kept his head down, not looking from the road, not even for the mill, which flamed and billowed up ahead in the late afternoon sun.

The next day was a scheduled day off. It was a Thursday. The weekday idleness that was an occasional part of the spread-work was hard on Jeremy and he slept late and Deborah moved about the house very quietly. After making her own breakfast and sweeping away the grit from the mill, she sat on the top step of the front porch.

A dragonfly hung in the yard, then it darted away and then back and then hung motionless again, only a few feet from where it was before. Deborah turned her eyes from it and drew her knees closer to her. She felt a chill, a vague sadness. A whistle cried at the mill and she thought of Jeremy and she uncoiled; she straightened her legs and put her feet flat on the ground. She was angry and this surprised her. At first she thought she was angry at Jeremy's silence. He was silent last night—utterly silent after coming home from visiting the family of the hanged man and seeing his friend who'd been hurt at the mill and laid

off. He'd looked troubled and had been silent and she hadn't
had the courage to force him to talk and now he slept and he'd
probably go off somewhere in the afternoon in still more silence.
She thought: That's why I'm angry. She grew restless and the
anger persisted and she realized she was wrong. It wasn't Jeremy's silence. The anger had something to do with hanging here
on this June morning like that dragonfly out in the yard. And
the whistle at the mill: she had no work to do, no real work, no
work that produced something tangible, that fed them or clothed
them, something that could let her say, This is what I do. Did
she need another child? Yes. Maybe that. A child was a beautiful
gift from God. A child. She rubbed hard at her knees with the
palms of her hands, stirred her bare feet on the hard ground.
The thought of a child rippled darkly in her: death, impotence,
passion unreturned. And it wasn't just that she needed a child.
That wasn't all of it. People troubled her, people she loved.
Jeremy: and there was nothing she could do for him. Aunt Berenice: and there was nothing she could do for her. Her mother.
Her other aunts. These people were what filled her mind each
day. They were her work, in a way. But what was it she was to
do about them?

After a time, the screen door opened and Jeremy stepped
onto the front porch. Deborah turned her face and before she
raised her eyes, she saw his hand. The knuckles were raw,
bruised. She did not look up; the surge of pain she felt for the
wound brought words that she spoke as if to the hand itself, as
if it would accept the attention that her husband would not.
"You're hurt," she said. The hand was jerked away before she
could touch it, kiss it. She looked up. Jeremy was gazing out
into the yard, his face hard.

"What is it?" she said.

"Nothing," he said.

"Your hand."

"I did it on the coke oven door."

She didn't believe what he said, though she couldn't say
why. Maybe it was because the wound was on the back of the

hand. But she couldn't let herself think any more about it, she knew. There'd be no answers. She wrenched her mind away, pushed it into triviality. "Do you want me to make you some breakfast?"

"No," he said. He closed his eyes briefly and he said it again, very gently this time, "No," and Deborah nearly wept with gratitude at the gentleness, nearly wept with love for Jeremy, nearly wept, too, with anger at him at his keeping her isolated like this in her love, wept with pity for this man whose own life had made him so reticent.

"I'm going out for a while," Jeremy said and he went down the steps. But he did not walk away at once. He seemed to be waiting.

Deborah stood up. "You're off work again on Saturday, aren't you?"

"Yes."

"I'm going to make a picnic basket. Can we go out somewhere and be together for a while?"

"Okay." He turned and he nodded at her and he moved off. Finally Deborah did weep. First in joy at the prospect of Saturday, then in anger for having so little control of herself. She wiped her eyes and wondered what she would do with this day. The only place where she'd felt comfortable in the past few weeks was at Grandma Birney's. She decided to go there.

Deborah stepped inside, put on her shoes, and she went out quickly, walked fast past the North Plant, the downtown shops—half of them closed up, the others with few customers—and she crossed the railroad tracks into West Wabash.

Soon she saw the high, false horizon of the levee and she turned on the gravel road. She walked to Grandma Birney's street and paused a moment to gaze far down the way at the shantytown. A thin wisp of smoke was rising from the clutter of odd shapes there, structures too small for people, it seemed. And indeed she saw no people. Not from this distance. Only the sinuous line of smoke like dark blood flowing from a puncture wound.

She went down the rutted street to her grandmother's house,

and she knocked only once this time before opening the door and stepping in. "Grandma," she called.

There was no answer. She called once more, but her grandmother obviously wasn't in. Now Deborah listened for the rats. There was no sound at all except from outside—children laughing somewhere; sparrows squabbling in the front yard. The rats, too, seemed to be gone. Deborah had a quick vision that made her smile: her grandmother and the rats were out somewhere together, settling their score on the levee, the old woman brawling with the animals, in complete control, booting one rat after another off the berm and into the water.

Deborah thought to leave, but at the moment she felt more comfortable here than in her own house. She moved into the parlor and looked about, deciding—a decision delicious in its calm triviality—whether to sit on the couch or on the chair. In looking about, her eyes fell on the little desk with the coal-oil lamp. There were papers with writing on the desk top. She crossed to them.

At the top of the first page was the salutation: "Dear Rats." A new letter. Deborah picked up the sheets and read.

Dear Rats,

It's me again, the woman whose house you're in and whose warning you ignored. I said I'd get myself some strong poison for you if you didn't leave and I still intend to do that. It's not a pretty sight. I've seen animals die of poison and don't think that just because you're used to eating all manner of junk that you can survive. You can't.

But I figure you deserve another chance to be reasonable. That's because I'm a reasonable woman. I always have been. People sometimes think I'm not, but what do they know? My husband never took time to even ask me what was on my mind. Not that he'd ever tell me what was on his. Maybe nothing was. I figured that out only in the last year or two. But I might be wrong about him. It's too late now. I should have written him a letter and greased it up with maple syrup which he liked a lot and put it on his pillow.

But that's not what I wanted to tell you. The main thing is that it's a special problem for me having rats in my house. That's because of my daddy. I loved my daddy very much. Now *there* was a man who'd listen to me. He knew how reasonable I am. He'd put me on his knee when I was just a little slip of a girl and he'd ask about things that were important to me, like who I was mad at at school or how my doll had misbehaved, and I'd tell him all about it. I'd explain everything and he'd listen very carefully and after I'd spoken my piece, he'd say, I can understand that, you're a smart girl and I know just what you mean. Well, my daddy was a very strong man. He was a logger and a farmer and later on a steelworker and everybody respected him and no man would even so much as look cross-eyed around him because they were scared of him. But there was one thing my daddy couldn't stand and that was rats. They made him real nervous so that he'd even break out in a sweat and his voice would get real tight. Do you understand what I mean? My daddy was always in command and I loved that about him and the only time he ever showed any weakness at all was around rats and that's a very painful memory for me. That's why I just can't let you hang around here. I have plenty of memories of my daddy to keep me going both happy and not so happy but I don't want any rats around here when they made my daddy feel so bad.

Now, don't you get uppity at what I'm saying. It was just something from his childhood, I'm sure, and if it came down to it, he'd stomp on your little skulls easy enough. And don't go thinking that I somehow inherited that skitterishness about your kind. I'd fight you toe to toe if you ever had guts enough to come out and face

me and I'd whip your fannies too. But that's enough of
all this. You've had one more chance to do what's good
for you. Now get on out of here while you still got life
in your filthy little bodies.

Elvira Birney

Though the combative close lifted Deborah a bit, she was
most struck by a sense of vulnerability in her grandmother's
words. She returned the letter to the desk and stepped into
the kitchen. Then she went back to the parlor and crossed into
the bedroom and only as she entered the room did she fully
realize what she was doing. She was looking for her grandmother's body, hurt, unconscious, maybe dead. She felt foolish as she
looked at the neatly made bed spread with a patchwork quilt.
There was no one in the house. Her grandmother was alive. Her
housework done, she was out somewhere, sure of herself whatever she was doing. The letter was full of memories, which was
something Grandma Birney valued, good or bad.

Deborah returned to the parlor and sat on the chair and she
listened to the house ticking faintly around her. As if from an
absentminded clock, the ticks came regularly for a few moments,
then there was a period of silence, a tick, nothing, a tick, another,
the clock starting again but stopping at once, tick, tick, silence,
darkness, and Deborah slept, her head falling softly against a
wing of the chair. She slept and the room grew noon-dim and
she did not dream, but when she woke she thought she was
dreaming.

She opened her eyes and she was looking at the couch,
looking at one of the arm doilies, its delicate web of white, the
holes suddenly seeming nibbled there, eaten through by insistent
little teeth, and her attention was drawn down to the floor, to
the center of the large, round rag rug, and there was a black
shape there, upright. Deborah thought at first it was a crow—
not quite the size of a crow, but nearly—a young crow, very
black, that had come in through an open window. But then she
knew it wasn't a crow. It was a rat, sitting up on its haunches.

Its blackness wasn't sleek, she saw now, but mottled with scummy brown. A rat and it was watching her. Her heart was racing but she could not move. A dream, she thought, but felt her eyes flutter and she knew she was awake and the rat was still there and it moved its head, sized her up. She gasped now and drew her feet up onto the chair and with the movement the rat was gone, a quick rush toward the kitchen and it was gone.

Deborah sat for a long while on the chair, her legs clutched tight to her chest. She caught her breath; her heartbeat slowed; the space before her remained empty. She heard no sounds in the house and she wanted for her grandmother to come in now, to please come through the door. But the silence persisted and she sensed it full of rats waiting for her to sleep and she could not stay any longer. She got up from the chair and moved quickly across the parlor and out the door. When she reached the street she felt like a coward, but her grandmother was nowhere in sight and she did not go back.

O n Friday morning Jeremy went to the labor shack. Skinner's name was skipped without comment on the roster and Jeremy was assigned to the ovens again as if nothing had happened. Jeremy felt the release of a tension in him that he hadn't quite realized was there until it was gone. But when the gangs were dismissed and Jeremy reached the labor shack door, Spud's voice blocked him. "Cole."

Jeremy turned. The last of the other men moved past, the door clicked shut, and he was alone in the shack with Spud. Now the moment of ease seemed foolish. Of course he couldn't beat up the company spy and expect nothing to happen. Now Jeremy assumed he'd have to fight Spud. Right here. He was almost relieved at this. Get it over with.

But Spud didn't make a move. He stood as still as a barrel of nails under the SAFETY FIRST sign and he was watching Jeremy

closely—studying him, it seemed. Jeremy kept as still as Spud.
Finally, Spud said, "Heard you had a little trouble the other
night."

This was a critical moment, Jeremy sensed. If the mill bosses
already knew why he'd beaten up Skinner, they wouldn't be
playing this game. Jeremy said, "I didn't have any trouble."

Spud hesitated and then he smiled. The smile was a surprise
to Jeremy. It seemed almost friendly, even admiring. He said,
"But you dished out some trouble."

"You mean Skinner."

Spud nodded, a residue of the smile on his face.

"He got too close to me."

"You hurt him pretty bad."

Jeremy felt a stutter of regret at this. He thought of Nick—
also hurt bad—and the regret stopped. Then he felt the urge to
tell Spud why he'd paid back his spy. And he fought that feeling,
as well. Nick wanted him on the inside. Jeremy said nothing.

The earlier smile had finally disappeared entirely and Spud
was studying Jeremy again. He said, "Skinner's a good man."

"He's a careless man. He got too close to me when he
should've known not to."

"I never pegged you for being that touchy, Cole."

Jeremy strained at these words, listening for the suspicion
in them, and it was there. "Look," Jeremy said. "I had too much
to drink."

"Didn't peg you for a drinker, either."

"That's why I maybe got a little crazy when I had a couple."

Spud didn't answer this right away. He grew still again and
the two men stared at each other and then Spud said, "Skinner
thinks you might've had some other grudge against him."

"Is that what he said?"

Spud's mouth stretched a little bit at one side—the faintest
of smiles, perhaps—it was hard to tell—and he said, "He's not
talking very clearly at the moment . . . It's not easy to figure."

"People start figuring too much, they always make big mis-
takes," Jeremy said. "That's the way I look at it. That's why I'm
working in this place."

Two thoughtful creases shot up Spud's forehead from his brow. After a moment, they faded. He said in a flat tone, "You just a good hard steelworker, are you, Cole?"

"Thought you would've noticed that already, Spud."

"Maybe I have."

"I got drunk." He heard Nick in his head: Stay on the inside; you can help us there. "Maybe I made a mistake. I can't remember the whole thing very well, is the truth of it."

"You've always been okay in my book, Cole. I've always liked the way you've handled yourself." Spud turned slightly and dropped his clipboard on the bench behind him. Jeremy tightened. It seemed an ominous gesture, in spite of the words being spoken. It seemed a preparation for a fight, like taking off a coat. Spud continued, "In some other situation I'd even have some respect for what you did to Skinner. Not that you should have done it, but before this happened I figured you were just a little too—I don't know—too much a good guy to be somebody I could really understand."

Spud folded his arms across his chest. Jeremy felt his own chest filling, clenching. He was ready to fight this man. Spud said, "These are hard times. I'm the first to admit it. But hard times brings out the mongrels, the guys who like to feed on others. Like at this mill. I think there's probably some Bolsheviks around here, believe it or not. Some guys who'd like to destroy this place and the good men working in it."

Spud stopped speaking; his arms stayed folded; he did not move. Jeremy wondered when he would bring up the unemployed council meeting. That was the only thing that would give Spud a reason to question his motives for the beating. After a moment, Spud said, "These Bolsheviks like to take advantage of good guys. Make them think they're doing something good when they're really doing something bad."

Jeremy heard in this an invitation to play the innocent dupe. Maybe Spud did like him enough to want him to clear himself. Or maybe it was a trick to win a damning confession. There were risks either way. Jeremy smiled a slow, confident, friendly smile. "Like I said before, Spud. These guys who figure too much are

likely to be wrong. Couple of out-of-work friends of mine per-
suaded me to go to some damn meeting the other night. It turned
out to be run by some guys who definitely had that problem.
I'd've liked to bust their heads to shut 'em up, but they seemed
to have a bunch of friends around."

Spud laughed, a sound as hard and sudden as a punch, and
he laughed again. "Okay, Cole. Just watch your temper around
your own kind. It ain't like I'm short of labor, but Skinner was
an okay guy, useful to me, and you gave him a pretty good
working-over."

"I'll stay away from the home brew," Jeremy said. "Especially
somebody else's."

Spud laughed again and Jeremy turned and opened the door,
half expecting to be hit from behind, but Spud apparently was
satisfied because Jeremy went off to the ovens and his name
wasn't on the layoff list that afternoon.

Jeremy went out the front gate and headed for Nick's. He
felt quickened by his deception of Spud, as if he'd hit the man
cleanly and knocked him down. But he recognized the danger
of smugness and he looked behind him to make sure he wasn't
being followed. He resolved, too, not to tell Nick about Skinner.
Nick had been emphatic about not taking any action against the
man and it would only make him nervous, Jeremy decided.

At Nick's screen door the voice that answered the knock was
clearer now. It said, "Come on in," and even sounded a little
impatient, to Jeremy a good sign.

But the face was much the same. Nick was struggling to sit
up on the couch and both his eyes were open, but they were
still sunk deep in purple swelling. Jeremy looked away. He saw—
through the inner door, through the bedroom and into the
kitchen—a woman. She stood at the kitchen door, a small, spin-
dly, pale woman with a face that was full of freckles and set hard
against Jeremy, a hard, angry, but silent face. There was a whine
behind her and she turned and a boy appeared—a boy smaller
than the one Jeremy had seen here last time. It was Nick's second
son, also round-faced, and the mother cupped the boy's head in
her two hands and she bent to him and spoke intently.

Jeremy moved to a chair beside the couch and sat. "Are you all right?" he said to Nick.

Nick nodded. "Better. I ache more, I think, but I don't feel like I'm in pieces."

"Are they getting food for your family now?"

"They?"

Jeremy didn't know quite how to describe what he had in mind. "Your . . . comrades. You know, your other Communists."

Nick laughed, a sound shaped like the ridge of broken teeth he showed as he lifted his face.

"Look," Jeremy said, "I just don't know that much about this yet. But isn't that what all of you are supposed to believe?"

"I'm sorry," Nick said. "I wasn't laughing at you. It was the ones you're talking about that made me laugh. Sure, a guy like you—a pure man of the working class—would expect a Communist to act like one. It just shows me the theory's right and even worth getting beat up for. But these are mostly selfish, self-seeking people who are leading us. Even us, the shapers of the new society. We've got to wait till *everybody's* a Communist and the right way is the law before any of it will really work."

"So you're not eating?"

"We're eating some. I had a little bit of money left. I'm a good thrifty Red."

"How much do you have, Nick?"

"A little."

"How much?" Jeremy demanded.

"Not much."

Jeremy felt restless with concern. "What are you going to do? How are you going to feed your family?"

"By overthrowing the government."

This answer stopped both men for a moment and then they laughed. There was a movement nearby and Jeremy looked and the younger boy had drifted into the room. He stopped to study the stranger and his face was as hard as his mother's now; the whining had been only for her.

"Stop it," Nick said sharply. Jeremy assumed he was referring to the look the boy was giving him. But Nick's voice grew even sharper and he shouted, "Dammit, Sean. Stop it. Stop that scratching."

Jeremy realized, just at the moment Sean did, that the boy was scratching his forearm vigorously. Sean jerked his hand away and there was a large red mosquito bite on the arm. "Get on outside," Nick said, his voice still tight with anger, and the boy was gone.

Jeremy turned and Nick's face was angled away. Nick tried to take a deep, calming breath, but his hand jumped to his side and the breath popped out. "Dammit," Nick said.

Jeremy didn't say anything. He didn't understand what Nick had been so angry about, and the man still seemed preoccupied. Jeremy waited and finally Nick said, "I'm too hard on him. I love him too much. I love both of them too much." Nick paused and Jeremy waited some more, began to wonder if he should leave. Nick said, "It's bad to scratch those things . . . He scratches and it makes *me* itch." Nick tried to laugh at this, but it seemed to hurt him and he cut it off. "It's those damn mosquitoes," Nick said. "I get so angry at them, when I see one of them I go crazy trying to kill it. The idea of those things sucking my boys' blood . . . It drives me crazy, you know?" Nick's fists were before him, clenched; his face was red and he began to cough.

Jeremy stood up. Nick was turned away, spitting into a handkerchief. But Jeremy couldn't leave. He waited. Nick laid his head back against the crest of the couch and he said, "I'm sorry . . . Do you have any kids, Jeremy?"

"No." The word was soft as the pricking of a mosquito.

"Then you wouldn't understand what I'm talking about . . . I love those boys."

"I understand."

Nick lifted his head and sat up straight. "There's better things for you and me to talk about. Did you tell anybody today about the march on the Fourth?"

"Not today. I didn't see anybody today but Gus."

"It's okay. Gus knows. He says he won't come, but he'll be laid off before the end of the month. Mark my words."

"Is this march going to really do something?"

"Sure."

"What?"

Nick looked up at Jeremy and he smiled faintly. "You keep challenging me, Jeremy. Good. I want you to."

"So what's this march going to do?"

"We've got to suck at 'em a little bit. Like we were one of those mosquitoes. Suck even just a little bit of their blood. Make 'em itch."

"What's that mean?"

Nick's smile disappeared. For a moment Jeremy thought the man finally had had enough: he accepted only so many straight questions. But then there was a change. Nick's face was hard to read through its bruised puffiness, but the man nodded and now it seemed that he approved the question. He said, "It means we make Hagemeyer and his goons look to the world like what they are. Even just for one moment, in one little place. Other people will notice. The word will spread. We do it again, another time. And another. Eventually people will understand that there are bad guys behind this whole Depression. And there are some good guys too."

Jeremy smiled at this. He remembered Spud's calling him a "good guy," a term of contempt for Spud. Nick was silent but he was looking away; he couldn't see the smile. Nick seemed to brood for a moment and then he said, "You know what Hagemeyer's doing?"

"What?"

"He's starting to call in rents in Hungry Hollow."

"He can't."

"He owns most of the place. His father bought it all up with the vision of a company town in his head."

"I meant he can't because those people have no place to go."

"They go to shantytown. Or on the road."

"That's no place."

"Out of Wabash is all he cares. Hagemeyer's using the times to purge the mill. I think he's got himself a plan to bring in a bunch of real cheap labor from somewhere when this is all over."

Jeremy struggled to speak calmly. "He's going too damn far."

"There's another reason he wants those people out."

"What's that?"

"To take their votes away."

"Their votes?" Jeremy realized he was still on his feet and he sat. He was caught by Nick's words, by the man's air of having a special knowledge, of seeing connections that were simple and logical once spoken but which only he knew to speak. "How do they lose their votes?"

"They won't vote as hobos. They don't even have an address."

"Hoover can't win anyway, can he?"

Nick shook his head. "Hagemeyer doesn't care about Hoover. Hoover's a lost cause."

"Then why does he want to uproot those votes so bad?"

"You haven't seen the Post-Dispatch this afternoon?"

"No." Jeremy almost added, I don't read the papers, but he felt suddenly ashamed of it. For several years he hadn't given a damn what happened outside the mill and his house. But he knew that he should change that now. Nick was calling him to find the larger connections.

"Interesting bit of news," Nick said. "Guess who's running for the Congress as a Republican in this district?"

"Who?"

"John J. Hagemeyer."

Jeremy laughed. "Who'd vote for him?"

"Don't laugh, comrade. Hagemeyer's a shrewd man. I hate him and you hate him and some others in Wabash hate him—Hungry Hollow hates him, certainly. But he still owns half this town and you'd be surprised how many people hold him blameless for the hard times. It's not *his* fault the country went bad, they say. It's those stuffed shirts on Wall Street. Hagemeyer's own stock in the company fell real low, they say. He got hurt like the rest of us. He *wants* us to work. He's going to give us jobs again as soon as he can."

Jeremy jumped up. "That's damn stupid. It's Hagemeyer's kind . . . " He had no more words, only two hands clenched in the air before him. His hands seemed to him foolish, pitiful in their uselessness before this problem.

"And don't forget," Nick said, "this congressional district holds more than Wabash. It goes all the way up to Lawton. Lawton is full of bourgeois families. River shipping people, wealthy farmers, retired businessmen from St. Louis living up there on the bluffs and ready to send a man like John J. Hagemeyer to Congress. And then who knows what? Hagemeyer still believes in capitalism. He thinks things will swing back his way. He thinks his time will come and he wants to be in the center of power in Washington when it does."

"Stop it," Jeremy said, loud, as if he were angry at Nick. Nick smiled at this, a smile of control that Jeremy didn't like. Jeremy said, "I'm not your crowd of bindle stiffs in a packing house for you to play with."

The smile vanished. Nick's mouth tightened. "Look," he said. "Those people weren't bindle stiffs."

"Don't pick at my words," Jeremy said. "I'm just saying I don't like being worked up. You were talking like the other side to make a point, but it went on too long and I didn't like what it was doing to me."

"I'm sorry," Nick said softly. "You're a good man. You feel for the workers. I guess I didn't realize how strong that feeling is."

"It's strong."

"I'm sorry."

"I want to *do* something."

"You are doing something. Stay at the plant as long as you can. Listen for us. Tell people about us. Be careful."

"That's not enough."

"It's all we need for now. After the Fourth of July, maybe there'll be more. The Fourth may surprise a lot of people. Maybe even us."

While Jeremy slept the next morning, Deborah packed a lunch for them. She'd saved some fruit; she'd bought a little cheese; the bread was day-old. There wasn't much, but it was enough to justify the trip to the big mound. They could even afford the trolley on the way out. It went along the highway to Lawton, and they'd get off beyond Caleb Hart's land and then walk south to Sun Mound. The morning was clear and already hot. Deborah had gone to the window as soon as she'd risen. She wanted this day with Jeremy very badly. The sky was clear and she was going to have it.

Putting the food into an old straw basket made her sad. She didn't know why for a long while, not till she had finished the packing and had closed the lid. Then she realized that it was something she'd lost that was making her sad. It'd been a long time—three years or more—since she'd packed a lunch for Jeremy. She used to fill his black metal lunch box every day and it was a pleasure for her, as if she were lying in the grass and putting food in his mouth. But the lunch box was on the floor in the pantry now. With the short shifts, there was no chance for him to eat food at the mill and she felt sad, sad she couldn't feed him when he was apart from her, sad the town was this hard up. She laid her hand on the top of the basket and looked out to the morning glare of the backyard. Birds rushed through the light and she turned away. She wondered if she should interrupt Jeremy's sleep.

In the other room he was already awake. He lay staring at the ceiling and now that there was silence in the kitchen he expected Deborah to appear, ready to take them away to her little picnic. He found that he feared her coming in. The picnic seemed bizarre to him, given his concerns with Nick and the mill and Spud and Skinner and John J. Hagemeyer. Running for Congress. With a chance to win. Damn. This made Jeremy sit up in the bed. He couldn't just go out somewhere and lie in the grass and act like nothing was happening in Wabash. He felt intensely focused. All the time now. It was a feeling like his feeling before the ovens. But not as clean as that. This focusing had no clear action to release it. Stay at the mill, Nick had said. Listen. Talk. Be careful. What the hell kind of action was that?

And he couldn't break this concentration. Even in his mill work there was a time, when the ovens were just stoked, to lean on his shovel; there was a moment after, and it helped freshen the moments of exertion. He realized that for a few days he hadn't been able to let go. He blamed that on not having something specific to do. But pounding Skinner was specific and it had left him troubled. It scared him a little, this grip inside him. He turned and saw the twist of the sheet where Deborah had slept. He laid his hand there. He loved his wife. He did love her and he grew even more frightened of this preoccupation. He was distant enough from Deborah as it was.

He rose up and dressed quickly and he opened the door to the kitchen to find Deborah standing beside the table, her hand on a basket, looking at him. "Let's go," he said, and she smiled so beautifully that for a moment he was conscious only of her.

D eborah and Jeremy walked to the center of Wabash, the town square with its fountain that Deborah could remember as the place where all the horses were taken for water. The fountain was dry and the stone statue of Lewis and Clark standing shoulder to shoulder was black with soot and missing an arm, though no one could say if it was Lewis's or Clark's. There'd been talk of taking the statue down and putting one up portraying Sir Henry Bessemer, the father of modern steelmaking, but nothing came of it. Some said that if they wanted to honor steelmaking in Wabash, the statue should be of a Hagemeyer.

Deborah loved to ride streetcars and all the streetcars leaving Wabash originated at the square: the red cars went over the McKinley Bridge and down to the Twelfth and Delmar station in St. Louis; the larger yellow cars, which people called Yellowhammer, went out east of town and then north and up to the bluffs and terminated in Lawton, a hundred yards from the square where Lincoln once debated Douglas.

Deborah hooked her hand in Jeremy's arm as Yellowhammer came around the square, its bell clanging lazily, and she wished she were barefoot, she wished she could run with the car as it approached; she felt this even as she was happy to be holding Jeremy's arm and as she realized that for the moment she was happy Jeremy was the quiet man he was.

They boarded the streetcar and it took them out of town, over the Illinois Central tracks, along the scrubby green fields of horseradish and out to Indian Road. They got off the streetcar and walked south along the narrow dirt road, through the whisk of wind in the fields, and when they crossed the highway that led to Collinsville, Jeremy reflexively looked back west and he thought of the beating he'd given Skinner. He expected this thought to pull him away from Deborah, to focus him again on all the trouble. But instead he felt the same unease he'd had walking away from the beating and he turned his eyes to Deborah. She was moving ahead of him, the basket in one hand, her shoes in the other, and her hair was pinned up on top of her head. The free wisps of her hair made him restless—with what? Desire. Perhaps desire, though he still felt weary before that feeling; there was nothing he could do. He felt cut off from Deborah, as if it were she who'd died, as if this were merely a memory of his wife before him on the dusty road. But there was more to Jeremy's unbidden desire than the draw of her body; there was a gentleness to her apart from the softest parts of her flesh and it was this that he really desired, a gentleness that did not ask for his body to act. That desire was easier for him to nurture but harder to resolve. What could he do about it? Just be around her, was all he could think of. They moved along the dirt path and Sun Mound was before them; its grassy swelling loomed and called. He could lie up there with only the sky to see and he could be near her, and maybe that would be enough.

They passed through stands of hickory and cottonwood and they climbed the sheer path that led up the side of Sun Mound. Tight in chest and legs, they finally reached the top, the place where seven centuries earlier the king of the ancient Indian empire of Cahokia would stand clothed in a cape of polished shells and open his arms to the sun he took to be God. Deborah knew this story of the Indians and she stood at the edge of the broad plateau of the mound and she closed her eyes and lifted her face and she wondered what the lives of those Indians were like. She wondered how mothers and sisters and daughters loved each other. Her mind drew near to the women in her own life and this was not what she came to the mounds for and she turned away. She looked at Jeremy. He was lying in the grass beside the basket. She glanced out to the west and saw the mill in the distance, the blast furnace plant where Jeremy worked. White storm clouds of smoke poured from the stacks there, and Deborah looked back to Jeremy. He was not standing at the edge of the mound watching the mill, as she might have expected. He was lying beside her basket. She ran to him, happy, and she dropped to the grass next to him and she kissed him on the cheek and laid her head on his chest and he held her near him, tightly, and he wanted to do something, wanted very much to do something and he said, "I'm glad we came here." Deborah made a soft sound that touched him like a wisp of her hair, and he lay back flat on the grass and she moved up so that their faces were close. Jeremy tightened his arms around Deborah and she put her face in the curve of his neck and they fit together in an embrace that held a memory for them both, an embrace of grief. They'd held each other this way the night that Elizabeth was buried. Now, on the top of Sun Mound, Jeremy brought his hand up and he touched Deborah's hair and she knew that their daughter was in Jeremy's mind just as she was in her own. They clung to each other and their hearts slowed, their limbs grew heavy. Deborah remembered seeing Elizabeth across an open stretch of ground. It was out near the levee. They'd visited Grandma Birney and Lizzy had gone out to play and Deborah went to get the child. She saw Lizzy crouching down, swaying slightly, intent on something on the ground. Deborah wondered what could be so interesting and even before she drew near enough to see, she began to grow afraid. Lizzy was speaking to something, but she was stooped low and the angle was sharp and Deborah drew near and stopped. She could see what it was. On the grass before her daughter was a copperhead snake. It was curling up but it was a large one, she knew, maybe four feet. The bands—alternating chestnut red and copper red—were vivid and she'd known from her daddy to fear this snake. The copperhead could kill and it was meaner than any rattlesnake. It was slick and quiet and it could kill and Lizzy was talking to it, singing to it. Lizzy was singing a lullaby and the snake was gyring in the grass, curling and uncurling slowly, its head lolling back and forth. Deborah knew not to move. She could not make her voice sound, though she tried. But she knew enough not to move. The snake was charmed. Lizzy sang, Hush little snakey don't you cry, and the snake laid its head in the grass.

And Jeremy thought of Lizzy on a night in late fall. It was not many months before she died. He took her walking with him in the dark and she was very excited. Her hand was warm in his and he could feel her excitement. He took her through Hungry Hollow and out to the edge of the slag dump. From there they could see the furnace operation and it seemed to stretch across the whole horizon. The night was very dark and the mill burned on. This was the blast furnace plant and so its flaring and pluming were out in the open, not contained, not held in buildings like the North Plant. He could see the fires of the mill reflected in Lizzy's wide eyes—she was entranced by the sight. It's so beautiful, she said, and Jeremy lifted her and set her on his shoulders and she leaned onto him and put her arms around his forehead. He looked at what she saw—the place where he worked—and it was as beautiful as the child said. There were great clouds of smoke and steam and they swirled over points of light like nebulae spinning new stars and Jeremy could see dark forms there— the batteries of ovens, the smokestacks, the ore bridge. At first the swirl and flame of the mill was as silent as the sky, but now he could hear a hum, a sound like the sound of the horizon on a summer night.

Deborah waited motionless as Lizzy sang to the snake and

finally Deborah whispered, Come away now, and her daughter rose slowly and left the copperhead where it lay charmed on the grass and when Lizzy was near, Deborah grasped her hand and Jeremy reached up to grasp his daughter's hand and she said, What's that jelly fire? and he looked and he knew at once what she meant—the flame coming from the tall, thin stack. It's a bleeder valve, he said, and he felt her chin touch the top of his head; he could imagine her resting her head on his so that she could study this beautiful flame and when Lizzy looked up at her mother she smiled a smile that seemed full of some special knowledge and Lizzy's thoughtful study of the flame and her smile at the charming of the snake brought both Jeremy and Deborah to the same tremor of grief. They each felt it in the other's body and to feel the other's grief was too much to add to their own and they pulled gently apart. Jeremy rose and walked to the western edge of the mound and he looked off to the mill and Deborah lay flat and closed her eyes against the sky and she thought she heard a gliding nearby in the grass but she did not care and did not move.

O n Sunday afternoon the women sat in Miriam's parlor, all the women in the family except for Grandma Birney and, of course, Effie. When they all first sat down and Miriam remarked that it was difficult to get their mother to visit anymore, Adah said, She's home listening for the rodents in her wall, and Della said, At least she won't try to marry one of 'em, Adah honey, and there was a long period of bickering. They hadn't been together five minutes and they were already fighting and Deborah wondered why she came here when the sisters were together. She decided to see them only one at a time from now on. She didn't have the strength to listen to this. But the bickering finally faded, and Aunt Berenice, who'd been very quiet, said, "Joe killed a rabid dog once near our house. He didn't hesitate a minute. He saw the dog and took a piece of firewood off our pile and he went up to the dog and beat it to death."

In response there were no covert glances between the other sisters, no patronizing swoops in their voices. Della said, "You've got yourself a brave man," and she sounded like she meant it.

Miriam said, "That's right, Bunny. That takes guts, to kill a rabid dog."

Even Adah said, "You're a lucky woman," and she didn't undercut it in the next breath; she said no more.

Deborah appreciated the sisters' words to Berenice. They were being kind to her, at least here, for the moment, in her presence. Deborah knew it was wrong to avoid her mother and aunts when they were all together. If she loved them—and she did love them, especially now, stirred by the struggle in them between gentleness and cruelty—she had to try to deal with them at their worst. And what could she possibly do? She found that she had a crazy hope that she could change them, make them act only on their kindness. But she was sitting in a chair beside the window, apart from the sisters, silent, without the slightest idea how to influence these strong-willed women before her.

Berenice said, "I think that dog had been bitten by a rat. It wasn't a bad dog. I used to scratch him behind the ears when he came poking around our yard."

The others had no more words but they waited with what appeared to be interest, and when it was clear Berenice had nothing else to say, Della said to the group, "So what shall we do?" She paused only slightly before she added, "How about the Ouija board?"

"I don't know," Berenice said. "I don't know what to think about that. Can't we play pinochle?"

"With Debbie here, we're five of us, Bunny," Della said, standing in the center of the room. "We can't play pinochle with five."

"I don't mind," Deborah said.

"The Ouija board would be fun for us all," Della said. "We'll take turns and it's fun to watch."

Deborah wondered what Della was up to. She didn't like the Ouija board; it made her feel—it was hard for her to say what—unclean, maybe. And Berenice didn't want it either. "Aunt Della," Deborah said, "I *really* don't mind sitting out a game of pinochle."

"Adah?" Della said, turning to her sister. Adah and Berenice were on opposite ends of the couch.

Adah glanced at Berenice and then patted at her hair. Her marcel waves were drooping slightly in the heat. "I don't believe in talking to the dead, of course," Adah said, though her voice quaked a little, probably from excitement; Deborah knew Adah was extremely superstitious. Deborah looked at Della and sensed the woman struggling not to make a sarcastic remark. Adah said, "It's okay with me, though."

Della turned her back on Adah and Berenice and winked a slow, conspiratorial wink at Miriam, who sat on a chair before her. Della said, "Fine, Adah. You and I can start."

All four sisters—even Berenice—rose and began to prepare. Miriam went to a cupboard and took out the Ouija board and Della and Adah set two straight-back chairs in the center of the parlor floor. Berenice drew another chair near. Deborah stayed where she was. This was a foolish game, she thought. And disquieting. Death as a parlor game. She thought of leaving, but Della and Adah were sitting before each other and Deborah thought of Effie—Effie was always near her thoughts now, when she was with these women—and she realized her mother and aunts did not know that Deborah understood the truth. She still hadn't decided how to approach her mother with what she'd learned from Grandma Birney. Now she got an idea, perhaps prompted by the anger she felt at these quarrelsome women. She did not leave; she waited; and Della said, "Who shall we contact first?"

Deborah answered at once. "Effie."

All four faces popped up before her, four wide-eyed, tight-jawed faces. There was a moment of silence while they tried to figure out how to react. First Adah, then Della, turned to look at Miriam, as if to say, She's your daughter, do something. Berenice's face was changing; the eyes grew quizzical, then fearful. Berenice said, "Is she dead now? Did you hear something?"

"It's okay, Bunny," Miriam said.

"Hasn't Effie been dead a long time?" Deborah asked, playing the role that would have been sincere less than two weeks ago.

"Is she dead, Miriam?" Berenice asked, her voice crimped in fear. Deborah suddenly regretted starting this. She hadn't taken Berenice into account.

"Nothing's changed, Bunny." Miriam's voice was full of the smooth-edged finality she might use on a frightened child.

Deborah said no more. She could have pressed her mother for the truth—at least a public admission that Effie existed. But she was alarming Berenice and she said no more.

Miriam said, "That wouldn't be a good person to think about now, Debby."

"I have it," Della said. "Let's ask the board who's there."

"Okay," Adah said and she bent over the board and when her eyes went down, Della winked again at Miriam. Miriam smiled and nodded toward Adah as if to say, Don't let her see you. Della turned and put her fingertips on one side of the planchette and Adah put her fingertips on the other side. The planchette began to move and the women all murmured in surprise and expectation. Only Berenice was quiet. Her face was still half turned to Deborah.

Deborah silently called herself a fool. Again she wanted to leave, but to do so now would make her mention of Effie look suspicious. She did not want to raise that subject with these women for the time being. She turned her head away, closed her eyes as if she were tired, and she waited for enough time to pass so she could leave.

Della and Adah were calling out letters and Miriam was repeating them and writing them down and Berenice was softly exclaiming as more letters emerged from the board. Deborah shut her mind to the details of the game. Occasionally an individual letter would break into her head, but she refused to follow the words as they were formed.

Then Miriam said, "Here it is. Here it is. I-T-S-D-A-D-D . . ."

And Della cried, "It's Daddy!"

Deborah's face jerked toward the women. Was this Della's game? Was this what the winking was about? The hands on the planchette were gliding quickly to a corner of the board. "Yes!" Della said. "He says yes!"

Berenice sat back in her chair. She touched her lips with her forefinger, a thoughtful gesture. There was no alarm in her face, as Deborah expected. Aunt Berenice seemed very calm. Adah was hunched over the board, her eyes wide, and Della was smiling at her hands. Deborah knew Della was consciously guiding the planchette. "What do you want, Daddy?" Della said.

The hands on the board began to move and Deborah looked toward her mother. Was her mother going to let this happen? She was. She was poised over her note pad, clearly absorbed.

Letters were being announced and Deborah tried to close her mind again, but the letters insisted on stringing themselves together. M-Y-L-I-T-T-L-E-A-D . . .

"Me!" Adah cried. "Me!"

"Yes!" Della said. ". . . A-H!"

"A-D-A-H," Adah spelled. "I'm here, Papa! It's me, your little Adah! What do you want?"

Deborah tried to rouse herself to leave. Stand up, she shouted in her mind. Walk to the door. But she couldn't. She feared for Adah and she couldn't move, couldn't speak. She looked and the planchette was moving. Adah's face was radiant. "S," Della said. And Aunt Berenice: Berenice was watching with a placid smile.

"I," Della said.

A smile that reminded Deborah of Aunt Berenice in the tree.

"N," Della said.

A smile that chilled Deborah.

"G!" Della cried. "Sing!"

Adah sat up straight. "Do you want me to sing for you, Papa?" Adah clearly felt honored. The planchette raced to the edge of the board.

"Yes!" Della said.

Adah straightened even further. She lifted the wave in her hair and she began to sing in a thin, quavering voice. " 'I'm forever blowing bubbles. Pretty bubbles in the air . . . ' "

Deborah stood up. No one noticed. Adah had forgotten the words and she was beginning to hum. She stopped and said, "I'm sorry, Papa. I forget the next line." Her voice was bloated with nascent tears.

"It's okay, Adah," Della said. "Sing what you know. Isn't that okay, Papa?"

The planchette ran to the "yes" corner of the board, though only Della's hands were on it. Adah sang. " 'I'm forever blowing bubbles . . . ' "

The tears were streaming down Adah's face now, and Deborah went to the door and out onto the porch. She paused only briefly and heard Adah's voice, a frightened bird trapped in the house, fluttering to find release. " ' . . . Pretty bubbles in the air . . . ' "

Deborah crossed the yard quickly, strode away. She passed her own house and cut through downtown and went on out to the levee, to her grandmother's house. She knocked once and opened the door and went in.

Grandma Birney was there, sitting at her writing desk, and Deborah was very happy to see her. She plopped onto the couch, and her grandmother said, "Hello, honey," without looking up from the paper before her. Deborah wanted to talk about the feelings she had, but her grandmother's nonchalance was a comfort, she found, and to preserve it she said nothing. She closed her eyes and listened to the scratch of her grandmother's pen. It went on fitfully for a time and then there was a long silence and a sigh. Deborah opened her eyes and her grandmother was holding up a piece of paper, reading it and biting the end of her pen.

"Is it for the rats?" Deborah said.

"Yes," Grandma Birney said, and she sighed once more. "It's not easy."

"Aren't they paying any attention?" Deborah heard the words as she spoke them; she knew they could be interpreted as patronizing. But they weren't. She was sincere. And this made her smile. Writing to rats. Deborah realized she was taking this seriously; she even felt a tweak of envy over her grandmother's project.

"Oh, they're paying attention, all right," Grandma Birney said. "They're just not doing the right thing."

"Can I hear what you've written?"

Her grandmother squinted at the paper in her hand. "No. Not yet. This one's not done. I've got to find a new approach."

Deborah was disappointed. She watched as her grandmother put the paper down. Maybe she'd finish it now. Then Deborah could read it. But instead, Grandma Birney put her pen down too and rose. She came and sat next to Deborah on the couch and said, "How've you been, honey?"

Deborah shrugged. "Okay."

"What's the matter?"

"I was with the sisters."

"Oh, them."

"They were at each other again."

"They're naughty, quarrelsome children."

"I want them to stop."

"Have you talked to your mama about it? She's got a little bit of sense, at least. Not as much as you, by a long shot. But a little bit."

Deborah laid her head against the point of her grandmother's shoulder. "I try to talk to her, but it's hard for me to know how. When I say it straight—why do you hurt each other all the time?—she either plays dumb—why, what do you mean?—or she just acts like it's not what it is. Why, we understand each other, she says. No one gets hurt. It's just our way."

"You don't believe that?"

"No."

"It *is* their way."

"But they do hurt each other. It's like they weren't sisters at all. It's hard to believe they all came from . . ." Deborah realized what she was saying and shied away from it.

"From the same womb," Grandma Birney finished. "I understand."

"Do you?" Deborah sat up again, squared around to face her grandmother. She hadn't expected this turn in her own feelings, but it had happened and now she would follow through with it.

"Yes," Grandma Birney said, seeming a little puzzled by Deborah's sudden intensity.

"Then give me Aunt Effie's address." Deborah braced herself for another display of harshness in her grandmother, but the woman's face did not change.

"Why are you so interested in Effie?" she said.

"She's my aunt."

"Do you expect her to be different from the others?" Grandma Birney said this gently.

"I don't know . . . I hadn't thought of her in that way . . . Yes. Maybe she's different."

"She's not." The grandmother's voice was still soft.

"When was the last time you saw her?"

"I don't know. A long time."

"Then how do you know?"

"She's my daughter."

Deborah wanted to ask Grandma Birney if she blamed herself, then, for how these women could rip at each other. If it merely had to do with being her daughters, then she had to accept the blame. But Deborah didn't say these things. Instead, she said, "Can you tell me where she is?"

Grandma Birney looked at Deborah for a moment and then sighed, a sigh that sounded like the one prompted by her struggles with the letter. "I can give you the last address I know."

"Please."

Her grandmother nodded and stood up and walked to her desk. She bent over, took her pen, and wrote something on a piece of paper. She brought it to the couch and gave it to Deborah. "Here it is," she said.

Deborah glanced at it—an address on Mallinckrodt Avenue. Just over the McKinley Bridge. Then something occurred to her. She looked up at her grandmother and said, "You knew the address by heart."

"I never forget a thing," the woman said, and her voice sounded hard.

Monday morning Jeremy climbed the ladder up the B-furnace with three other men. They were Gus and two men Jeremy didn't know very well, new men swung here from other parts of the plant. They were all assigned to poke out the B-furnace stove, a job that they'd work in pairs, alternating. It required going into the stove, and no one could stay in there for more than a few minutes. Each pair would work three minutes inside while the other pair rested outside. It was the most intense job at the blast furnace plant, but unlike the other men, Jeremy never complained about the assignment. Whatever was in his head from the outside world never survived a morning inside the stove. He still felt a clotting in his limbs from the memories on the mound yesterday, and the stove was a welcome purgatory.

He climbed, while off at A-battery the skip cars climbed with him, carrying white rock this trip—the limestone. Already inside the furnace was the rough red ore and after the limestone would come the coke. He looked to the top of A-battery and a skip car was dumping its load in the hopper.

A gassy smell turned Jeremy's attention back to his own ladder. It reminded him that there was always carbon monoxide up here. Every couple of years—sometimes more often—the mill would lose somebody to the gas. A man would linger too long in the wrong spot and at first he'd feel a little woozy, a little drunk, and then he'd sit for a rest; his body would fold itself up insistently and his judgment wouldn't be good at that point and he wouldn't even know to be afraid and he'd die.

The four men climbed through the smell and up to the metal platform circling the B-furnace hopper. They went around the hopper, stirring up the ore dust beneath their feet, and they climbed to the top of the stove, a tall circular structure, like a boiler. The bottom half of the stove was a brick-lined flue to burn the gas; the top half was shaped by a checkerwork of bricks that retained the heat. In the holes of the checkerwork were clogs of flue dust and it was these that had to be poked out with steel rods. To get to them, there was a trapdoor at the top of the stove that opened onto a space tall enough to stand in. The floor of the space was the brick checkerwork and it was here that the men would stand to clean out the flue dust.

Jeremy and Gus paired off automatically and the other two men leaned on the platform railing. Gus went to the trap and unscrewed it and laid it aside. He put their teapot lamp on one end of a double-hooked chain, lit it, let it down into the hole, and hooked the other end on the trap rim. Jeremy looked briefly out across the top of the furnaces. He could have looked out much farther from here, as far as Sun Mound, but he kept his eyes among the gas uptakes and bleeder valves and furnace stacks. He had no need to look farther: he was ready to crawl into the mill's most private place. He anticipated the sense of sufficiency he always felt in the stove. He would be there; the heat would be there; that was all he wanted.

One of the other men touched him on the shoulder, gave him the chain ladder, and he stepped to Gus, bent beside him, hooked the rim of the trap and let the ladder unfurl into the hole. Then Gus nodded and turned away from the hole and began to descend the ladder. Gus barely fit in the trap and he pinched in his arms and he disappeared. Jeremy turned and he saw the two men. One was leaning to the other and speaking into his ear, his eyes shifting to Jeremy. This was not what Jeremy wanted to see at this moment. He wanted only the mill. He paused and looked off to the long, neat line of coke ovens. A pusher was moving and Jeremy felt with his foot for the ladder and he went down, down, he felt as if he were plunging into deep water and then he was inside the stove. He stepped free of the ladder in

the hot, roiling darkness. The lamp flame was guttering frantically. The lamp itself was swinging and Jeremy touched it,
stopped its movement, but the light it gave off was slight and
still frantic. The hole above looked dark, as if the sky beyond
was fading toward night, though it was still morning. He had
very little time before the heat would overcome him. He turned
and from the dim interior of the space came Gus's hand to give
Jeremy a steel rod. Then the hand withdrew into the billows of
heat, into the blackness of the interior of the stove.

Jeremy stepped forward and plunged the rod deep into a
hole in the pattern of bricks. The dust was packed there and
thick and he flexed his arms, dug and pushed and twisted the
rod till he felt the clink of it against the brick. He did not bend
to his task. He kept his back straight. If he bent too close to the
heat rising from the oven below, it would sear his lungs. Already
his feet had begun to burn, even through the layers of rubber
laid inside his shoes. He did one hole, another, and his pores
burned as if a pin were being eased into each one, each pore
had a pin. He poked out a third brick hole, the normal quota;
he'd been in the stove nearly three minutes. But he liked this
work—his body and mind and memory had been wiped so clean
in here that he wasn't even conscious of its having happened—
and he knew Gus liked the work and they'd stay a little longer,
to do a fourth hole. Jeremy took a step forward and plunged the
rod into a clogged hole and he glanced up to see Gus. He could
see the Hungarian's shape farther in, near the edge of the checkerwork, near the place of the greatest danger in this job. The
combustion chamber was in the darkest place, waiting for a mis-
step: before the chamber was a clear shaft down to the bottom
of the furnace; a man falling in would be sucked down into the
oven and then out through the hot-blast valve. Some had fallen
over the years and it was very difficult to deal with the body of
a man who died like that. Jeremy was anxious for Gus, though
he knew the Hungarian was conscious of the danger, was as
experienced at this as Jeremy. But Jeremy resolved on the next
entry to go first and make Gus work nearer the trapdoor.

The air was very thick now. The heat felt as if it were no

longer external but something being generated from within Jeremy's body. The fourth hole was cleared. Gus was turning, coming out of the shadows. Jeremy turned, too, hung back to let Gus go past him and up the ladder first, and Gus let Jeremy grant him that; he went up the ladder quickly and Jeremy followed, the back of his throat liquid with heat, his bones dissolving, and he was in the air, rising into air that felt cool in spite of the hot June sun, a sun that had burned him before but was no threat to him now, not as he rose from this place of true heat.

And Jeremy stood with Gus at the railing as the other two men went into the stove. Jeremy and Gus leaned on the railing and did not move, did not let the flare of heat in their bodies show in even the tiniest movement. They did not move and did not speak and they both understood that this was an expression of respect for each other and for their work.

They descended into the stove many times through the day and when the shift was done, they went to the locker room and changed and Gus nodded at Jeremy as he left. Jeremy lingered. He was tired at last from a day's work, excellently tired. Finally he went out and he stopped at the personnel shack and on the new layoff posting he found Gus's name.

While Jeremy was going into the stove for the first time that day, Deborah boarded a red streetcar at the square. She sat by the window near the front of the car and the heat of the velour seat burned through her dress. She leaned forward for a moment of relief but she did not move to an inner seat that had been shaded from the sun; she wanted to watch out the window and she sat back again. It was still hot, but not as bad, and she concentrated on the twin metal sounds, the thin whipping of the overhead wire and the low blade-whine of the rail.

Outside, West Wabash went by—a run of shops, most of them boarded up; overgrown lots scattered with rocks and rubble and raggedy children; tar-paper houses with men on their front stoops. Deborah felt sad for men who had only their stoops to go to in the middle of a Monday morning, and she turned her face from the window. She thought about Effie, about what she could say to an aunt in exile from women who included Deborah's own mother. She could think of no words, could not even clearly picture the moment of meeting.

After a time, the street began to rise. Deborah looked outside. Ahead was the dark arch of McKinley Bridge and below it was the river, wide and brown like a summer-tanned child. She liked the river, and the car would soon go down the center of the bridge, too far from the sides to see; so she rose up a little to look at the river for a few moments more. Its surface was smooth except for the wake of a boat that looked like stretch marks. Then the river disappeared and there was the flashing of shadows from the superstructure of the bridge. Deborah leaned back and waited, her eyes closed, until she heard the clang of the bell and felt a turning.

The streetcar screeched its way off the bridge ramp and onto elevated tracks that curved and curved until the car was running parallel to the river. Deborah was on the right side of the car and below her was a tangle of pipes and metal shapes that looked like a shelf of pots and pans. There was a powerful odor in the air—a stink that could not be compared to anything in a human body or an animal body or even the foulest, slowest waterway. This was the Mallinckrodt Chemical plant and she looked beyond it, across a distant highway, and up a slope to a neighborhood of brick row houses on a hill. Near the front edge of the hill, in the center of the houses, was a massive gray stone church with twin spires stretching up high, each narrowing to a fine point, as if listening for something from very far away.

Deborah assumed it was a Catholic church; it had to be Catholic and she knew it must be Aunt Effie's church. This excited Deborah. It was as if she'd just caught a distant glimpse of Effie herself. The streetcar clanged the excitement out of her, but the sound was an alert for the approaching station—Mallinckrodt Avenue, which ran past the south edge of the plant and up the hill. Aunt Effie's street.

Deborah rose and the streetcar stopped and she gave her ticket to the conductor on the way off. She went down the steps of the elevated platform and hurried past the hiss of the chemical plant. Then she could see the church again, almost straight ahead, perhaps a block or two north of Mallinckrodt. She crossed a wide street that ran south to downtown St. Louis. Mallinckrodt Avenue climbed the hill and she kept her eyes on the church, which was growing in her sight. There were figures in stone in the facade of the church, beneath the spires and over the wide series of dark wooden doors, but she couldn't make out the figures from this distance.

Aunt Effie was near, a woman Deborah felt she knew, through the kinship of blood, even if she had no memory of ever seeing her. She didn't even know when the rift had occurred, when Effie had become Catholic. How did her aunt's religion make her different?

Deborah was at the top of the hill and the church was off to the right—spires only, from this angle, rising above the house-tops. She went along the street and as the number she sought grew closer, she felt a trembling begin inside her. She refused to plan what to say. That would only make her sound stiff. She would depend on the moment; she would let her feelings at confronting her aunt give her a voice.

Then she found the address: the right half of a brick two-story semidetached. At the windows were white lace curtains. There was a flowerpot on the top step with a thin green plant inside. Deborah went up the steps and the inner door was closed, the shade drawn. Deborah opened the screen and knocked on the glass of the door. She waited a few moments and knocked again. Then there was a rattling inside and the door opened.

The woman who stood before Deborah was small and very thin—willfully thin, Deborah felt, as if the woman had decided there were parts of herself she had no use for and so she'd gotten rid of them. But the face held the traces of the family's women.

Indeed, the high cheeks and the wide-set eyes were exaggerated in the thinness of this face. "Aunt Effie?" Deborah said.

The woman cocked her head. "I'm Effie Birney," she said.

"I'm your niece. I'm Miriam's daughter, Deborah."

"Oh my," Effie said, and though Deborah's hands were at her side, Effie found them, raised them, clasped them in hands that felt cold and bony but full of a fervor that made Deborah worry about weeping. She didn't want to seem mad to her aunt and she feared that her tears, though prompted by gratitude, would do that. "Oh my," Effie said again. "Come in. Please."

Effie turned and led Deborah inside, still holding one of her hands. The room was dim, and candles in shallow red jars flickered on each end of the mantel. Hanging over the mantel was a large wooden cross and Deborah was struck by the figure there. The crosses in the churches she'd always gone to were empty, as if Christ had been taken down already and been buried. But on this cross Christ was still there, still suffering. The face was clear even in the dim light: there were cuts on the cheeks and brow, bruises, tracks of blood from the crown of thorns; the eyes were half-closed, cast down; the mouth was opened slightly from the pain. Effie's hand was gone from hers and there were words being spoken but Deborah could not listen, could not take her eyes from this suffering man. She felt a crowding in the room, presences of the past hour: children moving in rock-strewn lots; men sitting on stoops, their hands drooping over their knees; the men in her own block who were laid off from the mill, their women with tight faces and clinging children; and she sensed Jeremy nearby, struggling with the short hours, aching in his silence for more work, aching too for their daughter. Even Lizzy was somewhere close as Deborah looked at this anguished face on the cross before her, this occupied cross, a cross for hard times.

"Deborah?" It was Effie's voice, the same voice that had been fluttering against her for the past few moments in vain.

"Yes," Deborah said, turning. The room was empty, except for herself and Aunt Effie, who seemed not quite so thin in the flickering candlelight; her eyes seemed to catch all the light and what was faint in the setting of the room was bright in the circle of these eyes.

"Would you like to sit down? You're very welcome here."

"Thank you. Yes." Deborah sat on a wing chair and Effie sat on a settee across from her.

"I can see your mother in you," Effie said.

"You can?"

"Perhaps not too much," Effie said. "Perhaps I was just wishing it were so."

Deborah nodded and took this to mean that Effie was sad at the separation from her sisters. This made Deborah yearn to have something to say that would comfort Effie: they send their love; they ask how you're doing. But there was nothing like that to say, and Deborah's eyes shifted away from her aunt's expectant gaze.

Deborah saw a large statue next to the fireplace. It was of a beautiful woman in a long, blue, hooded cloak. She assumed this was the Virgin Mary and she realized she did have at least one vague notion about Catholicism. She couldn't remember where she'd learned it, but the Catholics were supposed to have a special devotion to Mary, a devotion the church people she'd always known frowned on. The face of Mary had a faint smile, as if she would be very gentle, even with her critics.

"That's my mother," Effie said.

For a moment Deborah tried to understand this literally: somehow Aunt Effie saw Grandma Birney in the statue. Deborah looked at her aunt.

Effie was smiling faintly. She seemed to read Deborah's confusion. She said, "That's Mary, the mother of God."

Deborah looked back to the statue. The phrase sounded odd to her, though she knew it meant the mother of Jesus. She pictured, instead, the God of her childhood imagination, God the Father—the gray-bearded old man—running home to his mama, this beautiful woman in blue, and jumping up onto her lap. Deborah was lifted by this image: there was a woman who could comfort even God. Deborah was happy for God and happy that someone knew how to do this impossible thing and she was happy it was a woman.

"She's my mama," Effie said. "And she's yours, too. She's everybody's mama. God chose her for that."

Deborah smiled at Effie and she didn't want to talk the life out of this image and she said, "I'm so happy I'm here."

"I am too," Effie said.

"I only just learned . . ." Deborah stopped. She realized how this truth—she'd only just learned of Effie's existence—could hurt her aunt.

"It's all right," Effie said softly. "I understand that over in Wabash I'm not officially alive anymore."

Deborah braced herself now for an attack by Effie on the other women. But it didn't come. Effie fell silent and Deborah stood up and moved to her and bent to her and kissed her on the cheek, hoping all the while that Effie's silence would continue, that she wouldn't prove her mother right by being like the others. When Deborah began to draw her face away, Effie leaned forward and returned the kiss and she said, "What made you come to me?"

Deborah sat beside Effie on the settee. "Because you're my aunt."

Effie smiled. "That's not exactly a reason. Blood kin can hate and . . . worse than hate. They can be indifferent to their own blood. They can forget very easily."

"I can't."

"No?"

"Maybe it's not just the blood kinship that made me come here . . . I don't know. They're not a pretty sight, sometimes, my mama and her sisters."

"You must love them very much."

Deborah did, of course, and she was fully conscious of that love. But Effie's perceiving it through Deborah's anger at them surprised her. "I do," she said.

Effie nodded, but the animation had vanished from her face.

Deborah guessed at her thoughts: If the girl loves her mother and aunts so much, she'll ultimately side with them against me. Deborah was so certain that this was what her aunt was thinking that she answered as if it had been spoken. "But I came here."

Effie said, "So you did," and she seemed to exert her will— the life came back into her face. "Who told you where I am?"

"Grandma."

Effie closed her eyes briefly, half smiling. "So she's still alive?"

"Do you think they wouldn't even tell you if your mama died?" As soon as Deborah asked this question, she feared that indeed they wouldn't.

"Oh, I guess they'd tell me," Effie said. "Write me a letter or something. But only after she was laid deep in the ground and the new grass had taken root."

"She's alive," Deborah said. This was what Effie had smiled about. "She's going strong."

"Why did she give you my address?"

Again Deborah was tempted to make something up. But before she could think of anything, Effie said, "Tell me the truth now."

"I insisted on it."

"Nothing's changed."

"No."

"Nothing's changed for me either," Effie said, and Deborah decided it was foolish to expect Aunt Effie to be any more anxious to reconcile all the women than the others were.

"I still believe what I believe," Effie said. "And I still can't watch people close to me leading lives of ignorance or petty worldliness and say nothing about it."

Deborah had no answer for this. She felt a weakness in her limbs and she turned away from her aunt and leaned back on the settee. She still yearned to make peace among the sisters, but she had no idea how. She'd expected that just coming here would make a plan clear to her, but there was nothing. She felt Effie's hand patting hers.

"I understand how things are," Effie said.

"But I want it all to be better," Deborah said. Effie's hand grew still on Deborah's and then it squeezed her hand gently. "We get distracted, living on the earth," Effie said.

"That doesn't tell me what I should do about it."

"So it doesn't . . . Did you come to me to answer that question?"

"Not exactly."

"Because I don't have an answer."

"But if they're just distracted, at least that says there's something in them that would want to make everything all right again. If I could just get their attention back."

Effie laughed gently, like the flicker of the red flame on the mantel.

"You don't think so?" Deborah said.

"I'm sorry, Deborah. That's not what made me laugh. It's just that all of a sudden one Monday morning after thirty-odd years of estrangement, the child of one of my sisters—a child I've never seen—shows up at my door and within a few minutes we're talking as if we've known each other forever. In fact, we don't know the first thing about the lives we've led. But already we're talking about plans for some sort of reconciliation, as if you and I have been working on this for a long time."

"You must think I'm a little crazy."

"No I don't. It's just faintly amazing to me . . . You should meet Father Harrison."

"Is he your minister?"

"My priest. He'd know how to understand this."

"Is that your church a few streets over? The one with the two steeples?"

"Yes. The Immaculate Heart of Mary."

"Is that the name of the church?"

"Yes."

"An immaculate heart." Deborah looked back to the statue of the woman. That was what she was really seeking for her mother and for her aunts. An immaculate heart. Swept as clean as their houses, washed as clean as their laundry. There'd be no hard words then.

"She was a big problem between Mama and me," Effie said.

Deborah glanced at her aunt and she was looking at the statue of Mary.

"Mama didn't understand what Mary is," Effie said. "I guess I see why. In a way, Mama was no longer my mama when Mary came. She didn't understand. My sisters didn't understand. None of the church folks I grew up with understood . . . My sister Bernice used to be a tomboy. She'd get as dirty as can be during the day, but then an hour or so before our daddy was due home . . . "

"I know," Deborah said. She was instantly sorry for interrupting her aunt, but she was very glad to have a shared bit of family knowledge; she felt close to Effie because of it. "I know that story too."

Effie smiled. "Good . . . Well, that's what Mary means to me. I'm a sinful person. Willful and angry and unforgiving, for starters. Just like my sisters. Don't be deceived about me, Deborah. I'm no different from the others. But we're all full of sin—everybody on the face of the earth. We all want our own way and not God's. And I know this about myself very clearly. I know it even though he came and died because of it so I could be forgiven." Effie lifted her face to the cross over the mantel. "And I want to see him. He's the way we can see God, recognize him like he was walking down the street. But I'm still sinning right along. It's like I've been out playing in the mud and I'm dirty as can be and he's coming home soon. My daddy Jesus. What's to be done? I love my daddy and I'm so dirty that I can't let him see me like this, so I run to my mama. I run to Mary and I ask her for help and she takes me in and cleans me up, washes my face, puts me in a clean dress and sits me on the front porch. She makes me clean and pretty again for when my daddy comes walking down the street and up to the porch and then I can jump in his arms."

Effie was weeping now. Deborah bent near to her, patted

her hand, but she felt no strength in herself to console her aunt. She wasn't even sure Effie needed consoling. Deborah sensed that her aunt's tears were complicated, were like the soft thrashing that had begun in herself.

Effie continued to weep and Deborah knew she should go now.

"I'm so glad we know each other," Deborah said. "Can I come again?"

Effie nodded.

Deborah rose. She crossed the room with soft steps and opened the front door. She turned. But she did not look at her aunt. Her unspoken farewell was to the woman with the immaculate heart.

Jeremy waited until the next day to see Gus. He wanted to give the man time to tell his family and think on things. But the wait had made Jeremy anxious. He didn't want to come empty-handed, but he had almost no money at the moment. Payday was a few days off and he and Deborah were always short as it approached. Still, as Jeremy left the plant, he couldn't bring himself to face Gus without at least a token of help.

He turned east outside the main gate and before he reached the train tracks he found a wide dirt path and followed it north. Ahead, in a strip of land fifty yards wide that followed the Illinois Central right-of-way, he could see scattered women and men in gray furrows with wooden stakes. This was the community garden where Deborah had planted some vegetables.

Jeremy knew enough to be doubtful that anything edible was there yet, but he kept on. Maybe there was at least some leaf lettuce, he told himself. He wanted food for Gus. He passed through the ankle-high wire fence that surrounded the whole garden and he went to Deborah's plot on the far side, a few yards from the tracks. There were only the thin little scallop-leaved sprouts of tomato plants. "Damn." Jeremy said this aloud and he was angry at himself for thinking anything useful would be here. Plants took too damn long. These weren't times to wait for things to grow.

Jeremy strode out of the garden and he went to Hungry Hollow and he found Gus's street and he walked down it. Ahead, he could see a man on a porch. Children raced through the closing space, but as Jeremy approached, he kept his eyes on the man. It was Gus, sitting on his porch, motionless. Jeremy was drawing near Gus's house, and farther up the street, on the opposite side, a car stopped and a second car—a police car—came past and parked in front of the first. Men got out of both and moved briskly up to a porch where a woman was standing and beginning to shout.

When Jeremy stood before Gus's house, he hesitated. He knew an eviction was going on up the way. The cops were there and Hagemeyer's men were too. Jeremy looked at Gus. The man's face had turned to watch the eviction and swung back now to meet Jeremy's gaze. Jeremy wanted to go up the street and deal with the men who were putting the family out, but he felt restrained by a thought of Nick. Wait. Their time will come. Jeremy looked back and the cops were standing in the yard, their arms folded as Hagemeyer's men went into the house. The police were permitting this and nothing could be done for now. Jeremy crossed the yard and stood before Gus.

Gus was sitting on the top step of his porch. He nodded a greeting and slid to the side to make room. Jeremy nodded in return and sat down. He and Gus watched two evictors carrying a couch out of the house, a third following with an armful of clothes. All of it was dumped at the edge of the street. Jeremy felt himself beginning to grow animated with anger. He didn't want to do something foolish. He looked away.

Gus said, "When they do this thing to me I will have to fight them."

"When will that be?"

"Maybe the middle of next month."

"I will fight them with you," Jeremy said, thinking: That will be after the Fourth of July demonstration; whatever else Nick wants, I'll take time to do that, at least. The thought let him glance down the street. The clutter of objects was growing at the edge of the yard. The woman was bent into the pile, frantically searching for something. Two children were near her, standing very still. Jeremy wondered where the husband was.

Gus said, "You save your fight for when they are trying to take your house. We only are getting one fight, I think, if we are wanting to fight to the end."

"That's what they'd like. Take us out one at a time. They can handle us like that." This idea was shaped in Jeremy as he spoke it. He understood what Nick was driving at. "Come to the march on the Fourth. That's what they're afraid of. All of us together."

Gus didn't say anything. Both men sat in silence. Jeremy kept his eyes away from the eviction. He couldn't sit here much longer. He felt like a damn scrawny little tomato plant, sitting here. He looked at Gus and saw, beyond him, one of the cops jerking a shotgun away from the woman. She fell to her knees and buried her face in her hands.

"You be there?" Gus said, his face not turning, his eyes on the ground.

"At the march?"

Gus nodded.

"I'll be there."

"Okay," Gus said. "I be there too."

"Good," Jeremy said, but the satisfaction he anticipated at this did not come. Instead, unexpectedly, he felt restless. There was still nearly a week to wait. And even then—what would a march accomplish? Would they walk away from the mill gates in control of their own lives again? There was shouting up the street. Gus stared at the ground. Jeremy knew he'd better get out of this place now or he would do something—he'd go up to the paid-off cops and the company men and he'd bust some heads, he'd act, he'd get rid of this restlessness—and he knew that would just pull him up by the roots. He stood and said, "So long, Gus," and he strode away and the shouting faded behind him.

I t took two days for Deborah to face the women in her family after her visit to Effie. She felt powerless before this whole problem. And at the same time she sensed even more strongly the ideal of gentleness. With the opposing elements of her frustration intensified, she wanted to remain alone. But on Wednesday morning, the twenty-ninth of June, Deborah left her house and headed for her grandmother's.

There were thin tracks of smoke rising above shantytown and Deborah could see figures moving among the shacks. She turned into her grandmother's street. Somewhere near, a crow cried, but Deborah did not look. She felt anxious being outside, now that she was drawing close to the comfort of her grandmother's house. She walked faster and crossed the yard and did not knock at all. She opened the door and stepped into the frilly closeness of the parlor. "Grandma?" Deborah said.

There was no answer. Deborah was glad. She felt the rise and fall of relief in her, like a bird cry sounding and fading. It rose again, but now it was a harsh cry to her ears, like a crow's. It angered her to feel relieved that someone she loved was gone; it made her angry at herself and it frightened her. "Grandma?" she called again, louder, though she knew the house was empty.

She remembered the letter that her grandmother had been struggling with on Sunday. Deborah wondered if it was done. She crossed to the writing desk and found a letter there. She picked it up and began to read.

Dear Rats,
    You're still with me. I tried to write you to say you're fools not to listen to me. You're running a big risk and for what? I've been thinking and thinking about that.

Then it hit me that maybe you feel sorry for me. You think you've got to stay around because I'm all alone here. Well, you're still fools. I'm not lonely living like this. This is what I want for myself. I'm independent. That's something good. I don't need to be surrounded by my daughters and my granddaughter to feel like my life means something. This is the worst thing you've done around here. The devil's work, trying to make me feel sentimental. I don't need a thing but to be left alone.

Though there were still more words, Deborah lowered the letter and closed her eyes to stop her tears. She considered putting the letter down without reading on. She would leave the house and not return. But her grandmother had always seemed happy to see her. Deborah lifted the letter again to read on, to try to find out why Grandma Birney had veered into this mood. The letter said:

My papa always knew how to be alone. That's me. That's the way I am too. My papa gave me plenty of memories. Plenty, though I wish he was with me now. I really do wish that. Then you'd have to leave right away. I'd bring out the poison and there'd be no delay in killing you.

Do I want you dead? Is that something I dream about? I won't lie to you. I could have put out the poison before this. That should be obvious. No. I don't want you dead. If you're anxious to stay with me here—even if it's out of a false pity—I'm soft-hearted enough not to just kill you for that. I don't feel so good and I'm going to lie down now . . .

I just woke up and I still feel a little odd inside, but I'm better. I'm not sweating so bad. The heat has broken a little. I just read this letter over and I don't know what to make of it. I should just tear it up, I suppose, but I've done that so many times already and I can't face an empty sheet of paper again. Better for there to be some words on the paper, even if I don't know what to think of them. One thing, though. I know I shouldn't talk bad about my family. They're doing the best they can, my daughters. My granddaughter made me give her Effie's address. I didn't know what to think about that, either. Effie went away from me because she didn't like what I believed anymore. I was mad at her. But maybe I was to blame too. I never gave her a chance, maybe. I was just as bullheaded as she was. It's funny, though. Thinking about Effie now I feel like I never lost her. Those years apart just kind of fall away. I feel like she's still close to me . . . Am I going to go to sleep again and wake up and be just as baffled by that as I was about all my earlier words on not needing my daughters? I can't seem to settle on what's really true. Sometimes I can sit on my couch all alone and if you rats stop making noise like naughty children, I can feel like they're all around me, everybody, all my daughters, even Effie, and my granddaughter and my sons-in-law even, both of Adah's husbands included, also Joe, who has always hurt Berenice so bad but he's sitting real still and you can tell he's sober, you can tell he's feeling calm like he was washed in the Blood, and they're all calm, and Papa's there, of course, and Momma and my brothers and sisters, the room's full, like it was Thanksgiving Day or on the day of our Lord's birth and I don't say a word to any of them, I don't need to, cause we're all just so calm and peaceful and we all have sense enough to keep still.

I'm tired again and I pray to God I don't get up and find this is just the raving of a crazy old woman . . .

There was nothing else on the page and Deborah smiled. Grandma Birney had not returned to reject these words. This vision of peace remained unchallenged. Deborah was glad. It was her own vision. She put the letter down and turned. She tried to imagine the parlor filled with all the people from Grandma Birney's life. But the room remained empty. That was all right. For now, Deborah's own vision was focused on just six women. That was enough.

Then she had an odd feeling. She listened to the stillness of the house and she tried to understand it. She felt that the rats were gone for good. Then she wasn't sure. Then she knew that the feeling was something else. The stillness that had clutched her came from the bedroom.

Deborah crossed the parlor telling herself this was like her fear the last time her grandmother had gone out. But at the bedroom door she was certain of her intuition. She stepped into the room and she saw her grandmother in the bed and she knew as she crossed to her, knew even before she could clearly see the calm, still face, that her grandmother was dead.

The women sat in Miriam's parlor the next morning waiting for Zeigler's Funeral Home to finish preparing Grandma Birney for view. Adah wept noisily; Della, softly; Miriam's eyes were red, as if she'd done her weeping alone, before the others arrived. Berenice did not cry at all, and this frightened Deborah. Berenice sat looking out the window, only her eyes moving, following whatever went past outside. Deborah watched Berenice's eyes and she knew, from the sounds, most of the objects that drew her aunt's gaze: cars passing, children, the horse and cart of a ragpicker. There were movements, too, without a sound outside, quick movements of her aunt's eyes, and it took a while for Deborah to realize these were from birds rushing past. Watching Berenice's eyes entranced Deborah, finally made her forget her fear for Berenice, dulled even the pain of her grandmother's death. Deborah had done her own weeping in the night and Jeremy had stayed awake. He'd said nothing but he did not sleep. She had sensed his wakefulness as if it were a humming in the room and she'd understood it to be his way of consoling her. Now she watched Berenice's affectless eyes and she could not feel her own arms lying on the chair, or her hands.

But one thought did not fade in Deborah. Effie. No one had mentioned Effie and Effie's own suspicion burred in Deborah's mind: they wouldn't even tell her of her mother's death in time for her to attend the funeral. Deborah thought of Grandma Birney's last letter. In it she softened toward Effie and she never returned to deny the words. Deborah's hands clenched, feeling rushed back into her arms, she turned her face from Berenice and saw in her mind a reunion before the forgiving sleep of Grandma Birney. She saw Effie and Miriam and Adah and Della and Berenice standing before the coffin at Zeigler's Funeral Home, leaning together, gentle in their common grief.

Adah sobbed loudly, suddenly, and Deborah looked at her. The sound seemed harsh; Adah's face was more angry than sad; and she said, "I can't stand it."

"What, Adah?" Miriam said.

"I can't stand the thought of Elwood Zeigler putting his hands all over our mama's body."

"It's to fix her so she won't stink, Adah honey," Della said.

"You shut up." Adah's face snapped toward Della, and her tears seemed abruptly to have stopped.

Miriam rose and moved out of the room. Deborah rose and followed. They stepped onto the front porch. Deborah took her mother's apparent disgust with Adah and Della as a hopeful sign. She said, "Mama?"

Miriam turned. "Yes?" The word was faint and full of sadness, and it revived Deborah's own sorrow at Grandma Birney's not being there anymore. Her purpose faltered briefly, but then she focused again on the living.

"Did you read Grandma's last letter?" Deborah said.

"To the rats?"

"Yes."

"She was losing her grip at the end."

"For writing to the rats?"

"Not that so much," Miriam said. "Grandma Claire in the Ozarks used to do that. That's just a bit of hill-country superstition. It was all those things she wrote about the family."

"She felt close to Effie."

"What do you know about Effie?"

"I know she's alive."

Miriam's cheeks pulsed, as if she were gritting her teeth.

Deborah felt fearful. Her mother still could intimidate her when she wished. But Deborah said, slowly, with precision, "And I know where she is."

Miriam looked out to the yard. "I don't wish Effie any ill."

"Were you going to tell her about Grandma Birney?"

"Dying?"

"Yes."

"Of course."

"When?"

"At the right moment."

"Doesn't she deserve to see her mama before they put her in the ground?"

Miriam turned to Deborah with a puzzled look. "Why is this so important to you?"

"She's my aunt," Deborah said, but suddenly it didn't sound convincing.

"There are plenty of families with a relative or two who just never fit in. You've never even met Effie."

Deborah didn't deny this. She was snagged on the question of her own motive.

Miriam said, "If Effie came to the funeral, it would be bad for everybody."

"Just because she's a Catholic?"

"Did your grandmother tell you all this?"

"Yes."

"Being a Catholic was part of it. But mostly it was her being Effie. And my being Miriam. And Adah being Adah and Della being . . ."

"She deserves to see her mama a last time."

Miriam sighed and said nothing. Deborah decided it was the closest she would come to getting her mother's approval, and so she stepped off the porch and walked away toward the city square.

When she got off the streetcar at Mallinckrodt Avenue, she could hear bells ringing to the west, up the hill. They came from Our Lady of the Immaculate Heart. Deborah guessed that the time was around noon. It was a Thursday, but the bells were ringing as if there was a service.

Deborah went down the steps of the streetcar station, past the chemical plant and up Mallinckrodt Avenue to Aunt Effie's house. As she approached, her steps grew slower from the sadness she was bringing. As on the last visit, Deborah avoided trying to plan what to say. She stopped at the foot of the stoop and looked up at Effie's front window. The occasion of this meeting was sad, but Deborah felt certain that good would come of it. The women would be united in their grief, forgiving in their grief. Quickly she climbed the stairs and knocked at the door, propelled both by her hopes for a reconciliation and by her fear of losing her nerve. There was no stirring inside and Deborah knocked again, louder. She waited and no one came and then she thought of the church bells. Aunt Effie was at church.

Briefly Deborah considered waiting on the stoop, but the mystery of her aunt's religion, the strong feelings it stirred in the other women, drew her down the steps and to the corner. She turned north and the twin steeples were before her and they grew in her sight as she walked. She missed a curb, stumbled into the brick-paved street. There was another block to go and Deborah kept her eyes lowered as she continued, watching where she stepped but also saving the final vision of the church. She did not look again until the sound of a voice, echoing faintly as if from within a deep cave, lifted her face.

She was before the church. It filled her sight, and from where she stood she could not take it all in. The facade was vast, the color of a storm sky, and over the doors, pressing out of the stone, was Mary. Her face was large and gentle and her hands were spread and her heart was visible. From the center of her chest her heart emerged just as she herself emerged from the church facade and from her heart came flares of stone fire. Mary's heart burned in the stone and Deborah could not take her eyes from the heart, its nakedness, its burning, like the coal that touched Isaiah's lips.

The voice was still echoing in the distance, a man's voice speaking words that Deborah could not understand. She lowered her eyes from Mary and climbed the steps toward the row of tall wooden doors. The two central doors were open and Deborah approached them, stopped in their frame without stepping through. The air before her felt chill in contrast to the midday at her back. The voice moved inside and Deborah's eyes adjusted to the dimness and she could see in the distance a white figure before an altar, a massive cross above, and Christ hanging there, the cross canopied in dark wood, as if it were a throne chair. Candles burned on the altar. A second, smaller figure, a boy, knelt behind the man in white, the priest, and the words came from the priest, foreign words in a deep voice, not singing, exactly, but speaking in a cadence of virile respect. "Qui pridie quam pateretur, accepit panem in sanctas ac venerabiles manus suas . . ."

Deborah stepped inside as the voice rose and fell and she smelled a musky smell, like burnt flowers. She passed from beneath a low roof inside the door and she felt the lift of the nave and she stopped, her body rising, filling the vast space above her, though she did not look up. She held this expansive feeling inside, contained it, found a strength coming to her limbs and an eagerness to find Effie and sit with her.

She scanned the pews. There were perhaps a hundred people—mostly women—scattered through the church, but she could not pick out Effie immediately. Then all the faces were turning toward the altar; even the few bowed heads rose.

"Accipite, et manducate ex hoc omnes," the priest proclaimed. His back was turned to the pews. He knelt before the altar and then stood and his arms were rising slowly before him and his hands were joined in raising a large white disk. "Hoc est enim corpus meum," he cried and a bell rang—the breaking of a metallic wave on a shoreline—and it rang once more and then a third time.

The disk stayed aloft for a long moment, its whiteness clear in the dim light, and a chill prickled over Deborah's skin. She stepped into an empty pew and sat as the disk slowly descended.

Deborah's mind was wiped clear, her grief and her anxiousness and even the hope of her plan for her aunt, all disappeared. She sat and the priest's voice filled her and she felt herself following the rise and fall of the sound in the same way she'd expanded to fill the nave when she'd first entered, with her body, with the rhythm of her body and the pulse of her blood. A golden chalice rose as slowly as the white disk and the bell rang three times and the chalice descended. The prayers resumed and though the language flowed mellifluously, each word seemed to stand clearly apart from the others, a stately language, unwilling to blur itself, honoring every word.

Deborah closed her eyes and gave herself over to the cadence of the voice and she knew Effie was somewhere nearby, but she felt no urgency in locating her. Then at last there was a hush; the voice began to murmur. Deborah opened her eyes and found people filing toward the priest, kneeling at a rail that separated the pews from the altar steps. The priest was moving along the line of people, feeding them from a golden bowl. It was now that Deborah saw Effie. Her aunt was rising from the rail, crossing herself, moving up the aisle and into a pew near the front where she knelt again. She had not looked in Deborah's direction.

Soon everyone had returned to the pews and was kneeling and Deborah grew conscious of herself, sitting. She was an outsider. She had not been able to go forward, as the others had, to receive communion. So instead, she focused her attention on Effie. Effie was her link to this place, to the bread that had been given. Effie was kneeling with her head bowed and Deborah kept her eyes fixed there, letting the priest's voice drift up into the nave above her. Then all the people in the pews spoke, women's voices, "Et cum spiritu tuo."

The priest said, "Ite, Missa est."

"Deo gratias," the voices said.

The priest spoke again and the people's hands moved before them and they said, "Amen." Then the priest and the boy were gone and the people were rising from the pews and coming up the aisle and past Deborah. One was an old man, but the rest were women. Several of them glanced at Deborah and there was a severity in their faces, as if they knew that she was an outsider. Deborah fixed her eyes on Effie, who had not risen from where she knelt, and at last the church was empty but for the two of them.

After a time, Effie rose and when she stepped into the aisle she saw Deborah. Effie smiled, but the smile faded instantly into concern, as if she had guessed Deborah's purpose here. Effie approached, and before Deborah could speak, the woman leaned near and whispered, "Let's talk outside."

Deborah followed her aunt up the aisle. Effie was wearing a black lace scarf and it made Deborah remember something that she'd noticed—but without understanding—in all the other women leaving the church. Each of them had a covering for her head. Deborah realized that this was how she'd shown herself to be an outsider.

She passed through the large wooden doors behind Effie and immediately her aunt stopped and turned. "What is it?" she asked.

Deborah could think of no way to soften this. Effie already seemed to understand. "Your mama's passed away."

Aunt Effie closed her eyes, bowed her head, and crossed herself slowly, touching her forehead, the center of her chest— the spot where Mary's heart emerged from the stone above them—and the points of her shoulders. "Requiescat in pace," she said, low, and then she began to weep.

Deborah had no words to speak. She stood watching her aunt cry and she felt ignorant in her inaction, ignorant and once again powerless. Effie shivered faintly as she wept, and Deborah was drawn out of her self-consciousness by a surprising feeling. She was happy for her aunt's tears. They spoke of Effie's love for her

mother, in spite of all the years of separation. Deborah wanted
to hold her aunt, comfort her, and as she watched the woman
weeping she grew aware of her own passivity. She was a spectator
again, just as she always was in her mother's parlor. Deborah
wondered at this; it frightened her: did she herself have the crust
of her mother and her aunts? Was this inaction a reflection of
some hidden potential in herself that would accept the thirty-
year estrangement of a blood relative? Deborah stepped to Effie
and put her arms around the thin little woman, but Effie drew
back.

"I'm all right," Effie said, straightening up, wiping away her
tears with a handkerchief.

Deborah was stricken by these words. She'd wanted to comfort Effie in her grief, not take the grief away, not when it was
an expression of her love for her mother. The tears were stopping
now, even as Deborah watched. Effie's quaking had eased and
she was patting away the tears, calmly, patting away the love
she'd found for her mother, and Deborah's hands rose helplessly,
wanting to snatch away the handkerchief, wanting to take this
face in her hands and squeeze the tears out once more. It had
been Deborah's touch that had stopped the tears. She'd made
Effie conscious of what she was doing and the tears had stopped.
The very love had stopped. Deborah began to tremble in anger
at herself; in anger, too, at this woman who was the same as the
other sisters after all, just as her mother had said. Just as Effie
herself had said.

"Effie?" The voice was deep, precise in the shaping of the
name; the priest's voice. Deborah looked, and coming out of the
dimness of the church was a man in black, the white collar of
his priesthood circling his throat. He was a short man, wide-
shouldered, like one of the millworkers from the Hollow. He
had a handprint of baldness pressing from his forehead into the
center of his gray hair, and his face was square and pocked and
constricted in concern for Effie as he approached.

Effie turned to him and said, "Father."

The priest's hand came out and lightly touched Effie's shoulder, his head tilting in silent inquiry. Aunt Effie looked at Deborah and said, "Father, this is my niece, Deborah."

The priest looked at Deborah with eyes that were widening, as if in surprise. Then he smiled and said, "I'm Father Harrison. I'm very happy to meet you."

"I'm Deborah Cole. I'm the daughter of Aunt Effie's sister Miriam."

Father Harrison nodded and said, "I'm glad you've come to see your aunt."

Deborah sensed that the man knew the whole story of Effie's family. And so she listened for a trace of insincerity in him, some animosity toward her, but there was nothing like that.

"She's brought me news of my mother's death," Effie said and her voice was flat. Deborah looked at her aunt and the woman seemed very calm. It was as if she had never shed a tear. Deborah wanted to go down these steps now and escape. Her mother was right. This was a mistake. But what was her mother right about? That it was natural for bickering and bitterness and estrangement and hatred to exist in people who had clear reason to love each other, to draw together, to help each other always? Was it natural not only for those bad feelings to exist but to be accepted without struggle, even embraced? No, Deborah cried in her mind.

"Effie?" the priest said, and Deborah looked at him. She heard behind his word: What's going on inside you? Deborah felt she knew what Father Harrison was thinking. His thought was her own: Why aren't you reacting to your mother's death, Effie? Had the priest seen Effie's first rush of tears, now cut off utterly?

"Did they send you, Deborah?" Effie asked.

"Mama did." It was almost not a lie.

"Effie." Father Harrison's voice was soft. Deborah heard the name as a gentle command: Let go of your anger.

Deborah said, "Grandma wrote a letter just before she died. She spoke of her love for you. She said she felt close to you."

Effie forced a laugh at this and the sound cracked and briefly there was the promise of a sob, but instead came words. Effie said, very low, "Hail Mary, full of grace . . . " and she looked out toward the river. The words she spoke faded to a whisper, and Deborah looked at Father Harrison. He returned her glance and nodded once, his eyes closing briefly. It's all right, he was saying.

"Blessed art thou among women," Effie whispered and she paused. Then her words resumed but without sound until they surfaced once more: "Holy Mary, mother of God, pray for us sinners . . . " The words wavered, like rippling water. " . . . Now and at the hour of our death." And Effie began to weep.

"That's right," Father Harrison said, with a tone of approval for a favorite child. Deborah's intuitions were confirmed by this; he, too, desired Effie's grief, the love it implied. Effie turned to the man and drew near him and he put his arms around her and she cried and Deborah realized she should go. The priest turned his face to her as he comforted Effie and he said, "Thank you for letting her know."

With Effie grieving again, Deborah's hopes revived. She said to Father Harrison, "The funeral is at noon on Saturday at Zeigler's Funeral Home in Wabash. Please try to persuade her to come."

Father Harrison glanced down at Effie and then back to Deborah. "We'll see," he said.

"Please," Deborah said. "Maybe they'll all forgive each other."

Father Harrison smiled. "I have to be in favor of that."

Nick was forcing himself to walk around and around the room. He was sweating profusely from the afternoon heat and the pain. "It's been ten days," he said and Jeremy understood him. It had been ten days since the beating and Nick was explaining this seemingly purposeless circling. "Ten days," he repeated, low. "Ten days." And these were expressions of impatience, Jeremy knew, to drive him on. But it was hard for Jeremy to watch. Nick walked hunched over like a very old man and his face had lost its puffiness and was expressive again and the pain was clear there. Jeremy sat on a chair and watched. Nick was trying to walk the pain off, and Jeremy looked away; it was sensitizing his own body in an unpleasant way, like the hour before a toothache.

"Dammit," Nick said, and he stopped and held his side.

Jeremy said, "Sit down now, Nick. You've done enough for today."

"No." Nick said it sharply and he began to move once more.

Jeremy couldn't watch this any longer. He decided to leave. But first he'd report the little bit of news he had from the day. "Spud caught me after the shift today and he was real nice. Real nice."

Nick made a sharp, glottal noise, but Jeremy didn't know if it was from pain or from contempt for Spud.

"He said to me, 'Too bad about the Hunky.' I didn't say anything, and he said, 'You was his friend. Right, Cole?' and he did this with the niceness all stripped from his voice, like this was a suspicious thing, my being friendly with a Hungarian."

"So what did you say?" Nick was still moving.

"I said, 'Only friend of mine is my paycheck.'"

Nick laughed and he cursed at his side, stopping in the center of the room, and then he said, "You got angry at me a few days ago for talking like the other side. But that's a great thing to feed old Spud. It's just what he wants to hear."

"I know," Jeremy said. "It hurt me to say it."

Nick let out a careful laugh, and there were voices from outside. Not loud, but Nick stopped and listened hard to them and Jeremy followed Nick's attention. They were kids' voices. Angry talk. Nick crossed to the window and looked out. He grunted, as if in recognition, and Jeremy rose and joined him.

Across the street, in a vacant lot, Nick's older son was standing before a boy, a larger boy in a grimy undershirt with biceps like a man's. The larger boy was talking loud, poking his finger into the chest of Nick's son, who was inching backwards and putting a word in when he could.

Nick said, "That bastard has been after Brian for a while . . . Stand up now, Brian, dammit."

But Brian was clearly planning some other strategy. His feet were nervous and he was trying to ease away, though the big kid eased with him, kept him in poking range. Finally Brian said something sharp and loud and he turned and began to run this way.

"Damn," Nick said and he was gone from Jeremy's side. Jeremy watched Brian running across the street, through the yard, his face wide in terror, the boy with the man's arms three strides behind. When Brian reached the porch Jeremy glanced toward the door and Nick was there, closing it, locking it, keeping his son outside. There was a frantic rattle at the door, a knock, a yell. "Stand up to him, dammit," Nick shouted.

Jeremy looked outside, and the large boy was coming up the steps, grabbing Brian and pulling him away from the door, down into the yard. He threw Brian to the ground and Brian tried to rise and the large boy hit him in the face and sent him down again. Brian tried to curl up, but the boy pulled him by the shirt, made him stand, and hit him in the stomach, dropping Brian to his knees.

Jeremy wanted to go out and fling the big kid into the street, but this was Nick's son and Nick wanted him to learn to fight and Jeremy turned away from the window. His feeling was complicated: he wanted even more now to grab the bully by the throat and shake him hard; he wanted to yell at Nick to let his boy into the damn house; he wanted to grab Brian by the scruff of the neck and throw him into the big kid; he was angry at Brian for not fighting, for not doing something; and he was angry at himself for the same reason, angry in the same way, not for his own inaction before this child's fight but for his larger inaction, the fact that he was still playing footsie with the bad guys at the mill, with the whole damn problem in this town.

There were sounds in the yard. Cursing and crying and Jeremy looked toward Nick and Nick's back was to the door; his eyes were closed and he was standing very still.

Zeigler's Funeral Home was at the corner of a street of single-family brick houses near the square. It, too, was brick and

looked like one of the houses, except for the absence of a front
porch and the presence of a green canvas awning stretching out
to the street to protect the mourners from the rain or sun or mill
grit. Elwood Zeigler, a squat, thick-fingered man of Adah's age
with an annealed-gray pompadour, stood beneath the canopy,
near the front entrance, and he bowed, sweating in his black
suit, to the people arriving for Grandma Birney's funeral. Deborah looked away when he bowed to her and she hooked her
arm in Jeremy's.

Inside, the smell of flowers was as strong as cheap perfume
and the parlor was small and dim and hot. Jeremy pulled away
from Deborah and went to the back of the room, and Deborah
moved forward, toward the open casket. But her attention was
not on her grandmother's body; instead, she was noting the
mourners scattered about in the chairs. Effie was not there.

The front row was empty except for Miriam and Berenice.
Deborah drew near and her mother rose and they embraced.
Miriam was weeping. But Deborah's mind remained on Effie.
Even as she patted her mother in the embrace, even as she saw
Berenice on the chair—her eyes dry; her face, her hands, her
body very still—Deborah continued to think only of the possi-
bility of Effie walking through the door. It struck her that Adah
and Della weren't here yet either, and this encouraged her.
There was still time for Effie.

Miriam let go of Deborah and wiped at her tears with a
knuckle, though she was clutching a handkerchief in her other
hand. "She looks so beautiful," Miriam said. "Just like . . . I don't
know."

Deborah thought to turn now to Grandma Birney, but there
was a commotion at the door. It was Adah staggering in at the
back of the parlor, sobbing and leaning on Della, whose face was
scanning the parlor plaintively, as if she were seeking help with
the woman on her arm. Deborah looked past them to the parlor
door and into the foyer, watching for Effie, and in the back row
Jeremy was thinking of slipping out.

There was too much purposeless action here for him. The
tears and glances and hugging and low words made his hands

twitch. Especially with two days yet to go before the march. And the march itself was beginning to seem a pitiful thing. A woman— one of Deborah's kin—was sobbing in a side aisle; others were rushing to her, whispering; Jeremy was about to rise and go out. But then he saw, at the other end of the parlor, a face. The dead woman, in a light. Her face. There was suddenly a center to the room: this woman. Only this woman was real. She calmed Jeremy's hands. A dead woman. The body had a clean finality about it, and it had nothing to do with the past; Jeremy realized this and he felt glad, he felt a quickening. The face in the light at the end of the room was clear and final and decisive and suggested a course of action: someone could die. Jeremy set this aside by reflex. But the idea returned; it alone seemed uncompromised. People were being taken from their jobs, their homes; they were being put on the road and they had no work and no food and someone could die for this. A thought. Just a thought. But it made him calm. Somebody could always die. The flurry of sounds had moved away, toward the front, and Jeremy sat and waited now without being affected by the foolishness around him. His mind moved idly. He wondered how close he'd actually come to killing Skinner. He wondered: if he himself had a son like Brian who was being beaten by a bigger kid, could he go out and stop the kid without actually killing him? He would certainly stop the fight, he knew, and he might well go too far; he might kill the boy who was beating his son.

And in the front of the parlor Deborah wondered if she should go to the back row and sit with Jeremy. He was keeping to himself; she sensed that was what he preferred. But she couldn't stay where she was. The sisters were weeping and shushing and consoling and haggling—just the four of them; only the four; actually only three, for Berenice remained seated, quiet. Deborah moved away from them, toward the door, but the people who were coming in were neighbors, friends of the sisters; the thin little woman with the face of the Birney women was not among them.

Now Elwood Zeigler was entering with the pastor of the

Wabash First Christian Church, a pock-faced man with wire-rim glasses, and there was no one else in the foyer and Deborah glanced toward Jeremy. He was sitting in the dark shadow of the back row. Deborah looked at the sisters settling into the front seats and she turned and sat on the end chair of a middle row. She bowed her head and tried to shape a prayer. Dear Father, please forgive these women and forgive me and please bring Aunt Effie and . . . please.

She felt inarticulate before God. She always felt inarticulate in prayer. How could she say what she wanted? It sounded too simple, really, what she was praying for. And she remembered her mother's challenge: why was she doing this? Why was she trying so hard to force these women together? Why not let them be?

The pastor began to pray. Deborah wanted him to pray in her behalf; she tried to listen to him, to participate in his words, but the man's voice twanged in her and the phrases all sounded abstract—great reward, last days, the judgment seat—these were not part of her own inchoate prayer and her mind shut down, like Jeremy's mind, and she and Jeremy sat apart from each other and from the service and from the other people in the parlor. Deborah did look toward the door once more and a few moments later she looked again, but then she decided it was no use, and so she didn't see Effie come in during the song sung by Elwood Zeigler himself in a nasal tenor.

Jeremy glanced at the thin woman as she sat down in a seat near him in the back row. He saw that she was weeping, but she made no sound and he looked away from her; he focused on the face in the light at the front of the parlor, and he waited for all of this to end.

Elwood finished his song and the pastor spoke, his hands clasped before him, and he said nothing that would suggest that he even knew Grandma Birney and Deborah thought of slipping out. She was on the end of a row not far from the door and it seemed to her that nothing here had anything to do with her grandmother. And the four sisters side by side in the front row seemed far away from Deborah; these four hairdos were as still as the woman in the casket and as distant. But Deborah stayed where she was and at last the pastor stopped speaking and Elwood was singing again.

A faint peeping sound drew Jeremy's eyes to the thin woman in black near him and her face was bowed, her hands were clutching at her face; she was crying and Jeremy wondered who this was, who would be moved so deeply by the old woman's death and yet not be part of the immediate family, not be in the front row of mourners. He wondered if he should say something to this woman, if he should reach out and touch her arm. But what could he say? And to touch her might only cause alarm.

Elwood finished his song and the pastor invited the mourners to file past the casket for a last good-bye, the bereaved family first. The woman beside Jeremy rose instantly from her seat, but instead of going forward, she stepped toward the door, where she paused. Deborah, too, rose and she looked around, not expecting, this time, to see anyone, but there was Effie in the doorway of the parlor crossing herself and then she was gone.

The vision of Effie had been so brief and surprising that Deborah had to overcome the inertia of her expectation. But there was no doubt in her mind: moments before, Effie had been standing in that doorway. Deborah focused on her revived hope, and she was moving to the door, into the foyer, and now she was alarmed at her aunt's flight. This would be even worse—to bring Effie this far and then lose even the attempt at reconciliation.

Deborah was outside and she saw Effie dressed in black hurrying across the street to an old coupe parked at the opposite curb. "Wait, Aunt Effie," Deborah cried but the woman did not stop, did not even look back.

Deborah moved quickly into the street and Effie had circled the car, was getting into the passenger side. "Please," Deborah shouted and she ran toward the car.

Behind the wheel was Father Harrison, and he opened the door and stepped down from the running board as Deborah approached.

"Mrs. Cole," he said in greeting as she stopped before him.
"Can't I see my aunt?"

"I'm not here to prevent that," he said, his thick millworker
hands rushing out before him, open-palmed, as if fearful of being
misunderstood.

Deborah nodded and stepped around him and looked in the
open driver-side door. Effie was holding a handkerchief to her
face. "Aunt Effie," Deborah said. "Won't you come back inside?"

"I'm sorry," she whispered.

"Please . . . if not to see the others, at least to say good-bye
to Grandma."

"I've said good-bye to her."

Deborah had no more words. She wanted to invoke the
sisters, the family, love, forgiveness, but she felt as awkward as
if she were trying to make up a prayer. The car smelled of gasoline
and rubber and metal and heat pulsed against her face and she
was sweating and there was no more to say. Effie kept the handkerchief over her eyes and did not speak and Deborah backed
away, turned. She saw Elwood Zeigler spanking across the
sidewalk and opening a door on a waiting limousine. A policeman
sat nearby on a motorcycle. All of this blurred as Deborah's eyes
filled with tears.

"Mrs. Cole." It was the priest's voice.

Deborah turned to it.

"I appreciate what you tried to do," he said.

"Can't you persuade her?"

"I'm afraid not."

"You don't want to. Is that it?"

"Please, Mrs. Cole."

"Have I been wrong? Are my other aunts the ones who've
been cut off? Is there something about you Catholics that won't
let you love people like us?"

Father Harrison's hands came forward again. "Please don't
talk like this," he said. "No. Of course that's not true . . . There
are those of all religions who would twist what they believe into
a reason to hate. But they betray what they claim to believe
when they do that."

"Then won't you please make Effie cross the street? Maybe if the sisters just saw each other, God could bring them together. Can't you just make her cross the street?"

Father Harrison smiled faintly. "I can't make Effie do anything. Any more than you can compel her sisters."

Deborah felt a clutching in her chest. She looked over her shoulder and there was movement at the front door. The sisters would soon be coming out.

Father Harrison said, "Christ joined us all together, Mrs. Cole. We're one body in him. But each of a body's parts isn't joined directly to all the others . . . "

Deborah turned away. Miriam was moving beneath the awning. Adah and Della appeared at the door.

Father Harrison said, "Thank you for giving Effie a chance to weep for her mother."

Deborah strode across the street, caught Miriam at the door of the limousine. "Mama."

Miriam looked up, startled.

"Mama, it's Effie. She's across the street in that car."

Miriam's eyes stayed fixed on Deborah. "Debby, please. If Effie is here and had wanted to see us, she'd have done it in the parlor."

"She's afraid . . . "

"Please, honey. Come with me now. This is the time to think about your grandmother." Miriam entered the car and Deborah turned to Adah and Della as they approached.

"Aunt Della," Deborah said. "Can't you and Adah speak a word of condolence to Effie? She's in the car across the street and she's crying . . . She wants to see you."

Della said, "You've come unhinged, Debby." She turned to help Adah into the car, but the sister was suddenly standing upright.

Adah said, "I don't want to hear Effie's name again. You're defiling our dear mother. Effie is a thief. She stole stockings from me and other things too and I don't want to hear her name again."

Adah lunged into the car and Della followed and Deborah wondered if these women were all mad. She felt mad herself.

Now Berenice approached on Jeremy's arm. Deborah was suddenly buoyed by Berenice's meekness. She was quiet, contained; Deborah stepped to her and spoke low, "Aunt Berenice. Can you take a minute to see Aunt Effie?"

"She's dead," Berenice said.

"No she's not. She's in a car . . . "

"She's dead." And Berenice left Jeremy's arm, moved past Deborah, and entered the limousine. It struck Deborah that Berenice was confused or hadn't understood; Berenice was surely talking about Grandma Birney. She stepped toward the limousine to explain, but as she did, she glanced across the street and the car was gone; Effie was gone. Deborah made a pinched little noise in her throat, a sound of dismay, and Jeremy stepped to her side, drawn by the sound though his attention was elsewhere. He was staring at the cop, who was moving on his motorcycle to his place before the hearse. Jeremy thought he recognized the cop from the eviction near Gus's house and an anger began to thump in his head. The cop's hat was cocked to the side, an arrogant man doing the work of bad men, and Jeremy realized that if he'd gone down to the eviction and tried to do something, it might have quickly become necessary to kill this cop. This thought came upon him unexpectedly, but with the clarity of the dead woman's face. And it roiled his feelings, set a surface current running against a deeper tide: he was frightened by the idea of killing, frightened too by the momentum he sensed building in himself; but deep beneath his fear was an odd calm, a contradiction, a sense that he was being borne by a powerful inevitability. He even understood what the Reds might have felt when they spoke with passion about the course of history. He could feel something in his life, carrying him. He could knock the cop's cap off and it would lead to something drastic. Easily. He knew not to do it; he was in control of himself; but he felt dangerous. Then Deborah clutched his arm and he sensed her trembling and all the rest vanished. He held very still for her, let her cling to his arm, and he was relieved for now, not to be forced to act.

"I'm so sad," Deborah whispered.

On the next day—Sunday, July 3—Deborah did not want to see anyone, and so she went out to the levee and along the gravel road to her grandmother's house. As she approached the front door she had the sudden feeling that the woman was not dead, that Grandma Birney was waiting inside for her. The feeling faded at once and left behind only a heightened sense of loss. Deborah stopped and struggled to hold back the tears that threatened to flow. And she realized that this impulse to compose herself was prompted by the instant return of the initial fantasy: it was as if her grandmother was waiting inside and Deborah didn't want her to see the tears. Deborah whispered in her mind: she's gone. And she let the tears return.

Still, she had to suppress the urge to knock. She opened the door and stepped into the foyer, and she wondered if this was a mistake, coming here. There might be only a keener frustration at the failure of Grandma's Birney's last vision to do any good for those left behind. Deborah thought to turn and go out, but she felt the pull of the parlor and she stepped through the door.

Miriam was sitting in the wing chair. Deborah started. "Mama," she said, an expression of her surprise.

"Hello, Debby," Miriam said, and her voice was faint.

"Are you all right?"

"Of course."

Deborah found herself wordless before her mother; she had nothing to say and there was nothing she sought to hear. This alarmed her. Especially now; especially in this place. But the feeling did not change. She felt only fear at anything her mother might say. Again she thought to leave, but the sad faintness that had been in her mother's voice held her. Deborah crossed to the couch and sat down. The house was silent. Deborah knew the rats were gone. To where? They've come to me, she thought.

"Look what I found," Miriam said and she raised a closed hand from her lap.

Deborah thought of her grandmother's letters. Perhaps another letter. "What is it?"

Miriam rose from the chair with surprising alacrity, crossed the floor, and sat beside Deborah on the couch. "This," she said and she opened her hand.

In the palm of Miriam's hand was a gray curl. A lock of hair, Deborah thought. But she looked more closely, and it wasn't hair. It was a whorl of feathers, twisting and mounting into the shape of a tiny crown.

"It's a 'mother's crown,' " Miriam said.

"What's that?"

"I found it in the pillow from Mama's bed. The pillow she died on."

"What does it mean?"

The hand closed slowly and Deborah raised her eyes and her mother was smiling. "It means," Miriam said, "that she's on her way to heaven."

Deborah watched her mother's smile and it persisted. It was a smile of peace and Deborah looked at her mother's hand and it remained closed around the crown of pillow feathers. Deborah was glad for her mother's hope, but she felt a sudden sadness as well. She knew for certain there was nothing more to say about Effie. Her mother's feelings, the feelings of her aunts, were far beyond her power to control.

On the morning of the Fourth of July Jeremy rose quietly, not waking Deborah, who was sleeping at last. He stood naked beside the bed and he looked at her. She was lying on her side, her back to him, and she was curled tightly into herself like a child, the pillow drawn against her chest. Jeremy looked at her hair, undulant against the sheet and as soft as steam, and though he was naked and the July morning air was as warm as Deborah's skin, he felt no stirring in his body for her, only a pulling to his clothes folded over the chair. He had work to do this day. It was time to go. He moved to the chair and he wanted to dress as methodically now as he once did at the mill. But this was not the place; this place did not have a hard enough edge; and the shirt he held in his hands was thin at the elbows, nearly worn through. Things were different now. He dressed quickly and he went out.

He approached the town square along Grady Street and ahead he could see only a small slice of the square, a few figures, then Yellowhammer moving past, blocking his view. He put his head down and the morning was hot and he slowed with a sudden fear that all of this was just damn foolishness. He strained on this morning of laborless sweat to remember the hooting and stamping and applause of the night at the meat-packing shed. This didn't answer the fear in his mind, but the fear in his limbs lessened and then the cries in his memory echoed somewhere outside of him and he raised his face. The corner was near and the sound was from somewhere ahead of him and he stepped around the corner of a shop and the town square was full of men.

Ragged, faded, like the bunting draped on the facades of the shops around the square, the men were drawing together, a hundred men, more, two hundred, turning and applauding and crying out in words Jeremy couldn't make out. "Soon," said a voice tinny and pumped up by a megaphone. It was the man in the bowler hat standing on the base of the statue of Lewis and Clark, and the crowd was turning to him. The man was dressed in a dark gray worsted suit with a vest, and he had a white wing-collar shirt that made Jeremy think of Turpin, who always changed from a white shirt at the mill. The man in the bowler lifted his chin as he raised his megaphone, as if he were going to drink from it.

"Pull together, comrades!" the man cried. "We'll march in five minutes."

The men applauded and whooped, and Jeremy crossed the cobblestone square, the trolley wires humming above him. The sun was hot and he looked at the radical with the megaphone and the wool suit and Jeremy wondered if the man could feel the heat.

Jeremy drew near the men, and they smelled like a shift going off, tarred, sweating naphtha, sour, and Nick's voice said "Jeremy." He turned and Nick sidled up along the back edge of the crowd. His face was livid in the sun, but all the puffiness was gone and he smiled now; the web of minute wrinkles radiating from his eyes and mouth were visible again, even against the splotches of blue-gray.

"Nick."

"It's our day."

"Sure."

Nick looked over the crowd of men whose torsos were stretched toward the man in the bowler and his words.

"Who is he?" Jeremy asked.

"Who?"

"The guy in the suit."

"Chernowicz. He's from Chicago." Nick answered with a voice thin from distraction. Jeremy glanced toward him. Nick was looking away from the crowd, scanning the square.

"What is it?" Jeremy said.

"The cops."

Jeremy followed Nick's gaze. The sidewalk across the way, in front of Delmar's Emporium, was empty except for a couple of kids and an old man. "Where are they?" Jeremy said.

"There aren't any that I can see."

"So that's good."

Nick glanced at Jeremy and gave him a half smile, as if they were sharing a silent joke. "Yeah. It's good."

Jeremy was going to ask what was behind the smile, but Nick was scanning again and his smile widened and he said, "We did get the press."

Before Jeremy could turn to look at the newspaperman, he saw, beyond Nick, a figure moving. Thick-armed. Gus. "It's Gus," he said.

"Good," Nick said, flipping a glance over his shoulder. "Take care of him."

"Okay."

"I'll see you afterwards." Nick started to move away.

"Nick. What are we supposed to do?"

"Just follow the crowd. We'll go to the front gate of the North Plant and make some noise. Then we'll go home."

"Is that going to do a damn thing for us?"

"We'll give Hagemeyer a chance to be himself," Nick said, and his eye squinted as if he'd tried to wink but it hurt. "Let's just see." Nick laid his hand on Jeremy's shoulder and then he moved off.

Jeremy felt a ripple of restlessness and he clenched his fists. This was all too vague, too indirect. In spite of the voice rising above the crowd now. Chernowicz from Chicago crying, "You are strong."

Gus was looking around and his shoulders rolled as if he was ill-at-ease and Jeremy walked over to him. "Gus."

Gus nodded hello and his eyes moved to indicate the crowd.

"They're gonna march soon," Jeremy replied. "Over to the main gate of the North Plant."

Gus nipped his head in assent; his body grew still; he seemed to see some sense in all this. Jeremy was glad Gus was here.

"Anything on your house?" Jeremy asked.

"Nothing. Could be happening anytime."

"Hagemeyer owns it?"

"Yes."

"I want to . . . "

"You don't be worrying about me." Gus said it softly. "You'll have your own trouble."

The voice from the megaphone cried, "Workers of the world, unite!"

Jeremy wanted to answer Gus, wanted to convince him it was okay; Jeremy had enough strength to help both Gus and himself. But Gus's eyes had fixed on Jeremy and the two men looked at each other and Jeremy sensed Gus thinking: This is important to me, that I should face these men alone.

"You have nothing to lose but your chains!" Chernowicz cried.

Jeremy felt his jaw tighten and he wanted to say to Gus, as

the shouts of assent scattered about the crowd: We've worked together long enough so that you can turn to me without any hurt to your pride.

The scattered shouts grew insistent, pulling at the voices that were silent in the crowd. Jeremy and Gus looked at each other and still Gus would not yield; his eyes were stubborn. He's as stubborn as Cronin, Jeremy thought.

"Unite!"

More voices answered: "Unite!"

"March!"

Jeremy and Gus together glanced toward the crowd and then back to each other, their eyes moving with the ease and the silent accord of the minutes just after coming out of the B-furnace stove. Then the connections to Cronin made Jeremy look away.

At the back of the crowd, his head bobbing in an effort to see to the front, was Turpin. The sunlight made the immaculate white of his shirt seem liquid to Jeremy, white blood.

Now the crowd was moving, nudging at Jeremy, pushing him, as a corridor opened. Gus was pressed to the opposite side. From the opening flowed only a rolling applause, cries, then Jeremy saw Chernowicz coming through, men closing up behind him, following him.

Chernowicz had a hide-rough face, a worker's face, a worker's creases in his forehead, around his eyes, his mouth. The three-piece suit was wool, heavy wool, and the shirt collar was held tight at the man's throat by a steel-blue four-in-hand. With Chernowicz close now, approaching, the suit didn't seem as odd to Jeremy as it had before: he thought of his own work clothes at the ovens, binding him in, keeping him contained, focused.

But Chernowicz passed by and there was a smell of bay rum and Jeremy could see no sweat on the man. Not a drop of sweat, even in the hot July sun.

Then the crowd turned Jeremy, carried him along, and these thoughts—he didn't know what to make of them anyway—were left behind. He looked for Gus. The crowd had compacted, and Gus was several heads away and forward a bit. Ahead of Gus,

Jeremy could see Turpin, the flash of his white shirt. Jeremy wanted to find Nick, but his view grew more and more constricted; he could see only a dozen heads as the crowd drew tighter, and he tried to accept the crowd, he tried to wear it like the heavy jacket he used at the ovens; but there was no comfort here; he felt only bound in, felt he couldn't use his arms if he needed to. He struggled to keep from pushing men away, throwing them off, forcing open the space around him. He held back these impulses. He put his head down and held back, and he just moved for now with the crowd.

And the crowd crossed the square with no stragglers, no ragged edges. Behind and on both sides were a handful of men who signaled to each other with tilts of the head and who kept the unemployed moving tightly together. Signs were raised within the crowd, hand-lettered signs nailed onto posts of scrap wood: WE WANT OUR JOBS; HAGEMEYER, FEED THE HUNGRY YOU CREATED; THE WORKERS ARE THE MILL.

At the front of the men was Chernowicz from Chicago and near him was Nicholas Brenner and they led the men into Central Avenue and down the center of the street, the trolley tracks passing just between Chernowicz and Brenner and beneath the tight center of the crowd which bloated at its edges off the brick width of the street.

Ahead, a red St. Louis trolley turned the corner and moved toward the flow of men. The bell clanged and the trolley kept coming but the crowd did not miss a step. The trolley clanged hard and clanged again, then it slowed, still clanging, and it stopped. The men approached and the trolley was stopped and the men cheered and split apart; they engulfed the trolley, flowed past it, still cheering at the power they had, and the crowd reunited beyond the trolley to continue the march to the mill.

Ahead was the corner the streetcar had turned: St. Louis Avenue, which led past the North Plant's main gate and on through West Wabash and over McKinley Bridge. When the crowd flowed around the corner, the main gate was still not in sight. It was beyond a curve several hundred yards away, beyond the long stretch of the hot-strip mill, a corrugated building the color of a week-old bruise.

The crowd claimed the width of St. Louis Avenue as well. But there were no more confrontations, no trolleys, no cars; the street was empty as they moved along the hot strip. Jeremy knew where they were and he wondered why the street was empty. He felt hemmed in, trapped, with the men clotted all around him.

Jeremy pressed forward, wedged his way between the men in front of him, and there was another ring of men before him, and another beyond that, and another. But he pressed on and he could see between the heads now. The crowd was nearing the bend in St. Louis Avenue. Jeremy pushed through another ring of men and he was beside Turpin and he could see Chernowicz and Nick up ahead.

Then the front edge of the crowd turned the corner, the next ring, the next, and Jeremy looked as he came around the curve and he saw up ahead the mill's double front chain-link gate and it was closed and before it was a line of men, arms folded, holding clubs, maybe fifty men, Hagemeyer's men, and in front of them were a dozen horses with cops on them and a dozen more cops on foot with rifles across their chests and two cop cars blocking the street on the far side of the gate.

Jeremy felt a rush of strength, a hard-edged joy: something clear might happen after all. But the rush in him veered sharply: this crowd was unarmed, unprepared to fight for itself; they could be suckered badly by that line of Hagemeyer's goons and they wouldn't be able to do anything but get whipped. Jeremy looked around and he tried to see himself getting quickly free of the crowd, isolating the goons one at a time and making them pay. But he couldn't see how exactly to do it. He hated the crowd around him now almost as much as the real enemy arrayed in front of the gate.

One of the policemen came forward as the crowd approached and he held up his hand to stop the advance and Chernowicz held up his hand to stop the men. Everything was calm for a moment, the crowd still fifty yards from the main gate. The policeman was raising a megaphone, and as he did there was no sound, just the nickering of a horse and the whip of July wind, and Chernowicz nodded at Nick, who withdrew, disappeared from Jeremy's view to the side of the crowd.

"All right, you men," the policeman said through the megaphone. "I want you all to disperse and go home."

Chernowicz raised his own megaphone and said, "We are a lawful assembly and we have a lawful grievance."

"The men you see before you," the policeman said, "are all either police officers or special police deputies. I am John Briggs, sheriff of Madison County, and I'm ordering all of you to disperse at once."

Chernowicz cried, "The men you see before you are the unemployed of Wabash, the victims of the policies of the owner of this mill, and I call on all of you to join us in this righteous— and lawful—demonstration . . . "

As Chernowicz spoke on, the sheriff made a motion and the line of men began to move, the horses began to move. Half the men and half the horses crossed St. Louis Avenue and the two groups moved along the edges of the street, approaching the crowd, passing Chernowicz now and beginning to surround the unemployed workers of Wabash, who were starting to fidget and murmur even as Chernowicz spoke on.

This was crazy, Jeremy thought; this was no way to fight. And he knew the best thing was for the crowd just to back up, just to turn and walk away and figure out a better way to deal with these bastards. But Chernowicz was crying, "The workers are strong and the world will soon know what kind of men are presently in control of this country . . . "

Jeremy looked around him. Chernowicz was still talking, but he was moving; he had disappeared from Jeremy's view and his tinny amplified voice was moving toward the rear of the crowd. Jeremy could see three cops to his right, floating above the crowd, hard faces staring down like perverse angels. Briefly a horse's head came up to obscure the center face, but it nipped

down and Jeremy looked to the left and there were more horse-
men and he was still hemmed in by the crowd, though the bodies
were stirring, words were floating through. We're in for it. Oh
shit, this ain't what I come for.

Jeremy looked over his shoulder for Gus and he saw only
strangers. Turpin was next to him and the man was quiet, his
face was calm. Jeremy tried to see through the crowd to the
edge, tried to see Nick, but he only saw glimpses of the faces of
Hagemeyer's men, waiting, ready. Jeremy felt a clenching in his
chest and he peered again through the heads, looking for Nick.

But he could not see Nick because Nick had moved to the
back of the crowd and had taken a large, smooth stone from his
pocket. Before the line of police and Hagemeyer's men could
completely surround the crowd, and as Chernowicz came in
sight, moving quickly in his direction, and when none of the
cops were looking his way, Nick threw the stone hard. It struck
one of the mounted policemen square in the face and he fell back
and his horse reared up and there was a great shout and the
horses and the men with clubs waded into the crowd of
unemployed.

Jeremy felt the men around him convulse, swirl away; suddenly there was room to lift his arms and at first he didn't understand; this was welcome, this space, but he glanced and the
faces above the crowd were coming in and then Jeremy knew.
Cracks now, cries, the unemployed were scattering and cracks,
thuds, wood on flesh, on bone, arms swinging, the faces of Hagemeyer's men were drawing near. Jeremy turned to them and
the other men were falling, veering off. Jeremy was in the center
of a closing circle and he did not want to fight in this spot. He
had to get to the fringe, to isolate the enemy. He could handle
more than one of these goons, but not all of them at once. It
was madness to stand here.

Jeremy looked around and a horse broke through the col-
lapsing rings and brushed past and Jeremy moved with the horse
at its flank. Above, the cop was looking the other way, bending,
wielding a club and Jeremy saw a flash of white below, falling.

The horse was moving and Jeremy stayed with it but he turned his face back. In the center of the street amid the flashing of bodies, legs, gyring men, lay Turpin. His legs were stretched out flat—someone stumbled there and groped on—and Turpin was trying to raise his torso; he rose onto an elbow but he was shaky, his hand went up to his head, a flow of blood there from a dark gash as big as a fist, and Jeremy was pushed by a twitch of the horse and he looked up to see the cop leaning down with his club about to strike an old man who was jerking his head away.

Jeremy reached out to grab the cop's extended arm but even as he did he thought of Turpin lying back there in the center of the street with the horses and Hagemeyer's men raging through and he missed the arm, the blow fell, and Jeremy was turning. He pushed back toward the center of the street, spun off the rushing bodies. One man had a club and Jeremy grabbed him by an arm and flung him away and he moved for Turpin, the sound of deep cries around him, the hammer strokes of hooves.

Jeremy reached Turpin, who was still only propped on one arm, his face striated with blood, one hand touching there, just the fingertips, dainty with shock, and Jeremy bent and lifted at Turpin's shoulders but the man went slack and a broad shadow came over them and Jeremy ducked down, a whistling went by over his head, and he scooped Turpin up in his arms like a child from a cradle. He turned to the east and put his head down and began to stride away, back along St. Louis Avenue, down the center of the street, and he kept his face low and there was swirling about him, shadows, the thudding sounds that made Jeremy gasp each time, each stroke of wood on bone a gasp of anger, and Jeremy moved fast, he drove his legs, waiting for a blow. But none came and the shadows thinned and fell back and the hurtling bodies were gone and there was only his own movement. He passed the corner of Central and St. Louis and Jeremy sensed Turpin's blood. There was a stickiness against Jeremy's chest, but he sensed more, the actual flow of blood, sensed it at the back of his own throat, in a weakness now in his legs.

Jeremy looked and there was a yard, grass, and from a thin tree a swath of shade. He moved to it and he laid Turpin down. Jeremy stripped off his own shirt and rolled it and pressed it against Turpin's head, both the man's hands coming up to help; a good sign, good enough that Jeremy cursed the man silently: Damn you. Damn you, Turpin, you didn't even let me hit somebody. Jeremy said aloud: "Dammit." He felt a restless strength in him, a chest-filling anger at everyone back in that street, everyone, and he half rose up. The curse formed again in his mouth, but he looked down and he saw Turpin's white shirt, his immaculate white shirt, splashed with blood, swoops of stain like mill flames caught and darkened there against his white shirt. And Jeremy unclenched his fists. He opened his fists and he bent to Turpin, covered Turpin's hands with his own, pressed at the man's wound to stop this flow of blood.

Deborah sensed Jeremy trembling faintly beside her in the bed. She'd heard of the big trouble at the mill today. A woman from down the street came by—a woman Deborah had hardly ever spoken to—and the woman rushed through her news in broken phrases—police on horses, hundreds fighting, blood in the street—all the while twisting at the bottom hem of her apron, and then she went on up the block to tell the next person she could find. Deborah didn't think to ask if the woman had a husband in the fight, but a few minutes later she decided that the woman's situation must have been like her own, for Deborah was waiting for Jeremy to return from wherever he'd gone that morning—a meeting, he'd said, of some workers—and she knew it must have been connected to this big trouble and she was weak with waiting in fear and she, too, wanted to tell somebody about what had happened.

But then Jeremy came home and even though he was bare-chested he would have said nothing if she hadn't asked and then

he said only that he'd taken the shirt off for the heat and somebody must've swiped it who needed it bad. Then he wouldn't
say another word and now as she lay in the dark next to him,
she was angry. She tried to wring the feeling out of herself. She
didn't want any more anger—especially when it reminded her
of her powerlessness with the people she loved. But the day
would not fade: she and Jeremy simply did not go anywhere that
whole day. They didn't go to see the Fourth of July parade, and
so surely Jeremy knew that she'd heard something about the
trouble because she never even suggested they see the parade
like always. He couldn't think he was protecting her by not
speaking, but still he said nothing. There were no wounds visible
on him. When he came to bed there was moonlight in the room
and she looked for the dark shadows—signs of the violence—on
his body, but there was nothing like that and she only began to
be stirred by him and she had to turn away. She concentrated
on the silence and her nascent passion turned to an anger that
brought her to this moment.

His voice was as silent as his hands and she felt the anger
growing now in her. But he was trembling. Why? Was he afraid?
That thought made her anger at him subside.

But there was no fear in Jeremy. It was anger that prompted
his quaking, anger at the men he had not broken today, at the
strength that was left unused in his body, at his own damn softness. But even as this made him angry, the emblem of blood on
a white shirt ruffled in his mind and he knew Turpin could have
died beneath the horses' hooves on St. Louis Avenue and the
flow of his blood needed Jeremy's hands to stop it and the image
of the horses carried images of the cops and Hagemeyer's men
and his anger began again.

"Jeremy." Deborah's voice turned him back to gentleness—
a gentleness that entered him at his fingertips and flowed into
his palms—a memory of Turpin's cold hands beneath his own—
the old man was going to be all right, Jeremy thought; he'd left
him in the care of a doctor who'd asked no questions at St. Anne's
Hospital a few blocks away from the mill—and the feeling in

Jeremy's hands flowed now into his arms, asking to release the tension there, a release that would not involve his physical strength.

"Jeremy," Deborah said, "are you all right?" Her voice sounded as soft and fluent as blood.

"I'm okay."

"Were you there?"

Jeremy thought: A lot of damn good I was.

"Yes."

"Was it bad?"

He stirred, he turned on his side, his back broad and bare before her. She drew her face near and she could sense his skin— a coolness that she could smell, a faint smell, as cool as sheet metal.

"Bad enough," Jeremy said, low. And he wanted to kill someone. It came on him that abruptly. It was a thought more than a feeling, it seemed; there was no rush of anger. There was a calm opening up inside him: someone should be made to pay his life for all this hardship people were going through. He'd thought this once before, at the funeral on Saturday. Now it seemed clearer.

"Are you sure you're okay?" Deborah's hand rose, her fingertips drew near his back, wanted to run down the hollow of his spine. She heard words in her head: one body. Who said them? Father Harrison. And they made her think of slightly different words, also from the Bible: one flesh. These words had made her stir in the pew in church when she was fifteen and she'd heard them: the man and woman shall be one flesh. The words had made her move her shoulders, made her face bloom with warmth, and she hadn't quite understood; but she did now, even as she nearly touched her husband's bare back, nearly touched him but did not.

As she drew her hand away, Jeremy was thinking about Nick. Where was he? Where was Gus? What happened to them today and to Chernowicz? And to all those men, the ones he had left behind? Did any of them die? Clubbed to death by Hagemeyer's men? It was enough that they were hurt. Who could he kill? And how? He felt calm. He felt weary. He raised his arm and laid it over his eyes and he let go, he fell toward sleep and Deborah lay quaking beside him in the bed.

There was a movement nearby; a shadow passing; Jeremy—dressed for work—moving out of the room; the light was dingy; Deborah closed her eyes and realized that she'd been sleeping. The house felt abruptly empty. She felt its emptiness along her arms. The sheet was knotted at her feet. She'd been sleeping and this was how she always slept—realizing it only with a tiny surprise after she'd awakened. At some point in the dark early morning it always seemed that sleep would never come, but when it did, she yielded to it with no awareness of its taking her. The house was empty now and she moved her arms, raised them, encircled her head with them. Her movement made no sound. The house was empty and it was very quiet and she felt a slick oozing of fear flow through her, like the first flow of her monthly blood. She listened hard for a sound and there was nothing for a moment but then a faint scratching, a movement somewhere, contained, tiny claws. She rose up and dressed and went out and stood on the front porch.

She could sit down on the front steps or she could go to her mother's house. But those women frightened her too. She was afraid of the silence of her own house, the sound of her mother and her aunts, the silence too of Jeremy, and Deborah had nowhere to go. She felt tears creeping into her eyes like sleep and she knew they were for Grandma Birney and another silent house. She remembered waking in her grandmother's chair and the rat was watching her and she moved off the porch now. Deborah wanted somewhere to go. She was weeping now and yet her face, her hands, did not acknowledge the tears; her thoughts kept flowing, detached, calm really, and she thought of Aunt Berenice. She could go there.

At Berenice's door she knocked once and spoke her aunt's name through the screen and then entered. The living room was dark and she passed through and called once more.

"Debbie?" The voice came from the back of the house.

"Yes. Aunt Berenice?"

"I'm out here, honey."

Deborah went into the dining room. The shades were down in this room too and the dimness made Deborah anxious in the way the silence had and so she hurried through and into the kitchen. Aunt Berenice was sitting at the table near the back windows and the shades were open and the sunlight beyond surprised Deborah. She'd thought the day was gray and full of clouds.

She sat down across from her aunt, whose eyes were turned to the outside. Deborah followed Aunt Berenice's gaze. The backyard was splotched with bared earth and witchgrass was growing in the garden. Across the alley a woman was hanging her laundry. The clouds were moving fast and they had vast cracks in them. The woman disappeared as a sheet lifted from the line in the breeze and the movement—soundless from where Deborah sat—made her aware of the silence of the kitchen, of Berenice's whole house, a silence like that of her own house, a silence that nuzzled her like an animal.

"Are you all right, Aunt Berenice?"

"Yes, honey."

Deborah felt awkward. She laid her arms on the table and then laid them on her lap and then put one elbow on the table and brushed her hair back with her raised hand.

"I suppose I should do my laundry," Berenice said, still watching the woman across the alley.

Deborah almost stepped into this flow of small talk, but she remembered last time—it was the same subject—she'd only led Aunt Berenice to an expression of her difficulties with Uncle Joe. Deborah said nothing, but laid both arms on the tabletop.

"It's Tuesday," Aunt Berenice said.

"Yes."

"Yesterday was the Fourth of July."

"Yes."

"I listened to the fireworks. I don't like to watch them, but I like the sound."

Deborah nodded. Her mind was sluggish with the sense that she'd done this all before. And this house was like her own. She felt it had taken her up; the silence was its soft-tongued mouth, waiting to swallow. Deborah concentrated on her aunt's high-cheeked face, her mill-gray hair, but the concentration yielded no words. She felt that if she spoke, her voice would never be heard. Her mouth would open, her throat would contract and vibrate, but there would be no sound.

"Listen," Aunt Berenice said, turning her face from the window, to Deborah, to the far wall, to the kitchen door; she cocked her head. "Listen."

"What is it?"

"Can you hear that?"

"What?" Deborah listened but she heard nothing. Not even the buzz that silence sometimes makes. Nothing. She tried harder. Her aunt's breathing: she heard the faint slip of air moving through her aunt.

"It's nothing," Aunt Berenice said.

"Nothing," Deborah said softly.

"I'm feeling okay," Berenice said.

"Good."

"You worry about me, honey."

"Sometimes."

"I'm okay. I seem distracted sometimes. Like now. I know it makes me look crazy. But I'm not. You never thought I was crazy, did you, Debbie." This was not a question, as she'd said it. Her voice fell and grew gentle, thankful even, and Deborah's eyes filled with tears and she reached across the table to hold her aunt's hand, as bony and cold as her bare foot had seemed when she'd climbed the tree.

"I don't have any bad feelings toward Joe," Berenice said. "He's never had the gifts that other men might have. Gifts of talent or wisdom or a gift of how to show that he loves somebody and needs them. I can't blame him for something God didn't see fit to give him . . . Don't go blaming Joe, Debbie honey."

"I never really have."

"Good," Aunt Berenice said, and she took her hand from under Deborah's and placed it on top. "He tries, I suppose... When he dies a violent death—and I know that's what's going to happen to him, because he's got very bad friends—maybe he'll think of me. Just at the end. I was always quiet for him. That's what he wanted, so when things get bad for him, he'll maybe remember me for being quiet and gentle. He's going to die with all that noise around him and he's going to think of me, bending near, saying nothing."

Aunt Berenice's voice faded to barely a whisper, faded like Deborah's strength. Her aunt's phrases snagged in her mind and they made her weak with a sudden fear: bad friends, a violent death. Jeremy was involved in serious things now; Deborah could sense that much. And there was nothing to do but wait for him to come home each time he left. Wait and be gentle and silent, like Aunt Berenice. Deborah's strength rushed back into her, drawn by a helpless anger. She rose from the table. "I've got to go now," she said.

"I'll do the laundry tomorrow," Berenice said.

Deborah felt her anger veer toward Aunt Berenice. The woman's passiveness made Deborah want to shout at her. Dammit, Berenice. You can't let yourself go like this because of... because of what? A man. A silent man. Joe. Joe the drunk and bootlegger. Jeremy wasn't like that. But Deborah felt her anger lunge at Jeremy now anyway. She didn't want this. It was Joe she was angry at. It was Berenice. It was herself. It was the silence. Had she just spoken? Just now? Did she actually say the things in her mind to Aunt Berenice? She didn't know. She didn't think so, but she didn't know for sure. She was going mad. This was no good, being here. Her aunt was watching out the window and Deborah turned and left without a word.

Jeremy stepped into the labor shack and the half dozen faces that looked at him were all strangers. He had checked the layoff list when he reported for work today and his name wasn't there. He had wondered at that: hadn't they seen him at the demonstration? These men were from other parts of the plant. One man looked vaguely familiar—a long, gaunt face—but Jeremy couldn't place it. Maybe the man had wielded a club yesterday. Maybe they all had.

Spud was standing under the SAFETY FIRST sign and he nodded at Jeremy as if nothing was unusual. The other faces, too, had swung away from him, and the room was quiet. Jeremy stepped away from the door and leaned against the wall and he watched Spud as the man checked the list on his clipboard and looked around the room. Then Spud called a few names to see who was who and Jeremy folded his arms across his chest. Maybe he'd gotten out of the crowd without anyone really noticing him. Turpin had preserved Jeremy's job for him. Jeremy smiled faintly at this thought, but the edge of the smile hardened: what was next? His job was safe, but for what? That he should go back to work as if everything was okay again? Jeremy looked at his hands. Should he find Spud alone somewhere and kill him? A calm thought, but he did not put it aside at once. Maybe not Spud, who was a little man. But the principle of it still seemed appropriate, even now, on the next morning, in the place where he worked, where his strength was focused to make steel. It was time for someone to pay with his life. He thought of Nick. What had happened to his friend Nick? He wanted to talk about this with Nick.

"Cole," Spud said.

Jeremy shifted his eyes to the man.

"B-furnace stove."

Jeremy nodded and turned and went out the door. There would be three others for this job, but he didn't wait for them. He wanted at least a few moments alone in the changing room.

He sat on the bench near the lockers and laid the strips of rubber in his shoes. The others would be grumbling when they came in. This was the job Jeremy and Gus enjoyed: the descent into the stove, the purging heat, the private sharing of hard work.

Gus was gone now. Jeremy banged a locker open and pulled out one of the thigh-long heavy coats. He dressed quickly—putting on the coat, the gloves, the wrappings for the ankles and wrists and throat—without savoring the preparation but full of anxiousness over Gus. He'd not seen him after the violence had begun yesterday.

As Jeremy was dressing for the stove, the other men came in. They were quiet. They sat near each other and dressed quietly and Jeremy was glad. Maybe these men were at least serious about their work. But he felt restless now, unprepared. For the first time he left the locker room to work a stove-cleaning shift when he wasn't looking forward to it.

Jeremy led the way up the ladder and the silence of the men behind him let him squeeze at his mind, try to concentrate on the fire to come, the clogged checkerwork of bricks waiting to breathe again. The stove glowed in his mind and he needed purging today; he was glad again for this job. Across the way the A-battery skip cars were carrying the scab-red ore and the gassy smell came—the carbon monoxide—and Jeremy stepped up onto the platform level where the smell was the worst, the place where men had died, sitting down quietly, waiting to sleep, and he went up the next ladder quickly, hearing the metallic scuffle of the others' feet behind him.

He moved beside the hopper, the ore dust swirling around him, and he went up the wide curving side of the stove. At the upper platform level, Jeremy stopped and he glanced only briefly at the dark sprawl of the mill below him and he turned as the other three men came up the ladder and onto the platform, pulling the wrappings up over their faces for the stove work.

"I want to take the first shift inside," Jeremy said.

The men nodded and turned stiffly to look at each other to see who would pair off with Jeremy. They seemed instantly to decide: one of them, a big man, broad in the shoulders, taller even than Jeremy, nodded at the other two and the second of them said, "Okay," and the third nodded slowly that it was all right.

Jeremy turned and crossed to the trapdoor on the top of the stove. He unscrewed it and put it to the side. The other man had the teapot lamp and as he hooked it on the chain, Jeremy concentrated on the heat rising against him, nuzzling him, drawing him to the opening. The lamp was lowered and the other two men came near, let the chain ladder down, and the three faces turned to Jeremy, the three sets of eyes that were stripped into the swathed heads. They watched him for a moment and then the other two men stepped back. The big man nodded for Jeremy to go first. Jeremy took an iron rod and squeezed into the hole, the heat plucking at his legs, pulling him down, and his breath snagged as he was swallowed into the convulsive dark.

He stepped into the center of the brick checkerwork and the heat was groping up, clutching at him. His pores began to fling out the residues of the past few days. In this place he was wiped clean. Nothing had to be figured out. Nothing had to be done. Nothing except to ream the bricks, to make a path for the cleansing fire. Jeremy wanted the fuel in his head— the riot and Turpin's bloody shirt, the scuffle of horses' hooves and the whisper of murder—to burn away quickly and completely and so he moved deeper into the stove, almost to the open shaft that plunged down to the bottom of the furnace.

He remembered the last time he was in the stove. Gus had worked near this shaft and Jeremy had grown anxious for him. And yet the man was surely in more danger now. It was this thought of Gus that reminded Jeremy that he was not alone in the stove and he started to turn to look for the big man who was paired with him and Jeremy could see—even as he turned, even in the thrashing dimness—the upward movement and the falling of the rod and Jeremy knew to jerk away but there was still a glancing burst of pain in his shoulder and he staggered back— near the edge of the shaft, he knew—he threw himself forward to stop his motion and he rolled away, the brick touching, burning at him. He jumped up and the big man was coming at him again.

Jeremy saw the iron pole rise and he grabbed his own pole at the ends, arms spread, and he thrust it forward and took the blow—the clang muffled in the thick air—and Jeremy was forced back a step. Another quick rise and fall, the bar in his hands quivered and stung and he was forced back another step. There could be only one more step—at the most two—to the brink of the shaft.

The big man's iron rod fell again and Jeremy braced and as it hit, he twisted his own rod to the side, moving the man's arms with it, and Jeremy stepped forward, swung his leg hard for the man's crotch but the man was moving, the blow hit on his thigh and he was straightening, drawing his arms up again and Jeremy pivoted his bar, a short jab into the ribs. The man recoiled, dropped his bar, but Jeremy left his own bar idle a moment too long. The big man grabbed the end and pushed Jeremy backward one step, two, and Jeremy let go, stumbling, his center of gravity shot up to his shoulder blades and he felt a pull backwards, he was leaning toward the abyss, his arms swooping fast to hold him away from the fall, the suck of fire. The man—a shadow as big as the stove—rose up and he would lunge soon, Jeremy's arms swooped, his center crept down, down to the middle of his back and he bent forward, fell to the side onto the bricks as the man lunged. The fire scraped at Jeremy, his shoulder, arm, his back now; he was pressed hard against the brick, the big man on him, hands dragging him toward the abyss. Fast, skidding, there was open space beneath Jeremy's shoulder, Jeremy's hands were free, a last chance, up, and his hands groped at padding, padding. Jeremy strained hard to keep his body from the shaft and his hands found the big man's padded throat. A blow thumped against Jeremy's head, hard, a prickling there, and the burning in his back made him gasp and his hands could not grip hard through the padding. Jeremy was almost gone, it was almost done, but he cried no and his hands groped up from the throat— no time there—to the face. His thumbs found the eyes and he turned his nails in and he pressed deep, gashed deep, and a bellow filled the space and an easing up above Jeremy and Jeremy raised his knees and with a quick heave to the side the weight was gone, another bellow, distant, sucking sounds receding, and the furnace below was fed.

There was no time to stop now. Jeremy's lungs were lined

with the knife gashes of the burning air and he dragged himself up, moved toward the tiny shimmering dollop of light above. He could not draw a breath. The pain flared through him from his chest and into his arms and legs and he felt heavy. He could not move his legs. He stumbled. But again there was a cry in him: no. He drove on—the ladder—up—his breath was gone, he was drowning—a cool, clean, lazy moment—Lizzy reaching through a shaft of sun—her baby's paw stirring the motes of dust and then touching his cheek. Air on his cheek. The dazzle of the shaft of sun flaring in his eyes. He was coming out of the stove.

And he knew he still was not through. The other two men. He pulled himself out of the trapdoor and dropped to the platform. His legs buckled but he was gasping air now; the air was giving him a little strength, just enough to stand up straight and move past the wide eyes of the men and to the ladder and he was on the ladder and he said to the two men, "He needs your help inside."

Down he went, expecting the others to follow. Down, his legs wavering as he climbed, and he wanted to sit and rest on the first platform but he knew the gassy smell and his mind was clearer now. His back—where he had lain on the checkerwork—burned as if he were still in the stove, but his mind was clear. He even knew as he came down from the B-furnace and found Spud standing in the shadow of the stack, waiting, that the man would do nothing more for the time being.

"Your man's had an accident in the stove," Jeremy said and he walked away.

Jeremy stopped at the administration building and told the safety officer about the accident: a man was working too close to the shaft to the combustion chamber in the B-furnace stove; he was there one moment and gone the next; a damn shame.

And then Jeremy went to the locker room and left his furnace coat and wrappings and he went out the front gate and he paused. He looked across the highway to the vast, craggy range of slag: the hard, knotted rock left from the fires of the mill. And he felt a hardness too, knotted in his chest. He had gone into the fire and killed a man—a faceless, nameless man—and this death was not the kind he'd begun to plan. A crow wheeled over the peaks of slag and Jeremy thought of Nick. He should go and see Nick. But the bird swooped and disappeared and there was only this horizon of scoria before him, its jagged line impervious now to any fire, reduced as far as it could go, and Jeremy grew suddenly afraid. His back burned softly and he opened his hands at his sides and he turned instead toward home.

The sound at the front of the house brought Deborah to her feet in the kitchen, and when she saw Jeremy coming toward her through the bright morning shade of the bedroom, she knew there'd been trouble at the mill. He stepped into the kitchen, and for a moment she saw in this first glance of his a silent plea for help. She felt a lifting inside her, a hungry hope, but then his eyes seemed to go flat, his gaze slipped away; he turned and took a step toward the sink. But he hesitated again and came to her and she was afraid now and he kissed her on the cheek. His skin felt hot. He moved off to the sink and turned the water on.

Her face still felt warm from the touch of his skin. "Do you have a fever?" she said, her voice tiny.

"No," he said. He straightened and moved his shoulders slowly and she knew he was unbuttoning his shirt.

"Are you laid off?"

"I don't know."

"You're home . . . early."

"Yes."

His shirt was coming off now and she gasped: his back was checkered and smeared with red. Burns, she knew at once. His upper left side was cross-hatched with these shadows of fire and the red blurred as it swooped down and across his spine and flared on his right side. "My God," she said and she took a step toward him.

Jeremy's head turned to her, his eyes moved slowly and looked at her face, saw the focus of her gaze. He realized what she must be seeing. He felt a thin sheet of flame clinging to his back.

She laid him down on the bed and she got a stick of butter and sat delicately beside him and she began slowly to follow the burns with her fingertips, spreading the butter over the wounds, and she was breathless with shared pain and breathless as well to be touching him. She wanted to know how he'd been hurt, wanted to know what was going on in his life now, the danger that he seemed to be taking on, but stronger in her than this was her touching his skin. The burns weren't serious, she knew. They were superficial, an odd image of something; as if, she thought, the sun had burned through his clothes, ardent to touch him. She traced these sun marks on his body and she felt a stirring of his muscles beneath her hand.

Jeremy felt her hand against his burning skin and he lay like his daughter had perhaps lain beneath his own hands, radiating a terrible heat, and he grew conscious of Deborah, her gentleness, the timid pressing of her fingers, the slickness, spreading, muting the pain, and he had a flicker of an image: the fire of the furnace, swallowing the faceless man, his bulk vanishing instantly in flame. Jeremy felt his own body prickle with the touch now of the heel of Deborah's hand, the broader, harder touch. And he felt restless, too; he regretted the quick meaninglessness of the act he'd done. One of Spud's men, gone, Jeremy alone the witness, saving his own life, and nothing was different, no change was made in the mill or in the town, not one millworker freed from his hunger.

On his shoulder Jeremy felt the soft flash of a kiss and Deborah pulled back with no real hope that he would respond, but she felt an intense drawing inside her, up her legs, her thighs, a ravenous drawing and she moved her hands to his shoulders, holding the wide breadth of his back. She wanted what was

beneath her hands: strength; physical strength. If she could devour him, tear with her mouth at this broad back, perhaps she
could have this strength too, perhaps she could control the people
around her, force them to love. She yearned to hold him tight,
bite at him, devour his strength, and Jeremy felt a stirring in
the center of him, a faint groping in his body, unfocused still,
but then his thumbs remembered, his thumbs plunging, the
weight rolling off him and away and it wasn't enough. It was as
if nothing had happened. He yearned, the groping in him veered,
grew strong, moved up to his arms, his hands. He wanted to kill
someone, more than ever now, and his fists clenched on the bed,
and Deborah saw this and she felt a dry sucking inside her, like
gasping for air in a place filled only with flames, and she drew
back quickly from the man beneath her and she rushed out of
the room.

The next morning Jeremy was sleeping on his stomach when
Deborah came and stood beside the bed and whispered his
name urgently, her fear impressing Jeremy even before he was
fully awake.

"Jeremy," she said, and when he opened his eyes and twisted
up off his stomach to look at her—his back smoldering with the
memory of the killing yesterday—she said, "There's a man outside. He wants you. He scares me."

Jeremy rose and put on his pants and he almost moved toward
the door. But he hesitated and went back and put his socks on
and his heavy work shoes, lacing them tightly. "Was he a short,
hard-looking little man, big chest?" he asked as he cinched the
lace a final time.

"Yes."

Jeremy stood up and he knew who it was: he wondered if
this was the time he'd finally have to deal with Spud. Jeremy
moved through the living room and he stopped at the screen.

Outside, Spud was standing in the yard, near the street. Ordinarily this would seem a gesture of respect. One millworker having business with another and not wanting to track the grit of it into the man's home. But with all that had happened, Jeremy figured Spud wanted fighting room.

Jeremy took a deep breath and went out onto the porch, down the steps, across the yard, each stride a preparation now, a tightening. Spud crossed his arms as Jeremy approached and raised his chin a little. Jeremy stopped before him.

"Cole," the man said.

"Spud."

"Real bad accident."

"Could've been worse."

A smile flickered in Spud's face. "I always have liked you, Cole."

"That why you tried to have me killed?"

"Somebody got their instructions mixed up."

"Don't bullshit me, Spud."

"Not *much* mixed up. But it wasn't supposed to . . . "

"Come on, Spud. I get enough bullshit from the Reds."

Spud laughed, a laugh as stripped down and craggy as slag. "Maybe it was *easy* to get those instructions mixed up."

"What do you want?"

"If I wanted just what some of the others wanted, there'd be no reason for me to be here."

Jeremy didn't reply. He crossed his own arms and waited.

"You're laid off, of course," Spud said.

"You could've put that on the bulletin board."

"Listen, Cole," Spud said, uncrossing his arms and lowering his voice. "I'm gonna tell you straight. Some important people want you dead pretty bad. You've got your damn fool self mixed up with dangerous elements out to do this country real harm and you've beat the crap out of one good man and killed another. You can't explain self-defense to guys who wanted you dead to start with."

"I thought it was you, wanted me dead."

"We all got bosses. I wanted you on my side."

"It's Hagemeyer who wants me dead."

Spud laughed again. "Hagemeyer doesn't even waste his time thinking about scum like you and me."

Jeremy narrowed his eyes at Spud. He couldn't figure this man out.

Spud said, "He's got others who work out how to get done what needs to be done."

"Others like you?"

"I just do my job . . . I wish to hell you'd've been satisfied just doing yours."

"I don't like what's happening in this town."

Spud looked away and moved his mouth as if he was going to spit. But he just puffed a bit and looked back to Jeremy and then over Jeremy's shoulder to the house. "Who owns your house?"

"Not Hagemeyer."

"Not you either?"

Jeremy didn't answer. No. He didn't own the house. They had a fine little old man who they paid rent to, but the rent still had to be there.

"Look, Cole, you've got a nice wife and you've had some bad times losing a kid like you did. And you may not understand this, but I was glad to see you comin' down off of B-furnace instead of the goon they sent over from the North Plant. So I'm gonna make you a deal. For the next ten days I'm gonna forget you exist. We've got a lot of other things to take care of anyway. You just don't show your face around the mill or even anywhere near it. Drop out of sight and in ten days you and your little lady be a thousand miles away from Wabash. Okay?"

Jeremy didn't say anything. His body was letting go just a little bit—with some regret; he'd just as soon get this over with. He didn't really like Spud any better for all these special concessions, and yet he couldn't really finish with him either.

Spud was watching Jeremy's face and he waited and his eyes went cold and he said, "Ten days, Cole. After that, we'll finish the job. And listen, Cole. Don't get me wrong. I like you okay.

But if I find you in this town a week from Saturday, I'll kill you myself."

Spud turned abruptly and moved off with a quick smoothness that surprised Jeremy. When the man grew small against the distant hulk of the North Plant, Jeremy went inside and put on a shirt—the burning of his back reassured him now that something could be done—and he went out not seeing Deborah sitting at the foot of the bed.

In the street he paused. He would go to see Nick, but he thought of Gus. Two days had passed since the riot at the mill gate and Jeremy felt bad that he hadn't gone to see Gus before this. He headed for the Hollow.

The street Gus lived on was quiet. It was a hot July morning, but the quietness didn't strike Jeremy as odd right away. He was in front of Gus's tar-paper house and he saw at the street's edge a trampled dress, a broken broom, a lipstick, a cracked hand mirror, other pieces of things that Jeremy looked at in a swoop now, without seeing, and he turned to face the house. The windows were closed, the front door was closed; Jeremy strode up the lawn and onto the porch, but he knew what he would see when he peered in the glass panel of the door: an empty house, the floor scuffed and bare, the doors open all the way to the back and nothing inside but dust and a glint through the east windows. Had Gus fought? Why couldn't he have said something to me? Damn him, Jeremy thought. Damn me. I want to hurt somebody for all this, a simple target, a simple act, and I'm always too late or I get sidetracked. I'm no good to anybody I love. Never have been. They're all dispossessed or hungry or dead.

Jeremy turned. He wanted to know where Gus and his family were now and so he stepped off the porch, walked toward the next house. But he went only as far as the edge of the yard. The house to the east was empty too. The windows were closed and there were no shades and he could see into the empty front room. He turned and moved back to the west. But the house on the other side had its windows closed and its shades up and Jeremy stopped. The quiet. He looked down the street and then

in the other direction: there was no one. The children who'd
been here just a little over a week ago were gone. Hagemeyer
had cleared them all out. Hagemeyer. It was time to go to see
Nick, Jeremy knew.

And so he walked quickly east, through Hungry Hollow, the
silence persisting beyond Gus's block. Only a few families were
left in the streets that Jeremy walked and he hurried on, thinking
now that perhaps Nick was gone, too. Or worse. He'd lost sight
of Nick early in the demonstration. Nick didn't know how to take
care of himself. He'd gotten himself beat up after the meeting
at the packing house. How could Jeremy expect the man to
protect himself in a riot?

Jeremy walked faster. Soon the rise at the east end of Hungry
Hollow was visible, the tar-paper houses there. At least Hagemeyer didn't own Nick's house. But horseradish kings also insisted on rent being paid, and Nick had been out of work for a
couple of weeks already.

Surrounding the street where Nick lived, the horseradish plants
were green and broad-leaved. The white-petaled flowers were gone
and the fields were thick with green and stretched far away on all
sides. But there were still children in the street and near the end of
the block Jeremy saw a figure in Nick's yard, a woman; Nick's wife,
Jeremy realized, as he drew near. The woman's freckled face turned
to him as he approached the yard and she had the hard, challenging
look that she'd had when he first saw her.

"What do you want?" she said.

"Nick."

"He ain't here."

Jeremy shuffled his feet. This woman seemed to be blocking
his way to Nick. It wasn't that he didn't believe what she said,
but he just didn't know how to get more out of her. The simplest
questions refused to find shape in his mouth while her hard gaze
was on him.

"You're one of the Reds, ain't you?" she said.

No, Jeremy thought, but even this much couldn't move his
voice. I'm not exactly that.

"One of his buddies," she said, her voice husky with contempt.

Jeremy looked at his hands. They turned their palms to his gaze.

"Well, you just listen here. He's got a wife and two boys and if he cared about them even half as much as about his damn buddies, he'd be . . . " She seemed to be running out of breath, or out of anger. "He'd be a better man . . . " Her voice trailed off and then after a moment, after Jeremy's hands turned to show him their backs, corded with veins, she said, "We're not going to have a home after next Tuesday. What does he care? He'd rather be a martyr for the damn working class. What's a working class anyway? No working class suckled a child or did the wash and so who's gonna be taking care of me when all the men think they're a damn fool class?"

"You're losing the house on Tuesday?" Jeremy said.

"That's right. If we don't choke on horseradish root before then."

Jeremy didn't want to hear any more of this. He thought to walk away, but he heard Nick's voice behind him. "Jeremy."

Jeremy turned and Nick was coming up the street.

"Damn your eyes," the woman said low, but Jeremy didn't know who the curse was for.

Nick came closer and he looked at Jeremy and then past him, to the wife, and his eyes narrowed. "Go in the house, woman. You got no business talking to my friends."

Jeremy sensed the woman moving away, and he was surprised that she went off without a word of protest.

"Don't pay any attention to her," Nick said. His face looked the same as it did on the Fourth. Maybe even better. The bruises were fading now. And he was standing upright, loose limbed.

"You got out of it okay?" Jeremy asked.

"The battle of Wabash Steel?"

"Yes."

"Just fine, Jeremy. I'm okay," Nick said, his voice clear and strong, and in the same tone he added, "That's more than I can say for many of our comrades from the march."

"How bad was it?"

"One man's dead. Two more could die before the week's out. Scores injured. It's just what we expected."

Jeremy cocked his head at the word and Nick said, "*Feared.* We feared Hagemeyer might have something like that in him."

"You should have armed those men, if you knew."

"We had to be the peaceful ones this time, Jeremy. So we could show Hagemeyer clearly to the world." Nick smiled. "And that we did."

Jeremy was surprised at the smile, but he didn't blame Nick. "I don't understand all this real well, I guess," he said. "I just know I can't do it your way anymore."

Nick's face, which was fissured with all the tiny smile lines, went blank; the lines went smooth, then they reappeared in a thoughtful frown. "What do you mean?"

"I mean it's time to stop talking and time to stop marching around together like cattle."

"What do you think's next?" Nick said, his smile creeping back.

"I want to kill somebody."

Nick's face went briefly blank and then his head turned slightly to one side, his eyes staying fixed on Jeremy, as if he were trying to decide if Jeremy was serious. "I feel like that all the time," Nick said.

"It's not like that," Jeremy said.

"No," Nick said. "I didn't really think so, coming from you." Nick's eyes slid away to gaze in the direction his face had turned. "Maybe so, Jeremy. Maybe that's next. Who'd you have in mind?"

"You know who."

Nick's face came back to Jeremy. "Hagemeyer."

"Yes."

Nick grew very still and then he nodded minutely. "Maybe so . . . I'll talk to some people."

Jeremy felt like grabbing Nick by the shirt front, but he

forced himself to hold back his anger. "I'm not asking for your approval, Nick. And I'm sure as hell not asking for Chernowicz's approval or anybody else's."

"Okay," Nick said, his palms rising as high as his shoulders.

"Did Chernowicz make it through the riot okay?" Jeremy asked, partly out of concern and partly out of a suspicion that he was not quite conscious of.

Nick hesitated briefly, then he said, "A few scratches. He was lucky."

"Good," Jeremy said and he looked away, off to the north. All he could see was Caleb Hart's fields. Rows of green plants all the same, all growing evenly, stretched out to what seemed to be the horizon. He felt suddenly uneasy with Nick.

"So you're going to kill Hagemeyer?" Nick said.

"Yes."

"When?"

"I don't know exactly. Soon." With each word he spoke, Jeremy felt the field recede, felt Nick fade.

"So why did you come to me?"

Jeremy tried to shape words in his head: Because you're my friend. But they were faint; they were too insubstantial to survive speech. He himself felt insubstantial now; he felt utterly alone and he said, "I don't have a weapon."

Nick nodded. "Are you sure you want to do this?"

"I'm sure."

"Then I'll help you."

Nick's words came instantly and firmly and with no hint of reference to any other authority. Jeremy nearly gasped with thankfulness. Nick's face was smiling, his face was vivid before Jeremy, the spoor of his beating clear to Jeremy now, refreshing his anger for the man who had to pay. Jeremy thought: I came because you're my friend. Still the words wouldn't yield to speech; but now it was because they were too full of substance.

"Thanks," Jeremy said, and Nick said "Kill the son of a bitch," and the two men shook hands hard.

S oon after the short muscular man had come and Jeremy went off again without a word, Deborah sat on the front porch steps and for a time she was conscious of her bare feet. They made her feel naked. She drew her feet together and she wanted to go inside and lie in the morning light on the bed and her breath was short and then she felt like weeping, though there were no tears forming. She prayed briefly, a spontaneous prayer and so she found words. She asked God for the gift of Jeremy's hands on her, her husband's hands, and she prayed for no more men to come to her house, no man. Her feet were naked and her legs, but she stayed where she was on the porch in the sunlight.

Later she heard her mother's voice say, "Debbie." Deborah opened her eyes and her mother was before her but not as near as she'd expected. Her mother was standing only halfway up the walk and her hands were clasping each other as if they were cold.

"Mama?"

Her mother came near now. Her face was drawn tight with strong feeling and Deborah rose. "Debbie, honey . . . " she said.

"Who is it?"

"Berenice."

Deborah sat down before she fell. Every pore opened and released her strength to the indifferent air and her head sank forward with the image of her aunt at the kitchen table yesterday. In her mind Deborah looked intently at her aunt's face and tried to see the warning there. I should have known, Deborah cried to herself. I should have done something.

A hand was on her own. She raised her head and it was her mother. "I know, honey," she said. "I know."

"What happened?" Deborah's voice sounded to herself as if it were from a third person, standing nearby.

Miriam's eyes closed for a moment and she turned her face

away. "A neighbor found her. Mrs. Noelke. Berenice did all her laundry this morning but she hung it in the basement, even though any fool could see it's sunny today and there's no sign at all of rain." Miriam's voice had risen in what sounded like anger and now it dissolved into sobs.

Deborah patted at her mother, pulled her down to sit next to her on the steps, put her arms around her, and all the while Deborah's mind was broken off from these actions of her body and it waited with an odd calmness for the rest of the story.

Miriam cried for a while and then slowly the sounds stopped and there was only silence.

"What happened, Mama?" Deborah whispered.

"It seems that she finished hanging the clothes and then went up and had a bath. Bunny still smelled of the bath soap, Mrs. Noelke said. She went and had a bath and put on a clean dress, her nicest dress, and she put her dirty clothes in the hamper and then she went downstairs and . . . " Miriam's voice faltered again. Deborah squeezed her mother gently and Miriam took a deep breath and finished quickly. "Bunny took a sheet and stood on the hamper and she hanged herself."

Deborah closed her eyes and the calmness was still in her mind and she tried to understand it; she listened and its silence was like the silence of Aunt Berenice's kitchen and she understood: this was the calmness of despair; Deborah had no power to control anything important in anyone's life and it gave her this phony little posture of peace.

But then she began to weep with her mother; and part of her weeping was in anger at this feeling in herself and part was for Aunt Berenice, who had bathed and dressed for death as if it were for her father home from the mill.

Three days later, in the middle of a cumulus-stuffed Saturday afternoon, Berenice was laid out at the funeral home, ready to be put in the earth. When the service began, Deborah was already sitting at the back, alone. Jeremy wouldn't come; his quiet had taken on a sullen edginess and all he'd said was the one word, no. And Deborah wanted nothing more to do with her mother and aunts on this day. Her face still burned from words only a few minutes before: Adah saying how it was at least a good thing they'd found Berenice quick, before she'd begun to decay where she hung; and after an embrace with her mother, Deborah had asked if she'd found a crown of feathers in Aunt Berenice's pillow and her mother had said no, no she hadn't, and her voice and twisted face showed that she really believed that this was a sign that heaven might be closed to Berenice. Deborah blamed herself for provoking her mother; she shouldn't have asked about the feathers. But it was done and Deborah felt as if she couldn't breathe in the tight, dark parlor and she'd already brought her prayers and farewell to Aunt Berenice; so when Elwood Zeigler began to sing, Deborah rose and slipped out the door and into the tight, bright air.

For a moment Deborah stood on the street, dazed as a woman who'd been evicted by the cops. She didn't know where to go. But she'd noticed Effie's absence and though she wouldn't expect Effie to come to a funeral here again, Deborah couldn't calm the restlessness in her at the thought of Effie not even knowing about Berenice. And she didn't know. Deborah was sure of that. If the women hadn't told Effie about her own mother's death, they wouldn't tell her about her sister.

Deborah moved off quickly. She caught a red trolley and it went up onto McKinley Bridge. Below, the river was rumpled like casket cloth but Deborah felt a surge of strength. She was putting a river between herself and Wabash. She closed her eyes and concentrated on the car sliding on its steel rails, carrying her away.

Only when the streetcar had come to her stop did her mind begin to drift back across the river. She got off and went up the hill. Her eyes fixed on the twin spires of the church and she wanted them to lift her up, to sharpen her senses with the attentiveness they seemed to have when she first saw them. All of this—the enmity of women linked by blood, the death of a mother even as she seemed finally to be making her way toward a reconciliation, the death by her own hand of a woman who seemed to suffer more from the silence of a weekday afternoon than from the mistreatment of her husband—all of this must have some sense to it. And her own failure. Especially that. And her husband; and her child. My God, she whispered in her mind. Deborah found herself trembling, standing at the top of the hill on Effie's street and trembling, and she wanted to pray but there were no words. Only her aunt's name: Effie.

She went to the house and up the steps and spoke the name loudly as she knocked on the glass of the door. "Effie. Effie."

But there was no answer. No one came to the door. The curtain did not stir. Deborah kept her eye on it to plead with Effie at her first timorous glance outside. But there was nothing.

Deborah went down the steps and she knew where she was headed: the church. She walked quickly and she watched the spires growing above her, shaping her feelings, focusing them, drawing them up to a fine point. At the foot of the steps she paused and looked above the door at the bas-relief of the Virgin, her heart—her immaculate heart—thrusting from her body, as if it could be seized. It was so vulnerable there, Deborah thought. But it was accessible, too. Deborah felt she might reach up and simply touch it and her own heart would be burnt free of its dross like the ore in Jeremy's ovens. A figure passed by Deborah and the movement drew her eyes down to the church doors. They stood open and a man and a woman came out with a child walking between them.

Deborah went up the steps and she hesitated at the door. She remembered her naked head. She felt in the pockets of her dress and found a few coins and then a handkerchief, and she spread it and laid it on her head and she entered the church.

The place drew her forward at once, bringing her from beneath the low roof at the back and into the lift of the nave. The space above her made her calm. It was empty, unreachable. No human quality—no hatred, no despair—could be brought into that space. But the emptiness had a shapely boundary, far off, implying the final orderliness of all things. She closed her eyes and felt the weight of the emptiness on her skin; it spread from her face and down her arms and her chest and it covered her like rain.

After a time, she lowered her head and opened her eyes. The altar was empty. But there were sounds behind her. She turned and saw at the back of the sanctuary two sets of three narrow doors. Perhaps a dozen people were lined up near one of the sets and Deborah moved closer and over the center door she saw a sign: FATHER HARRISON. As the man's square, mill-worker's face shaped itself in her mind, the left-hand door opened and an old woman came out and hobbled away while the first person in line—a man—stepped inside to take her place and the door closed.

In the image of Father Harrison's face there was an aura of sympathy: he, too, had wanted Effie to be reconciled to her sisters. In Father Harrison, Deborah felt she had proof that she wasn't mad, that this all had been worth striving for. She sat in a pew and waited.

The line moved person by person into the little doors to see Father Harrison—Deborah assumed he was inside the space, as well. Others came and joined the end of the line, but gradually it diminished and at last the final person—a middle-aged man in a white suit and tie but without a coat—came out of the left-hand door, closing it gently, and he moved away.

Deborah rose and approached the door and there was a fluttering inside her, but she breathed deeply at the marble-slick air and she opened the door and stepped inside.

No one was there. Nor could there be. The room was tiny, barely big enough for one person. On the side wall—blocking off, she realized, the space where the middle door was located—she saw a low, padded shelf—a place to kneel—and at what would be face-level for a kneeling person, a window shuttered by a woven wood screen. A faint light came through the screen.

Deborah felt the impulse to turn and go out. The place made her uneasy in its strangeness. But she hesitated and the moments dragged on. She was conscious of the doorknob in her hand and the strangeness of the room faded and now it seemed hidden, a secret place, and she pulled the door to and she leaned against it, tucked away, safe.

A shadow moved through the light from the inner window. Then a voice spoke from the other side. "Is there something you'd like to say, my child?" The voice was a man's, but extravagantly gentle. After the tremor of gentleness had moved through Deborah and passed from her, the voice seemed familiar. "Father Harrison?" she said.

"Yes?" the voice replied.

Deborah moved to the window and she bent to it. "Father Harrison, it's Deborah Cole. Effie's niece." And she knelt.

"Mrs. Cole? I . . . this is a surprise." His voice became at once conversational. Not hard, but the specialness was gone.

"I wanted to talk with you," Deborah said.

"Of course . . . You're not Catholic, are you?"

"No."

"That's what I thought . . . Would you be more comfortable talking in my office?"

Deborah straightened and she considered this. But she liked the clarity of this room and the feeling that no one could find her here. "I'm all right . . . May I stay?"

"Of course." The priest's voice grew suddenly gentle again and Deborah nearly gasped in appreciation. She laid her palms before her on the wall, on each side of the window.

"I went to Effie's house. She wasn't there."

"Wasn't she?"

"She didn't answer the door."

"Mrs. Cole, you need to understand something about your aunt. Normally I couldn't talk like this to you, but Effie asked me to explain when you returned. She told me to tell you some things about her . . . She has a very keen sense of her own shortcomings."

"I could feel that. I admire her for it. My other aunts and my mother don't have any idea anything's wrong."

"It's stronger than you might think. Perhaps even stronger than it needs to be . . . But your aunt believes that these short-comings—I'm changing the way I speak for you, Mrs. Cole; I shouldn't do that—Effie has a keen sense of her *sins*. Those she's committed—for which she has long ago been forgiven—but also for those she knows by her temperament she will inevitably commit in the future, given the right circumstances. She be-lieves—*we* believe—that this is the most dangerous thing in our life on earth. That we should sin. That we should willfully cut ourselves off from God . . . I don't mean to preach to you, Mrs. Cole. I'm just trying to explain Effie. Why she might not answer the door to you."

"She was there?"

"Perhaps . . . I'd say probably so."

"She doesn't want to see me anymore?"

"It's not that. She loves you, I'm sure. Just as she loves her sisters. But she's trying to avoid the near occasion to sin. She has been given such a strong personal sense of sin that she has felt the need to withdraw in order to keep herself pure. In another time, if she'd had her feelings earlier in her life, she might have become a nun of a certain sort. One who seeks a severe austerity in this earthly life in order to preserve herself from acts that could jeopardize a life that is more important to her."

"I don't understand. She's never going to answer the door to me?"

"It's all that you would have her return to that she can't face. She feels as dismayed as you about the way her sisters treat each other. But she knows that those same feelings are in herself. She could not avoid becoming one of them again."

Deborah pulled back. Her hands fell to her sides. Perhaps Effie was right, she thought. Deborah herself had felt the promptings to withdraw.

A shadow darkened the wooden weave of the window. Father Harrison had drawn very near. His voice grew softer still. "Mrs.

Cole, perhaps my own story would help you understand. When I was a young man I worked the mines out west and I was a hothead, to be frank about it. I was given considerable physical strength and I got into a lot of fights and one night in a little town in Colorado I almost killed a man with just my hands. The beating I gave him was no different from the ones I'd given others who'd tangled with me in the past, but on that night I had a very strong realization of what I could do. I had to hold back from continuing the beating—he'd started it, you see, and I felt no restraint in that way. He'd pushed me too far." Father Harrison seemed short of breath. He paused. Then his shadow grew larger and his voice grew smaller; it receded to nearly a whisper. "I'm the same man even now . . . I always believed in God. My parents were devout Catholics and they brought me up to believe, to know that there's more to us . . . I came to know out there in Colorado that I was a certain sort of man and I had to either embrace that or reject it utterly. For me there was nothing else. It didn't happen all at once, but the final solution was the life God finally led me to. To be a priest. To spend every waking hour focused intently on gentleness. If I were not this single-minded, I could kill someone. Even now."

The voice ceased. The shadow withdrew. Deborah put her hands on the wall before her. She yearned to touch Father Harrison's hand. As if he were speaking, she understood his present silence: he was a man struggling not to inflict pain. Were these the words of Jeremy's silence, as well? She bent near to the window and whispered, "I understand."

On Monday morning Nick appeared at Jeremy's door and he and Jeremy walked away down the block. Nick had a brown parcel under his arm and when they were out of sight of the house, Nick handed it to him. It had a hard center. Jeremy held it with both hands.

"It's a .30-caliber Luger," Nick said, smiling broadly. "It's a few years old, but that's an expensive weapon. You've got a box of fifty cartridges . . . Obviously we're all behind you."

Jeremy looked at Nick and he didn't like Nick's going to Chernowicz and the others, even if they did approve. But he said nothing. He was glad to have the pistol.

"Have you got a plan?" Nick said.

"Not yet."

"You want help?"

"I don't know. Let me think about it."

"Jeremy." Nick squared around to face him. "I'm with you on this. Anything you want from me, anything I can do, you just name it."

Jeremy looked at Nick's face—steady-eyed and webbed with sincerity—and he said, "Thanks, Nick," and he did feel grateful. He put his hand on Nick's shoulder and shook him while concentrating on the heft of the pistol and its ammunition in his other hand.

"Let me know," Nick said. "But I've got to head home now. We're leaving the house. Hart's throwing us out."

"Where can I find you?"

"The shantytown out by the levee."

Jeremy felt a twist of anger at this: Nick and his boys and his wife having to go down to shantytown. Jeremy turned away; he put both his hands on the parcel and his fingers spread around it.

"Find me," Nick said.

"Okay."

Then Nick moved away, back up the street, and Jeremy was left with the Luger and only the vaguest stirrings of a plan. Maybe it's simple, he told himself. Just find Hagemeyer. Jeremy felt a rush of strength at this thought. He was conscious of the placid weight in his hands. He looked around him. A house off to his right was empty. He walked into the yard, around the house, and back to the stained wood building that held the coal shed and the privy. There was a ragged hedge at its side blocking the view from both the alley and the yard next door, and Jeremy went into this enclosed space and sat down with his back against the shed.

He held the package for a moment and he measured his breaths, kept them slow; he cleared his mind; he prepared himself as he would at the lockers, before going to stoke the oven. When he felt still inside, he carefully unwrapped the parcel, the paper crackling into his hands, and he saw the Luger. All his life he'd been around guns and he had even fired an automatic pistol before. But he'd never seen a Luger and its lines made his breath catch. The pistol was hard and dark, and its mass was bunched up above and behind the trigger, big-shouldered, but its lines were curved. The high back, the toggle lock, the trigger and its guard, the top of the grip and the butt were all strikingly curved; and the barrel was slender and tapered. Jeremy felt the way he did looking at Deborah's profile: her soft mouth; her strong, man's jaw. Jeremy held the pistol, the grip in his palm, and he put his finger through the trigger guard and he felt a trill in him, a delicate physical pleasure with the Luger in his hand. Luger. He said the word in his mind; even its name was both hard and soft. "Luger," he said aloud, and he scanned the sky with the barrel.

Then he lowered his hand and touched the release catch and the empty clip came out. Jeremy laid the pistol gently beside him and he opened the box of cartridges. He clicked them into the clip, eight of them. Then he lifted the Luger and turned it over. A deep and empty place: he pressed the clip into the handle and it went in with a suck and a snap and he turned the pistol right side up. He put his hand on the slide and he pulled it, its mechanism knuckling, and he let it go and it snicked flat again and the Luger was ready to fire.

Jeremy looked at the pistol in his hand and he laid his head back against the shed and briefly he closed his eyes. He felt ready to act but it was not clear what he should do. There was no oven to stand before. But the Luger in his hand made his feet stir.

Jeremy thought of the Wabash Steel administrative building just off the town square. Hagemeyer must have an office there. Jeremy jumped up. He looked around him. The parcel paper was on the ground along with the box of shells. He bent and with one hand—not putting the pistol down—he took the other cartridges out of the box and stuffed them into his two front pants pockets. He straightened and with the toe of his shoe he nudged the empty box and the paper under the hedge. He looked a last time at the pistol in his hand and then he untucked his shirt and he stuck the Luger into his pants, the barrel sliding down against his skin. The shirt fell lightly over the butt of the gun and this cool, hard touch was his secret.

Jeremy strode away. The street passed, the North Plant fences, the rumbling inside the mill—this was his place no longer; he was laid off; he walked faster—and he crossed St. Louis Avenue. He went over a block and up Central and at the southern edge of the square, on the corner of a side street, was a wide two-story brick building with an American flag flying on a pole angled from the front edge of its roof. A black Packard limousine sat before the building and Jeremy drew back. Surely this was Hagemeyer's car. One of his goons, dressed up in a gray chauffeur's uniform, was near the curbside fender and Jeremy looked around.

Off to his right was the side of a frame building, the first store on the square, and there was a door and stoop. Jeremy moved to it and sat down and he looked across the way. The angle was severe, but he could still see the tire-rounded rump of the Packard and its slick stretch of side doors up to the front whitewall, and he could even see a few feet of the front yard of the administrative building. The goon was on the far side of the car, looking in the other direction. If Jeremy kept his eyes fixed on the space leading to the Packard, he would be able to see Hagemeyer when he approached the car. Then it was just a short sprint from this stoop to easy firing distance.

Jeremy was gasping for air. He struggled to slow his breathing. Just a short sprint. He touched the Luger and he felt reckless. He could see himself running across this space, the pistol coming out, Hagemeyer turning—Jeremy had never seen Hagemeyer, never even seen him; the man would be in a suit, a three-piece suit; he would be getting into the Packard; Hage-meyer—and Jeremy saw himself raising the pistol, the man's face fleshy in fear.

A trembling had come to Jeremy. His hands were trembling. Was this the hour? He himself would die. The chauffeur was probably armed. He'd kill the chauffeur, too. Jeremy was ready to die. He realized this with a leap in his chest. This was never a thought before. But he was no good for Deborah anyway. He couldn't even put his hands on her, even when he truly wanted to. And Lizzy was long dead. And Cronin. And maybe Gus. And his own father, ringed in fire. And this had to be done. Done right.

There was movement. Jeremy jumped up. Yes. A man in a suit was crossing the space. The goon was running around the back of the car. The man in the suit—the glint of a bald head, a wide-shouldered man but thin—this man was waiting for his goon to open the door; Hagemeyer couldn't even open his own damn door. Jeremy took a step, another, his hand moved to the Luger, touched it. He took another step as the door of the Pack-ard opened and he thought to run, but touching the pistol he realized he'd never even fired it, not once; he hadn't fired any pistol in years, he didn't even know if the damn Reds' pistol would fire. He didn't want to get nabbed trying something that he'd then never be able to finish.

Jeremy took another step, but he stopped in the center of the street. Hagemeyer was bending and disappearing into the backseat of the Packard and the Luger stayed where it was, under the shirt, nuzzled down near to Jeremy's crotch.

Deborah angled her head to listen. She was sitting at her kitchen table and it had been more than an hour since Jeremy had gone off with some man she'd never seen, a man with a face stained with yellowing bruises. She had cleaned the house—mill

grit, harder to take now that it no longer tokened their liveli-
hood—and then she'd sat at the kitchen table, suddenly very
weary.

Now she listened. Was there a sound? Could she hear a
scratching in the walls? She strained and all she heard was the
slip of her own breath. The house was still; the morning was still.
She felt the sweat oozing from the pores of her forehead. She
listened harder. There'd been a faint scratching sound, a swift,
sharp-pawed movement. She suddenly snapped upright in her
chair. Was she going mad? Aunt Berenice had been listening
like this. But so had Grandma Birney. She'd heard the sounds.
Deborah thought of her grandmother's letters, their crankiness,
and she smiled, briefly, the smile passing like a sound in the
wall. She thought of the rat sitting before her as she awoke in
her grandmother's parlor, a dark spirit, tiny but malevolent.

Deborah tried to smile again at a thought that scrabbled into
her. But she couldn't smile because it would trivialize—make
impossible—something that promised a release: she could write
her own letter. Deborah rose and went into the bedroom and
bent to her chest of drawers, listening all the while, hearing
nothing, but from the lowest drawer she took a writing pad and
a pencil. She returned to the kitchen table and sat down and she
began to write.

Dear Rats,
I'm not even sure you're there . . . That's not true.
Something is there. I've felt you around me for a long
time. What I want to figure out is if it has to be this way,
if you're in all the walls in all the houses in all the lives
in all the world. God help us if you are. But I'm not
talking like Grandma would have me do. Elvira Birney.
You remember her. She didn't give in to you. She told
you how she loved her daughter Effie and you couldn't
make her take it back. And Effie loved her too. She came
to the funeral, didn't she? At least she came. So get out
of my walls, get out of my house. You've got no place in

my life . . . When I say that, I can almost see you looking
at each other, your dark rats' eyes rolling in mockery at
me. You do have a place, you're thinking. I can't even
talk to my husband. I can't even be part of him. Not just
at night, when you're awake like me and you're watching
in your damn silence and there's the man I love lying
beside me dreaming his secret dreams and there's nothing I can do to bring him and me together. Not just then.
Anytime. In the daytime too, when he goes out to do
God knows what with the men you send. I know his
goodness. Jeremy's a good man. But I know you too. I
know what you can do. You think you've got a permanent
place here. Well, Grandma told me you've got to be
made to understand that you're not wanted. I'm going
to buy some poison. Something that you won't even know
is poison. I'll get something sweet-tasting, like all the
nice words of my mama and my aunts, but if you eat it
(and you won't even know not to eat it since it's so sweet,
since it's so clearly meant for you, since it's there in the
walls you think you own) then you'll die a terrible terrible
death and I'm just going to sit at this table and not even
say a word, not give you a look as you die. Then you'll
have to let go of Jeremy. This is our house, isn't it? You'd
have to give him up. You've carried away everyone else
I've loved, but you can't take Jeremy. If I can't have my
daughter and if I can't have my aunts, I can at least have
my husband. Please give him back to me. Please.

Deborah drew away from the piece of paper. She sounded
weak at the end. But she signed her name to it—Deborah Cole—
and then she added Mrs. in front and she folded the letter carefully. She rose and looked around the kitchen, thinking to put
the letter in a place where the rats would find it. But there was
a sudden ceasing inside her and then a feeling about these rats,
an understanding, and she thought: They know already. As I
wrote the words they were listening. They know.

The next morning Jeremy set out for the shantytown by the levee to find Nick and talk to him about the best way to finish with Hagemeyer. Time was running out: soon Jeremy would have Spud and the boys coming after him at home and that was something that would end badly, he knew; and worse, it would draw Deborah into the center of things.

Jeremy saw the levee up ahead and he walked faster. There were just a few houses out this way and the levee brooded like an Indian mound up against the sky. Jeremy turned onto a gravel road and focused on the sight before him. Half a mile off was a cluster of huts broomed up against the bank of the levee. Jeremy grew anxious for Nick and his sons and he couldn't even picture the angry woman, Nick's wife, being able to live in that place. Jeremy walked faster still.

Drawing near, he could see the shacks clearly—made of old packing crates, cardboard, flattened metal cans, scrounged wood, old tar paper—and though the empty strip of land along the levee stretched several miles in either direction, the shacks were all huddled close to each other. In the doorways were figures as motionless as the found objects around them—the bottles and cans and rags and scraps of lumber—and Jeremy was moving through the settlement now, the eyes at the doorway turning to him slowly. A pair of dirty children dashed past. Jeremy looked for Nick's sons, but he didn't see them.

Jeremy began to scan the faces to find Nick himself and the strangers fell away—he did not let himself linger on these eyes; he knew his purpose was somehow connected to them, but for now Nick was the only one he could let himself be interested in. Jeremy passed an old man chopping wood with the muffled thump of a dull ax and he passed a young boy sitting on a crate with a stripped tree branch across his lap and the empty eyes of a hobo. Jeremy kept walking through the narrow meanders of

the settlement, but he was ready to flee. Sad children, desperate
men: Jeremy had had as much of this as he could bear for now.
He touched the Luger through his shirt.

Then at a turning he saw Nick. The man was sitting on an
upturned can before a lidless kettle hanging over a fire. He had
a tin cup lifted to his mouth and he was mirrored in the act by
another man sitting opposite him, a middle-aged man in a kersey
cap.

"Nick," Jeremy said.

Nick looked up. He did not smile but gave a minute nod.
"Welcome to Hooverville," he said.

Jeremy glanced at the other man, who was staring into the
steam rising from his cup. Jeremy turned back to Nick. "Can we
talk for a few minutes?"

"Sure." Nick put his cup down and he stood up. "I'm glad
you came."

"Are you okay?"

Nick shrugged. He looked down at the man by the fire. "See
you," he said and then caught Jeremy's eye and he flicked his
head toward the north end of shantytown. He and Jeremy began
to walk.

"This place makes me . . ." Jeremy didn't even try to find a
word. The feeling was too strong and there'd been too many
words already.

Nick said, "This is what we're all gonna come to, if something's not done."

Jeremy nodded. The two walked in silence for a time, weav-
ing along the mud-trough pathways, and then they were out of
the shantytown and walking through the high grass at the foot
of the levee. Finally Nick said, "She took my boys."

Jeremy stopped. "Your wife?"

Nick took another step and turned. "I don't blame her," he
said. "Ain't no life for a woman and kids."

"Where'd they go?"

"I don't know."

"You gonna try to find her?"

"No. I'm going to Chicago."

"That's where Chernowicz is?"

"I'm no good for her and the boys anyway. I'm gonna get them hurt sometime."

Jeremy looked away. The gravel path went up along the levee a hundred yards more and ended at a fence. On this side of the fence, and off to the east, were a boulder-strewn field and a small wood, bur oaks and locust trees. On the other side of the fence was a field of horseradish.

Nick said, "Yeah. Chernowicz is there."

"Sorry about your family," Jeremy said, low.

"A family's a corrupt idea anyway. Capitalism in four walls."

Jeremy was grateful for Nick's turning to the ideology. It put him at a distance. Jeremy didn't hurt so bad for him when he was like this.

Nick said, "It's true. It even turned me into a damn tyrant."

This made Jeremy feel his friend's loss again and he looked off to the east. Crows were haggling out of sight somewhere in the trees.

"You want to go with me?" Nick said.

"To Chicago?"

"Yes."

Jeremy hesitated. He wanted to consider this idea but the answer was already on his lips. "I want to kill Hagemeyer."

Nick nodded once and lowered his eyes briefly. Jeremy sensed the man's disappointment and he appreciated that, but surely what Jeremy was going to do was the true consummation of his friendship with Nick. From the beginning Nick had identified Hagemeyer as the enemy of the workers of Wabash. Let others march in Chicago.

Then Nick said, "When do you plan to do it?"

"Soon. I can't wait past Saturday because that's when Spud and his boys will be coming for me. He's no fool. He's gonna make sure that it doesn't turn out wrong for him."

"Saturday?"

"That gives me four days."

"It's gonna have to be public," Nick said and his eyes grew very still; they focused intently on Jeremy, as if to stress the unspoken implication: You'll probably die doing this.

And for the second time Jeremy confronted with instant acceptance the possibility of death. He was ready; he could see no purpose for himself other than removing Hagemeyer.

Jeremy and Nick looked at each other in silence for a long moment and then Nick said, "There's something going on Thursday morning up in Lawton. Hoover's coming through and Hagemeyer's making an appearance with him in the square where Lincoln and Douglas debated. You know the place?"

"Yes."

"And, Jeremy. When you go up there, you're gonna need to do a better job of hiding your pistol than that."

Jeremy looked down. The butt of the Luger had worked its way out from under his shirt. He flipped the shirt over the pistol and said, "Okay."

Nick looked off toward the wood. Jeremy knew at once that there was no more for either of them to say to each other. Not now, not ever. He knew Nick had been his friend, but Jeremy felt nothing except the churn of impatience to get on with the work he had to do. Nick had his own work; Nick would be all right: Jeremy ran these things through his mind and he thought they were true. But they didn't explain why he should have no feeling for Nick at this moment. Perhaps this was part of his preparation for work, like methodically dressing for the ovens. Perhaps he had to strip down his feelings now so he could kill Hagemeyer.

"Good luck," Nick said, still looking away, his voice gassy from what seemed to be strong feeling.

Jeremy waited for some response in himself, but all he did was look off to the wood and the field nearby and think that he'd better practice with the Luger when Nick was gone. But after a moment he did force his attention back to Nick and he made himself say, "Good luck to you too."

Nick nodded at this and then he walked off without even

glancing at Jeremy again, as if Nick were a mourner moving away from an open casket that he couldn't bear to look at one more time.

Jeremy turned to the field and took the Luger from under his shirt and he crossed the gravel road. He picked his way through the rocks in the field and up ahead he heard the crows in a tree at the edge of the wood. He drew near and stopped. There was a cluster of bur oaks before him and the leaves were thick and the birds within were only dark scraps of shadows and a raucous scattering of sound.

He waited. He watched the sky above the trees and he held the Luger at his side and he flipped the safety off. There was a faint stirring of the hot morning air and he smelled the leaf mold from the wood and the river water beyond the levee and he looked at the tops of the bur oaks. They were thrashing from the birds within and he thought simply to fire into the shadows. But that wouldn't practice his shooting eye and he had only a limited number of cartridges.

Jeremy lowered his eyes to the trunk of the nearest oak. It was perhaps thirty feet away. Surely he could get this close to Hagemeyer. On the trunk was a scar, an oval bare spot the size of a cantaloupe. The size of a man's head. Jeremy raised the pistol, squared around, steadied it with both hands, and he squeezed off a round. The gun kicked and the sound was throaty and hard and to the right of the scar, maybe two inches to the right, a gash of bark splintered up from the impact.

Jeremy looked up at once to watch the crows fly. Only one rose above the tree and it went up, angled, hung there for a moment, a jagged black gash in the sky, and the Luger rose, too. Jeremy sighted and squeezed off a round, the pistol kicked, but the crow did not fall. It swooped and disappeared into the trees.

Where are the rest of the bastards? Jeremy cried in his mind. The trees were full of crows, he'd thought, and only one had become visible. Jeremy waited. He listened. The trees were silent. Maybe a rushing sound deeper in the wood. But nothing else. He had missed the spot on the tree, Hagemeyer's head, and he had missed the crow. Jeremy cursed softly and he squared around to the trunk again and his hands came up and he calmed himself, held his breath—it was okay; it'd been a long time since he'd fired a pistol. The next shot clipped at the edge of the bare spot, would have taken Hagemeyer's ear off. And the Luger was feeling lighter, was feeling like an extension of Jeremy's arm, a part of his body, a sinew.

Jeremy held the Luger straight out without using his other hand to steady it. He grew calm. He looked down the barrel, through the notch of the front sight, and he squeezed again and caught Hagemeyer in the center of his forehead. Jeremy lowered the Luger slightly and the pistol kicked once, twice, three times: a tight, quick cluster in Hagemeyer's chest.

There was a flutter nearby, off to Jeremy's left. He spun and against the sky, very close, was movement and his Luger came around and he tracked the spot quickly and even as he squeezed off the round he knew it wasn't a crow, it was a much smaller bird, a soft little whorl of a bird and it leaped in a spattering of feathers and fell like a chunk of slag.

There was a spike tumbling in Jeremy's chest and it spun up into his throat. The sky before him was empty. He wished the thing he'd killed had been a crow. The tiny bird was still exploding in his mind and he turned away. He concentrated on the tree. The Luger would do what he wanted it to do. There were four kills before him in the trunk of the tree and the dead bird flipped out of his mind like a spent shell.

On the following night, the eve of Herbert Hoover's appearance in Lawton, Illinois, Jeremy lay fitfully sleeping in bed and Deborah, unable to sleep at all, sat at the kitchen table, the door closed, the light on, a blank sheet of paper before her. She picked up her pencil and instantly the welter in her began to

shape itself into words. She bent over the paper and she paused—
but only for a moment, not really doubting what she was doing—
and then she began to write.

Dear Rats,
   Just because you are quiet in the walls doesn't mean
you're fooling me. You're running even now. You're running out there in the dark, all around my house and my
mother's house and Della and Adah's house and you go
across the bridge and up the hill to Effie's house. But
Effie's inside, hidden away, and she's not coming out.
Is she safe? Is she really safe from you? If she decides
not to come out, does that mean there's no way for you
to get in? I wish I knew. I'll never see her again, I guess.
But why can't I let it go? Why can't I just let her withdraw
like she wants and be at peace in myself with that? Am
I like you then? Am I one of you? Lurking around outside, looking for the cracks, insisting on coming in even
when I'm not wanted inside? Maybe that's why you can't
fool me. I know where you are. You're running in this
house now too. You're running in Jeremy's dreams. He's
been uneasy in his sleep tonight. I want to touch him.
I want to crawl inside his dreams too—just like you—
and does that make us the same? But I'll stroke him
inside there. I'll make his arms grow still, his hands ease
open. I can be strong for him in his dreams because I
think he's afraid in there. He's weak in his dreams and
I love him for that.

With her love curling onto the paper, Deborah paused and
she felt briefly calm, and beyond the closed door, in the dark
bed, Jeremy was coiled in sleep and in readiness to act as he
saw Hagemeyer's Packard slide into the square in Lawton. The
car came up into the middle of the grassy lawn and there were
people cheering and crowding near but there was a corridor
through the bodies that led from Jeremy to the back door of the

car. Jeremy was holding the Luger and he raised it and he strode
forward to the door and the window was down and Hagemeyer's
face appeared there, a round face with liver spots, and his eyes
blinked without comprehension at Jeremy and the pistol. It was
time, Jeremy knew, and he raised the Luger and laid the tip of
the barrel in the center of Hagemeyer's forehead and his fingers
began to move but there was a voice, a child's voice, and another
face appeared from the dimness of the car. Just behind Hagemeyer was a child, a little round-faced girl, and she said, Grand-
father, who's this man? Jeremy looked at the girl and she was a
stranger, an odd little face, clearly kin to this still uncompre-
hending man, but Jeremy watched the child's face rumple in a
sudden fear and Jeremy turned, he ran, he tried to run fast, but
the child behind him was beginning to cry, to sob in fear, and
Jeremy could not move his legs and he awoke.

Jeremy sat up in the bed and the girl's weeping was gone,
the dream was over with the abruptness of a shooting death, and
Jeremy's heart raced—in fear, he knew, in fear of himself. He
did not want the burden of this act, he did not want to strip
himself down to this murderous hardness; he yearned for a soft
place and he felt a drawing in his groin, his body was flexing in
desire, and he turned and his hands came out to find Deborah,
to hold her, to place this yearning gently inside her and he
wondered—his mind working from a great distance, as if in a
dream—he wondered if in touching Deborah this burden would
fall from him, if he could just lie in this bed with her all through
the night and then into the morning and afternoon and on into
tomorrow night, holding her.

But his hands groped in the dark and found only rumpled
sheets and he heard the child's voice again now, crying, a thin
sound, tearless from fear, and his desire vanished, his body went
slack, a bleeder valve flared in him, the jelly flame, but the flame
was cold, as cold as his daughter's hand, and he wanted her fever
to return, the fever was better than this coldness.

Jeremy lay back and he stared into the dark. Tomorrow he
would go out. The flame of the bleeder valve dissolved against
the night sky. Jeremy thought: I have my work. And in the

kitchen Deborah decided that she'd said enough in this letter. She had come to a moment of love and she thought: It is enough for now; I can sit here alone and I can love.

At ten thirty-five the next morning, Thursday, July 14, 1932, Jeremy Cole looked from the dimness of the bedroom into the kitchen and he saw his wife, Deborah, sitting at the table, her back to him. By moving slightly to the side he could see that she was writing something. Whatever she'd been writing the past couple of days, it was absorbing her for long periods and Jeremy felt he could prepare now without fear of interruption. The meeting started in Lawton at noon and he would catch Yellowhammer at eleven. The trip took half an hour and that would get him to the square in time to shape a plan.

He went to the dresser and opened his drawer and un-wrapped the Luger from the clean undershirts Deborah had put there on Monday. He unwrapped the cartridges and he counted out eight—enough for one clip; he would not need more than this, he decided. He eased the drawer shut and he moved across the floor, into the living room, to the far side and a wing chair. He turned the chair around to face the wall and he sat in it.

He was calm. His hands were steady as he placed the car-tridges in his lap and held the Luger before him. He waited, breathing lightly now, a little fluttery now in the chest, and he pressed the clip-release stud near the trigger and the clip came out. He drew his knees together and laid the Luger across them. He held the clip in his left hand and pulled down the stud on the case and he heard the spring coiling inside. Then he dropped in one cartridge, two, another, another, counting them. The sixth he knew certainly would be fired and the seventh—this one, he felt, would be the one to kill—and the eighth—the first one out, the one to burn Hagemeyer, spin him, tell him it was all over while he still had ears to hear.

Jeremy paused. He felt his anger quickening him, making

his hands go hard. This was not the way to prepare, he knew. He had to restrain the strength, keep it focused, bind it in so it could be used all at once, at just the right time, in just the right way. He picked up the Luger and the heft of it wiped his mind clean. Focused as this steel barrel, he sat for a time holding the pistol in his right hand, the clip in his left. Then he gently eased the clip into the handle and it stopped and held and he drew his hand away.

One thing at a time. Jeremy felt calm. He pointed the pistol toward the wall and he touched the milled knobs of the toggle, squeezed them, pulled them back and up. He listened to the recoil spring tightening in the grip, whining into its place, and then the breechblock would go no farther and he released the toggle and it snapped forward. The first round was in the chamber.

Jeremy paused with his finger resting lightly on the trigger. He held the Luger and sensed its readiness as a faint fibrillation in the palm of his pistol hand. Then he drew his thumb away from the grip and hooked the safety and pulled it back and down. A word was etched there: *Gesichert.* The word startled him, as if the pistol had whispered to him, a foreign word but soft, a lover's secret.

He lowered the pistol and he breathed in slowly, deeply. He was almost ready. He couldn't carry the pistol under his shirt today. He laid his head back against the chair to think and at that moment Deborah was putting her pencil down on the kitchen table. She felt a little tremor of foolishness. These feelings came from time to time as she wrote her letters, but she simply waited them out. There were things to say. She picked up what she'd written so far and she read:

Dear Rats,
    I've not spent enough time yet telling you that you're not wanted. Like my grandmother I'm too soft in some ways. I have this impulse to reason with you or feel sorry for you somehow. But you're not reasonable yourselves.

You yourselves have no pity. You are only interested in taking over our lives, finding the darkness and living there and when you run we can only just barely hear the clicking of your claws. You're out of sight, hidden away, but you're running. I sometimes realize how much energy you must have. But you can be killed. I can get poison and kill you. This is no empty threat. You can't be allowed to go on. You get away from here and you go and tell your friends to clear out of Effie's house, too. I know you're there. That's why I can't just forget about her. The body is broken. The one body that Father Harrison talked about. Effie is broken off from the body and you're running around in her walls and she can hear you.

This was all she had written this morning and she put the paper down before her. She picked up her pencil again and bent to the letter and she continued to write:

But maybe she's not broken away. She's in some distant part, performing some necessary function—with her prayers?—that is far from my own necessary function . . . Listen to me. I'm beginning to think of myself in ways that . . . Well, this is the most foolish I've felt in these letters, saying that I'm useful in the body of Christ . . . I'm not even useful in my own body . . . Jeremy has just come into the kitchen. I heard his step and he's standing behind me now, I think. This is how useless I am. There's no reason for me even to turn to him. He's moved away, to the sink. No. Not the sink. I can hear him opening the pantry door. What does he want? Nothing from me. I can't even turn my head, can't even look over my shoulder. I hear something metallic. What is it?

Deborah put down her pencil and turned around and she found Jeremy standing in the center of the kitchen floor, his black metal lunch box in his hands. She could see nothing in his face, no feeling, just the inertness of his black eyes, like coke long after the fire had formed its hardness. She trembled at this, though it didn't show, trembled even as Jeremy was trembling. Jeremy's chest had grown suddenly hot and liquescent at this turning of Deborah's face to him and he yearned no longer to touch her but to want to touch her. It had always been his body that would not yield, but now the failure had shifted to his will and the Luger drew him, only the Luger could lead him to act. Deborah did not move and Jeremy did not move and the Luger lay waiting in the indent of the chair cushion and Jeremy had nothing in him for his wife now, nothing for Deborah. But he yearned for the yearning that could restore him to life, even as he knew that he had a job, he had work, and it was time to turn to it.

Then Deborah said, "Where are you going?"

And Jeremy said, "Lawton." The word wisped from him like smoke from an oven door; but the fire was invisible and the smoke vanished and he knew he had to go. Deborah sat with this word in her head—Lawton—and she didn't know what to make of it. Then she saw Jeremy's eyes close slowly, stay shut briefly, then open. He came to her and bent to her and kissed her on the forehead and he turned and disappeared into the bedroom.

Deborah's trembling persisted and she took up her pencil and bent to the paper, her face drawing very near, and she wrote:

> I hear him now in the living room. More metallic sounds. The lunch box. What does he want that for? . . . And now I hear his step and the front door closing and his step again, faint. Now he's gone. He's gone and I can smell you. I can feel you watching, listening. He's gone and dear God I feel so empty. Dear God I feel like I'll never see him again.

Deborah stopped writing. The trembling had faded and she had no strength. Not even strength enough to hold her pencil and she laid it down. She sat at the table for a time and she felt as still as the trees outside, as bland as the sunlight. Bland and the time passed and the house ticked and she did not move. But then her mind began to resist. She could not accept that they were all lost. Her mother and her aunts, perhaps. But not her husband. They were one flesh. The word stuck in her: Lawton. The name of the town on the bluff. The town at the end of the line for Yellowhammer. She wished now that she'd pressed Jeremy for more than just this name. She found her pencil in her hand. She wrote:

> Why should he tell me the name of that town? Why didn't he just say he was going out...I'm going out. That's the most I've been getting lately. Now he looks at me for a long time and he says Lawton and he takes his lunch box. Why the lunch box? Not since things went bad three years ago has he needed his lunch box. He hasn't touched it in three years...There's something very wrong. Something wrong. He's in danger. The men he's been involved with. The men who even come to my front door. There's some protest or something in Lawton. But why the lunch box? What's in the lunch box?

Deborah's hand was racing now, the words were sprawling onto the page and she wrote: Damn you. Damn you back to the hell you came from. And she was done with the rats. She jumped up from the chair and she wondered how much time had passed. She knew she had to catch Jeremy quickly.

Deborah moved through the house and out the front door and into the naphtha smell and grit of the morning air. She turned and began to run along the street, past the shotgun houses and then the high cyclone fence at the mill and across St. Louis Avenue and up the nearest street, Grady, running past houses with lawns. Ahead was the square and she ran hard and she burst into its openness and Yellowhammer was sitting under an oak tree at the far side.

Deborah slowed, thankful; the streetcar to Lawton was still here. She walked past the statue at the center of the square and across the street. She looked closely at the windows of Yellow-hammer as she approached, but on this side of the car she could see only a woman in a large hat. Time had passed at the kitchen table before she'd decided to follow Jeremy: maybe she'd delayed longer than she'd realized. This thought rushed her around the back of the streetcar and a conductor in a blue uniform was stepping down from the center doors. Deborah scanned the windows and there was only an old man toward the front. She moved past the conductor and onto the steps of the car and she looked inside. There was no one else.

"Yes, ma'am?" the man said behind her.

Deborah stepped down and she was floppy-limbed with panic. "My husband. He was supposed to be on this streetcar."

"Coming or going?"

"Going to Lawton."

"You may've just missed him." The man took a gold watch from his pocket and flipped open the case. "It's eleven-oh-six. A car left at eleven for Lawton."

Deborah held back a gasp but it hissed in her head and she tried to steady her voice to speak. "When's the next one?"

"Eleven thirty."

"Tell me," she said. "Is there something special going on today in Lawton?"

"Yes, ma'am." The man smiled. "Wabash's own John J. Hagemeyer is going to be appearing with the president of the United States." At this he flipped up the lapel of his uniform jacket and revealed a "Hagemeyer for Congress" button; black, serifed lettering on a field of red.

A man and woman appeared at the conductor's side and he turned to them and his change machine began to click at his belt and Deborah's hands rushed into the pockets of her dress. There were a few coins inside. The remainder of her food money from Jeremy's final paycheck. She drew out the coins even as her mind spun around the event in Lawton. Hoover and Hagemeyer appearing together. A hard little nut of a conclusion would not move from the center of her thoughts: Jeremy was part of something very bad that would happen at this political rally.

In Deborah's hand now were five coins. She needed twenty-five cents. A dime. Her hand trembled. Two nickels. A penny. And the fifth coin was dark, old. What was it? She held it up. Under the patina was a buffalo. Three nickels, a penny, a dime. She could take the eleven-thirty car. The man and woman eased past her and Deborah gave the money to the conductor, who thanked her and said, "You'll only be a few minutes late to the rally."

Deborah turned and she started to move to the back of the car to be alone. But the conductor's words finally sorted themselves out in her head, the frightening word first: late; a few minutes late; the rally. Deborah sat down in the aisle seat just across from the door.

She had nothing to do but wait. She was forced to feel passive again, even now, when she knew she must act. Once more she had to tell her feelings of love to be still. If she let herself consider what might happen in the next hour and a half, she would go mad. She could only sit on this seat and fold her hands and wait, as if she were sitting on her mother's porch, as if she were sitting beside her daughter's bed. Or her husband's bed. No more thoughts, she cried to herself, and she began to rock faintly forward and back and she said in her mind "Dear God" over and over until the words blurred and there was no thinking at all. The time passed and then at last the doors closed and a bell clanged and Yellowhammer began to move out of the Wabash city square.

At the same moment, a Yellowhammer was clanging its way to a stop at the foot of the bluffs near the center of Lawton. Stepping off the car, Jeremy looked at the brick streets going up the side of the bluff, up through the strata of frame houses, the trees all growing at severe angles to the ground they were planted in so that they could stand straight before the river. The maples by the station were strung with the filmy sacks of tent worms and the sound of cicadas whiplashed in the hot noon air, louder here by far than the murmur of a crowd to the north.

Jeremy turned to this milder sound and he saw the square a hundred yards away. The oaks there were massive and hung with banners. Hoover and Hagemeyer. And people were gathering and there was a large platform at the far side.

Jeremy's thoughts felt simplified now. He held the lunch box at his side by the handle, easily, naturally, as he began to walk toward the square. But he had the gravity of an approach to the labor shack at the beginning of a shift and he knew that this was a mistake. He slowed; he made himself stop and look about idly; he resumed his approach with a casual saunter. Only his eyes remained intent.

The shuffling, eddying crowd was still diffuse; the square was big; the platform was wide. There would be no problem with access, Jeremy knew. He scanned the sides of the crowd. Out in the street a mounted policeman stroked his horse's mane. Leaning against a tree at the back of the crowd on the bluff side of the square was a policeman flipping his nightstick. Jeremy saw no other cops. But there were some men in work clothes scattered around the edge of the crowd; Hagemeyer's goons, he knew.

Jeremy drew nearer and he entered the square, moving through the middle of the crowd. Plenty of empty space. The crowd could double in size and there would still be room to wait in the center and move quickly to the front edge when the time came. The platform was perhaps thirty feet away now—just like shooting practice near shantytown. He could even stand here in the center of the crowd and kill Hagemeyer.

Jeremy looked now for Hagemeyer himself. On the platform several men in suits were talking near a row of folding chairs and a third cop was standing at the back corner. Hagemeyer hadn't arrived yet. Or he was out of sight somewhere. That was all right. He would be here soon. Jeremy stood motionless, his mind flowing into his right hand, the box there, holding the Luger; his arm was faintly tensive; he told himself he was calm.

And Deborah looked through the windows in Yellowhammer's doors. She could see Sun Mound against the sky, far off, moving slowly, and she drew her gaze nearer to the car. The posts flickered there; a fallow field drifted by, then a field of corn. Deborah turned to look out the front and she could see the distant rise of the bluffs. She knew this was dangerous, following the landscape; it was making her think, and she felt questions pressing into her. What was the lunch box for? Not for food. And she'd heard another metallic sound, from the front room. He'd put something into the box. Something metallic. She thought of the Reds. Was it the Reds he was involved with? She thought of the Reds because in the metallic sound she'd sensed a bomb. Madness. She couldn't imagine Jeremy with a bomb. Maybe a gun. Jeremy could use a gun. What was he going to do?

Deborah's hands and feet were stirring but there was nowhere to go. Only this slow slide across the river bottoms in a streetcar. She clenched her fists and her mind flailed about for an image, something to hold onto for a time: she saw a woman in a cloak, her heart exposed, flames of stone.

In Lawton there were sirens. And a band began to play, marching from behind the platform. There were cries scattered through the crowd—Hoover's name and Hagemeyer's and loud huzzahs. Ringers, Jeremy thought. He remembered the night at the unemployment council meeting and he was glad that he was acting alone. To hell with them all, he thought, and he almost cried this out loud amid all the commotion. But he held the words in, just for himself; he'd take no chances now.

The band played and the crowd stirred and it was clear that things were happening, but it was all still out of Jeremy's view, somewhere off to the right, in the street. The band thumped and blared along and then finally people were turning sharply, necks were stretching. Two men in gray suits and fedoras came up onto the platform and between heads Jeremy could see more cops at the steps. Then there was applause and a man was rising from among the cops and he was a surprising figure to Jeremy, a man in a three-piece suit and a high white collar, but his neck was thick, his shoulders were broad, his face was mill-ruddy. He stopped and smiled and waved to the crowd and there was applause. This was Hoover, Jeremy knew. But he looked like a millworker. One of Hagemeyer's boys.

Another cry came from the ringers—"Hagemeyer"—and Jeremy's head jerked toward the platform steps. Only the policemen were visible, but they were themselves turning and the blare of brass rushed by Jeremy but the drum thumped in his stomach and behind him, in the distance, there was a clanging. Yellowhammer was rolling into the station and the conductor had come forward and was tattooing the bell and grinning back into the car as if in great excitement.

The doors opened and Deborah was out of the car and running toward the square. A crowd was before her. Where was Jeremy? A band was playing. Nothing had happened yet. But she couldn't see Jeremy, just a hedge of people and a policeman standing by a tree, another on a horse, banners, heads, hats, backs, a line of fancy cars off in the street. Near one of the cars she saw a short, thick-armed man with a massive chest, the same man who'd come to tell Jeremy he was laid off.

Now Deborah was at the rear of the crowd and she saw no protesters around, no picketing, no one who seemed to be anything but a supporter of this rally and a thought clutched Deborah, yanked her up straight: Jeremy was acting alone. He had a gun and he was acting alone. She looked into the crowd, entered it, there was room to move, and Jeremy could see Hagemeyer. The man was crossing to Hoover and the two shook hands. Hagemeyer was broad in the shoulders like Hoover and he was bald and he had a knife-cut smile that went straight across his face. He turned to the crowd and his face was raised and he had no eyes. The round lenses of his glasses were white with flame and Hagemeyer had no eyes and Jeremy felt tightly bound, felt a gentle pressure like heat on his body and the sounds faded in his head, the face with no eyes lifted, lifted and turned and the knife-smile stretched tighter, the face nodded down slightly, the flame flashing, and Jeremy felt strong, his hands were strong but still gentle, ready to touch the tongue of the Luger and he lifted the lunch box and held it in both hands and Deborah was pushing her way through bodies, sorting shapes, heads, shoulders, faces. Jeremy wasn't here, wasn't here, and the band was playing and the crowd was cheering and she glanced up and she could see straight ahead of her, above the crowd. Two men were holding their hands aloft, waving. She recognized President Hoover and she knew who the other man was, the sun glinting off his glasses, and there was a movement into the thin corridor of space before her and it was Jeremy, a few yards away. She cried his name but her voice was carried off by the noise swirling around her and she squeezed forward through the crowd and Jeremy touched the catches on the lunch box without taking his eyes from Hagemeyer, Hagemeyer and the flame there, sucking at Jeremy, drawing his careful hands, and there was a touch on his arm, a hand grasping. Jeremy turned to see and coming around him was Deborah—a vision from a fever, his wife's body coiling around him in a dream—he turned back to the eyes of fire—a place to aim. But there was a pressing on his chest, he was bumped backwards.

Deborah pushed at Jeremy's chest. He was not looking at her, he was looking over her head and she set herself square before him and doubled her fists and drove them into his chest, pushed him back and the crowd gave way, people moved, Jeremy's eyes came down. His eyes focused on the vision that persisted, that pressed at him. It was Deborah and his arms were tight, his hands were ready. He looked up and Hagemeyer was moving to the center of the platform, his chest was broad, easy, three quick rounds in the trunk of a tree. But Jeremy stepped back again, another step. Deborah was here and forcing him away and she didn't understand, she was a small quick bird, pulling his eyes, pulling his strength when he wanted to kill the crow circling the center of the platform, the crow not diving and disappearing but lingering, ready to be killed now, ready to die for Cronin and for Gus and for Nick and for Turpin and for all the suffering men and the suffering women and the suffering children and Jeremy was angry and yet still giving ground. Deborah was pressing him now, her hands on his chest, and she was digging at the ground with her feet and she was crying and Jeremy's anger was packed in tight in his chest, unvented fire in an oven, and he was ready and Hagemeyer was ready but this woman was pushing him and he twisted his body and he spun free of her. He turned to face the platform and his fingers went to the latches and there were other hands there, soft, fluttering hands, stripping the box away. The box fell to the ground and Jeremy's right hand clenched and went hard and he looked at the blur of this face before him and he drove his fist out, a hard crack, and the body flew away, tumbling, falling.

Jeremy stopped. He could see. There were people nearby, but he was in an empty space. Before him lay Deborah. Her face was turned from him. She was rising to one arm. There was a bursting and then a voiding in Jeremy's chest, like a cartridge flipped from a gun and falling to stillness. The crowd was silent. The band had stopped. Because of him? He looked at Deborah and blood was coming from her mouth and he felt the blood as if it were slipping softly from his own eyes, bleeding from his brain. He hadn't meant this. Not this. A voice was speaking behind him, crying out: Ladies and gentlemen. Only a few faces had turned to notice what had happened here. Jeremy looked at his hands. They were trembling. A man was before him. What the hell did you do, mister? Jeremy could not push this man away. Not even so he could go to Deborah now, though that was all he wanted. He wanted to go to her and take away what he'd done but he could not even lift his own arms.

I'll handle this. A voice, a man in a blue uniform, a cop was here now, and Deborah saw the cop push a man away and confront Jeremy. Her face was numb and the ground, the crowd, were tilting, but she rose and she stumbled forward, wedging herself between Jeremy and the policeman, falling against Jeremy's chest.

"It's all right, officer," she said.

A voice was declaiming from somewhere and the policeman glanced beyond Jeremy, toward the front of the crowd, and back to Jeremy and then to Deborah. Deborah laid her hand on Jeremy's chest, put her hands on him and she felt Jeremy's arm come heavily around her, felt his hand touching her shoulder, tentatively, like a blind man's.

The policeman said in a low voice, "Do me and the president a favor. Take your family squabble someplace else."

"Yes, officer," Deborah said. "We're sorry." She lifted her head from Jeremy's chest and took his arm and tugged gently at him to lead him away.

The policeman said, "Wait." He pulled a handkerchief from his pocket and handed it to her. "It's clean," he said.

"Thanks." She took it and touched it to her mouth and Jeremy looked down at her and her mouth was covered and he felt her guiding him. He tightened his arm around Deborah's waist and he felt heavy against her, like an invalid, and he realized what she was doing; she was getting him away from this place and he was thankful for that. Thankful now. The strength he'd had was gone. And this was not what he'd meant to do. Hurting Deborah was worse than what he'd intended. But he was glad his strength was gone. He was glad she had his arm and he looked at her and she was guiding him and then she straightened suddenly and stopped and looked back and Jeremy followed her gaze. The cop was standing over the lunch box and he was looking down at it.

Deborah broke away. The policeman was bending, his hand was going out, and Deborah ran. "Wait," she said. His hand paused and she pulled up to walk the last few feet. Calm, she told herself. Nothing suspicious. Faces had turned at her word and they vanished now toward the voice at the front, which proclaimed, With the same guts and drive that made this country, we can find our way again.

The policeman was still frozen, half bent; he saw her approaching and he bent down and grasped the bucket and she was there, her hands coming out, but he was holding the bucket, offering it to her. Then his brow crumpled and he shook the box slightly. Deborah's hands came out, lay on the box, and she tugged it gently. It did not yield. She looked in his face, held her eyes steady. "It's a thermos," she said, letting her voice be loud, drawing the faces again. "You want some coffee, officer?"

Shushing came from the faces. The policeman glanced at them and Deborah watched his suspicion droop into embarrassment. The voice at the front cried, Times change but people don't change.

"How about it?" Deborah said, loud. She tugged again and the lunch box came free. It was heavy and her breath snagged at what was in it.

"Get on out of here," the policeman hissed.

Deborah turned and she saw Jeremy waiting. He was where she left him, maybe thirty yards away, alone, in a lot across the brick street at the edge of the square. He stood straight and he smiled at her. The voice behind her shouted and the crowd applauded and Deborah began to walk toward Jeremy.

Then the short, broad-chested man spanked from the corner of her sight and was up next to Jeremy. She gasped and Jeremy had seen the quick movement and now Spud's face was as surprising to him as Deborah's had been a few minutes ago.

"What the hell you doing here?" Spud said and he came up to him, put his face up close, and he pushed Jeremy in the chest, backed him away from the crowd.

Jeremy was not ready for this. His arms were still balky from the pain he'd given Deborah. Spud pushed him again and Jeremy knew that a fight now would mean the cops and then the box and Luger and it would all come out and he'd lose Deborah.

"I'm gonna finish you now," Spud said, pushing Jeremy again. Then Spud straightened up.

Deborah was behind him and she said, "You know what this is in your back, don't you?"

Spud was rigid but his eyes were narrow. He was thinking of angles and Jeremy didn't know what to do about it.

"Step to the side, hon," Deborah said softly, leaning around

Spud to look at Jeremy. "This close, I'm liable to kill both of you."

Spud's eyes opened wide. "Look," he said. "Let's just call it a standoff."

A clanging drifted through Spud's words and Jeremy glanced over his shoulder. Yellowhammer was sitting across the way, its rear rod rising, its sheave nudging into place on the wire above the car. The conductor below hooked the rod chain on the side of the car. Yellowhammer was ready to leave.

"Over here," Deborah said.

Jeremy looked back and she was moving Spud into a space a few yards off, sheltered from view of the square by a boxwood hedge.

"Jeremy," she said and he followed her. She put Spud in the center of the space and Jeremy came over. Deborah backed away a bit and Spud watched the Luger withdraw. The streetcar clanged and Deborah nodded at Jeremy and Jeremy squared around in front of Spud and he let the man's face turn to him. Jeremy had good leverage; he set himself; he felt a quick bright flare of desire for the touch of his wife and he understood what they had to do and the strength poured into his fist and he hit Spud at a slight upward angle on the point of the chin and the man flew back and fell and did not move.

Deborah dropped the Luger into the lunch box and latched the lid and she and Jeremy turned and ran together across the grass. They ran and the conductor saw them coming and held the doors and they were inside Yellowhammer and beginning to glide away.

There was a spot of blood on Deborah's lip. She sat down on the narrow bed in the dim coolness of the basement room and for the first time since she'd begun her pursuit of Jeremy to Lawton, she felt safe. They'd stopped at their house and packed what was essential to them—very little, in fact—and they'd caught another streetcar, a red one, bound for St. Louis. In the center of the McKinley Bridge Jeremy had leaned from the window and thrown the lunch box into the vault of air beyond the bridge. The box had fallen out of sight into the river. They had climbed the hill and Father Harrison had asked no questions. He would help Jeremy find work. If not in St. Louis, then in the west. He had friends. And he'd taken them into the back of the church and down narrow, cool-breathing steps and he'd left them here and Deborah felt safe and she felt the blood on her lip.

Jeremy put the bags down. He looked at the pipes flowing through the ceiling and down into the furnace, a squat mass without fire. Cold. And the smells were cold: iron and coal and concrete. Jeremy turned and looked at Deborah sitting on the bed and his skin recalled her strength; she'd plucked him from his self-willed death and brought him to this place and there was a tongue-soft wisping of her power on his skin as he stood looking at her, even as she closed her eyes and let her head loll back, exposing the line of her throat, her hair falling softly behind her. She was softness too and she was his wife. This was his wife and the flame in him was undulant now. He drew near and he saw the spot of blood ready to flow and he sat beside her. She did not open her eyes. She did not move. She sat with her throat exposed to him and she felt her pulse there, quickening. She felt her husband's strength coiled beside her and then his lips touched her throat and Jeremy drew his face away. He looked at the spot of blood and he bent to it, kissed her gently there, the blood spreading on his own lip and he tasted it, the taste of flame, the flame that his daughter had loved as it thrashed against the night and then it was a different taste, his wife's body, the taste of her skin. Jeremy took Deborah in his arms and lifted her and then they were naked before each other and then hard to soft they were joined and hard to soft they billowed and hummed and Deborah's hands were corded from pressing at his back and Jeremy's hands were curled from touching her face. When Deborah heard the beating of a heart, at first the sound seemed to come from outside. She could hear it beating far above her, but then she thought it must be Jeremy's and then she thought it must be her own and then, as her body rushed like blood into the body of her husband, she felt the heart beating all around them both and she saw it flaring like a Wabash night, burning them until they were clean.

A Note About the Author

Robert Olen Butler was born and raised in Granite City, Illinois. He now lives with his 13-year-old son, Joshua, in Lake Charles, Louisiana, where he teaches at McNeese State University. He is the author of four previous novels— *The Alleys of Eden, Sun Dogs, Countrymen of Bones,* and *On Distant Ground.*

A Note on the Type

This book was set in a digitized version of Caledonia, a type face designed by William Addison Dwiggins (1880–1956) for the Mergenthaler Linotype Company in 1939. Dwiggins chose to call his new type face Caledonia, the Roman name for Scotland, because it was inspired by the Scottish types cast by Alexander Wilson & Son, Glasgow type founders, in 1833. However, there is a calligraphic quality about Caledonia that is totally lacking in the Wilson types.

W. A. Dwiggins began an association with the Mergenthaler Linotype Company in 1929 and over the next twenty-seven years designed a number of book types, the most interesting of which are Metro, Electra, Caledonia, Eldorado, and Falcon.

Composed by Rainsford Type, Ridgefield, Connecticut
Printed and bound by Fairfield Graphics,
Fairfield, Pennsylvania
Designed by Iris Weinstein